UNMARKED GRAVES

PROJECT DEMON HUNTERS: BOOK FIVE

CHRISTINE POPE

UNMARKED GRAVES

ISBN: 978-1-946435-30-9

Copyright © 2020 by Christine Pope

Published by Dark Valentine Press

Cover art by Christian Bentulan

Formatting by Indie Author Services

THE WORLD WAS A BLUR OF GLARING LIGHTS and harsh sound, a sharp wailing noise that felt as though it was drilling right through his eardrums. Will Gordon blinked, aware of a throbbing pain in his temple and the face of a stranger bending over him, his unfamiliar dark eyes filled with concern.

"William?" the man said. "Can you understand me?"

Will started to nod and realized even that slight movement hurt too much. "Will," he whispered, shocked at how weak his voice sounded. "Will is fine."

The man smiled. "Will, then. Do you know where you are?"

He blinked and saw a metal roof overhead, realized there was a second stranger, a woman, on his other side, her gaze fixed on a device that was monitoring his pulse and blood pressure and probably a few other vital statistics. However, none of that mattered to him right then.

Where was Rosemary?

"Ambulance," he said, realizing that he'd paused longer than he'd thought before answering the EMT's question.

Another smile, one with something of relief in it. "Can you tell me the year? Who's president?"

Will dutifully recited those facts, although it hurt more than he'd thought to utter the few syllables those answers required. "Woman...who was with me?"

"She's fine," the EMT said. "She's following us to the hospital."

In his car, Will assumed, since he and Rosemary had driven over to Colin Turner's house on Las Flores Drive in Will's vintage Challenger. Recalling that bit of information made other memories come flooding back...the confrontation with Caleb Dixon in the hallway of the house that Colin and his girlfriend Madeline Nash had bought together more than a decade earlier...the jeering expression on Caleb's face as he disappeared with the hard drive that contained the missing *Project Demon Hunters* footage.

No, it was Caleb *Lockwood*, Will reminded himself. "Caleb Dixon" was a fiction, an identity the man had made up to ingratiate himself with Rosemary and get her to help him find the files from Colin's canceled show. Caleb Lockwood was something infinitely more dangerous than a self-described indie filmmaker, a man who had the blood of demons running through his veins.

The mere thought of that footage being in Caleb's hands was enough to make Will move restlessly on his stretcher. He couldn't lie there while that demonspawn was off with the precious footage, might already be destroying it—

"Hey," the EMT said, putting a gentle but still inexorable hand on Will's sternum. "You need to lie quiet, Mr. Gordon. You took a pretty bad blow to the head."

"I'm fine," Will protested, although he wondered at that moment whether he actually was fine. Simply lifting his head an inch or two had increased the dull, throbbing ache behind his temple, and the interior of the ambulance seemed to spin around him.

"That's for the doctors to decide," the EMT told him. "Until then, you need to lie still. They're going to want to do an MRI to make sure you haven't suffered a serious head injury."

Under normal circumstances, Will would have agreed on taking such a prudent approach. Now, though, he could only chafe at his current weakened state. Who knew that Caleb would be so quick, so ruthless?

You should have known, or at least guessed, he told himself. *As soon as Rosemary told you who he really was, you should have been more on your guard. You knew you weren't facing an ordinary human.*

Well, he couldn't go back and change what had happened, so it seemed the smartest thing at the moment was to do as the EMT said and wait for a clean bill of health from the doctor.

"And the police will want to talk to you, too," the EMT added.

"'Police'?" Will echoed.

"When we arrived at the house, your girlfriend told us you were attacked."

Should he bother to point out that Rosemary wasn't his girlfriend? To be perfectly honest, Will didn't know exactly what she was. She'd come into his life and assumed far more importance in it than he'd expected…or should have allowed. He was supposed to be helping her, and what had he done?

Screwed up royally, and kissed her when she came to him at the church, scared half out of her mind because someone had been following her from the parking garage across the street. Will knew he should have been concentrating on locating her pursuer…although the stranger, whoever or whatever he was, appeared to have disappeared into thin air. At any rate, he should have remained focused on the situation with Caleb rather than giving free rein to his emotions and pulling Rosemary into his arms.

True, she had been more than responsive to his kiss, letting Will know that she'd wanted it just as much as he had, but still, she'd been upset and frightened and in need of reassurance. His timing had been terrible.

He shouldn't have kissed her. Not then, anyway.

But, just like his botched fight with Caleb Lockwood, it was over and done with, and the only thing he could do now was pick up the pieces as best he could and see what happened next.

It wouldn't be the first time.

"Yes," he said slowly, realizing that the EMT was still watching him intently, obviously waiting for some kind of response. "There was an intruder."

That was all he wanted to say, though. If he hadn't been knocked out cold, hadn't left Rosemary to handle calling the ambulance, then he would have told her that she should do whatever she could to leave any mention of Caleb Lockwood out of all this. While they would have had to report some kind of confrontation with an intruder in Colin's house, they could have been purposely vague, said he was wearing a ski mask or that it was too dark to see his face clearly. Will didn't like lying, but he understood that sometimes a bit of prevarication was necessary in pursuit of a greater goal. Michael Covenant had told him a long time ago that it was never a good idea to get the authorities mixed up in anything supernatural, since they would probably never believe the more outlandish aspects of those cases and often hurt more than they helped.

Because the EMT now wore an expression of curiosity, Will hastened to add, "But I didn't get a good look at him. He came at me from behind."

"Too bad. But I'm sure the police will want to hear your side of things."

Of course, they would. In fact, they'd probably have a long list of questions they wanted to ask him. Maybe the doctors would put the interrogation off for a while, since he guessed that any tests they'd want to run would take precedence over an interview with the police, but it wasn't the sort of thing he could delay indefinitely.

At least Rosemary apparently was all right. She had to be, or she wouldn't be following him to the hospital. Will wanted to know what had happened during those lost minutes after he blacked out, but that was yet another discussion that would have to wait. Why Caleb hadn't hurt her—why he hadn't tried to get rid of Will permanently while he was helpless and unable to fight back—he didn't know, but there had to be some kind of explanation. Maybe the part-demon had simply decided he didn't have the time, had thought it better to cut and run rather than carry out any further revenge against his adversary.

Or maybe...even though Will really didn't want to admit such a thing to himself...Caleb had realized that an Episcopal priest didn't present much of a threat, and therefore it was smarter to leave him behind and get out of there just in case the neighbors had heard something of the altercation and called the police. After all, while the authorities would of course investigate an assault, they'd be a lot more dogged in their pursuit of a murderer, and that was exactly the kind of attention Caleb had most likely decided he needed to avoid.

The ambulance turned and then slowed down, which seemed to indicate they'd arrived at their destination. Most likely Glendale Adventist; Will thought it was probably the closest hospital to the modest-looking house that had hidden such a terrible secret.

As soon as the vehicle came to a stop, the EMTs opened the back doors of the ambulance and pulled out the gurney he was lying on, and quickly and efficiently rolled it into the ER. He was wheeled off to a corner, and a moment later, a brisk woman with a lilting East Indian accent was shining a penlight into his eyes.

"Pupils responsive," she said, making a note on his chart. "Good."

"I'm fine," he said, although his head had started to pound again, and he knew the claim was probably more bravado than actual reality.

"Well, we all hope so, sir." She looked over at the male nurse who had come over to stand next to her, and he fastened a blood pressure cuff around Will's arm.

Weren't they monitoring my damn blood pressure the whole way over here? he wondered, but he didn't bother to protest. Now that he was at the hospital, he knew there was protocol to be followed, and better to let things run their course and act as cooperative as possible in the hope that they'd realize he really was okay and there was no need for him to remain here.

A few minutes later—after the nurse had removed his watch and his belt and taken his cell phone and house keys from his pants pocket, and put everything in a plastic bag for safekeeping—he was wheeled out of the ER and into the room where the MRI machines were located. He lay quietly while the thing banged away, his eyes shut, body tense with cold, worry for Rosemary mounting even though he tried to tell himself she was fine, that he just hadn't seen her yet because they weren't going to allow him any visitors until all the necessary tests had been run.

"All done," the tech announced, and then Will was whisked away and brought to the elevator, where he rode up a few floors before being taken to a room at the end of the hallway. Although there were two beds in the room, the other one was unoccupied for the moment. The two orderlies who'd wheeled his gurney into the hospital room transferred him to the bed closer to the window, informed him that a doctor would be along in a bit to discuss his MRI results, and then turned on the television overhead, although with the sound off.

"Try to stay awake," one of the nurses told him. She was pretty and blonde and probably a year or two younger than he was...not that he really cared about her appearance. Right then, the only thing he cared about was seeing Rosemary. Well, and getting out of the hospital as soon as possible.

He summoned a weak smile. "I'll do my best."

"We'll be by to check on you in a few minutes, bring you some ice chips," she said. "And the doctor shouldn't be too long."

Nodding hurt too much, so he only said, "Thanks."

"Just part of the job," she replied, and went

out, with the other nurse—who hadn't spoken a word—following immediately behind her.

Will lay in the hospital bed, staring at the bright images on the TV screen without really focusing on them, and wondered where Rosemary was.

———

She knew Will's tricked-out 1970 Dodge Challenger could have kept up with the ambulance without breaking a sweat, but honestly, Rosemary would have been frightened to put it through its paces even if she'd wanted to top off this gem of an evening by getting a speeding ticket. No, she knew they were headed to Glendale Adventist, and so she'd driven there at about five miles an hour over the speed limit, just enough to feel as if she wasn't dawdling, but not so fast that she thought she'd attract the attention of any police in the vicinity.

A sigh of relief escaped her lips as she pulled into the hospital lot and parked in the closest open space to the ER. Since it was a Saturday night, the place was busy—she saw a man covered in blood getting wheeled in on a gurney, and a pair of cops were escorting a disheveled woman who appeared to be around thirty or so, obviously high on something, who squirmed in their grip and wailed in syllables that didn't sound like any language Rosemary had ever heard.

Like she's possessed, she thought, and a shiver passed over her, even as she scolded herself for letting such a notion enter her head. No need to conjure demons when it was far more likely the strange woman was whacked out on meth or PCP or bath salts or whatever chemical cocktail people used these days to recreationally scramble their brains.

Ignoring the tumult, Rosemary headed toward the front desk, where a stern-looking black woman in her late fifties or early sixties sat. "Hi," she said as the woman glanced away from her computer to make eye contact. "I'm Rosemary McGuire. My friend William Gordon was just brought in by ambulance. Do you know where he is?"

"Just a moment," the nurse said, her voice far friendlier than her appearance had seemed to indicate. She typed in something—presumably, Will's name—and then added, "He's being taken to have an MRI."

"Is that bad?" Rosemary asked, hating how frightened her voice sounded. Wasn't she supposed to be tough and confident when horrible stuff like this happened? At the moment, though, she was mostly glad that she hadn't burst into tears.

"Not necessarily," the woman replied. "It's standard whenever someone's suffered a bad blow to the head. Just want to make sure he hasn't suffered a TBI."

"A what?"

"Traumatic brain injury." The nurse went on before Rosemary could respond, "But the notes on his file say he was conscious and responsive on his ambulance ride, so it sounds like he's doing well." Her brows drew together in a frown. "Glendale P.D. is sending a detective over to speak with you. Go ahead and have a seat in the waiting area." She pointed to a group of chairs upholstered in gray fabric where a number of people were sitting. They were all ages and races, but they all shared the same anxious expression, one that Rosemary guessed she wore on her face as well.

The last thing she wanted to do was talk to the police. Unfortunately, she had a feeling she wouldn't be allowed to opt out of that particular interview. If she'd been thinking straight, she should have realized the police would be involved at some point. When she'd made the initial call to 911, she'd only said that she was with someone who'd suffered a blow to the head, but when the ambulance arrived and the EMT asked her what had happened, she'd blurted out that she and Will had surprised an intruder, and it was while protecting her that he'd been assaulted. She guessed that one of the EMTs had contacted the Glendale police department while they were en route.

Okay, so, she'd have to think of a story to give the detective. More than ever, she wished she'd had a chance to talk to Will. They needed to make sure their accounts of the incident matched up. Somehow, she knew he wouldn't want her to tell the truth—not that the police would believe it anyway.

Yes, officer, Will Gordon and I surprised a man who's part-demon, and he attacked Will and tried to hurt me, only I summoned powers I didn't know I had and used them to protect the two of us. That's when the part-demon man gave up and disappeared into thin air.

You know, your usual Saturday night in Glendale, California.

Rosemary let out a huff of a breath and tried her best to corral her racing thoughts, even though her hands kept shaking and she felt as though she couldn't truly focus on anything until she saw Will again and was able to confirm that he really was okay.

Think, Rosemary, she scolded herself.

All right, the full truth obviously wouldn't work, and so probably the wisest course would be to use just a little bit of it to concoct a story that was both plausible and vague. There was no point in saying who the true culprit was, because "Caleb Dixon" wasn't even Caleb's real name. Besides—

"Rosemary McGuire?"

She looked up and saw a man in his early forties, slim and of medium height, with cool, piercing gray eyes, standing a few feet away from her. He wore a sport jacket and tie, which told her he must be the detective from the Glendale P.D., because she couldn't think of anyone else in Southern California who would wear that sort of an outfit on a Saturday night.

Feeling suddenly tired, she said, "Yes, that's me."

The man pulled a wallet out of his inner breast pocket and flashed a badge at her. Glendale P.D., just as she'd thought. "I'm Detective Phillips. Do you mind if I ask you a few questions?"

Actually, she did, but she knew that sort of response wouldn't earn her any points. She'd only just met him, but those coolly assessing gray eyes had already given her the impression that Detective Phillips wasn't the sort of guy who messed around. Instead, she responded, "Here?" as she gave a dubious glance around the crowded E.R.

His stern mouth relaxed ever so slightly. "Let me take you to the cafeteria, get you a cup of coffee."

"Sounds great." In all honesty, it really didn't, since she tried to avoid caffeine so late in the evening. This particular evening, though, having some coffee was probably a good idea. She had a feeling it was going to be a very long night.

She picked up her purse from her lap and slung it over her shoulder, then followed the detective as he led her away from the emergency room and down a hallway to the cafeteria. At that hour, they weren't serving food anymore, but the vending machines worked 24/7.

"How do you take it?" Detective Phillips asked as he fished some change out of his trousers pocket.

"Black is fine," she replied. She shuddered to think what that vending machine used for milk or cream.

Without responding, he got two cups of coffee —both black—and then guided her over to a table off in one corner. The cafeteria wasn't entirely empty, but no one else sat in that part of the room.

He slid one of the cups of coffee across the table to her and said, "Why don't you tell me what happened?"

Rosemary picked up the coffee and took a very small sip. It was too hot and too bitter, but it did do a good job of sending a much-needed jolt along her nerve endings. "Will and I went to the house—"

"The house at 1830 Las Flores Drive," Detective Phillips interjected, pulling out a notepad from his pocket. Irrelevantly, she wondered how much random stuff he kept in there.

She nodded and said, "Yes. It belongs to a… friend of a friend." Close enough. After all, she was friends with Michael Covenant, and he'd been friends with Colin Turner, so the connection wasn't a complete fabrication. "The owner passed away recently, and we were checking on it to help out the owner's sister." Again, not a total lie; now that she knew about the house's existence, Colin's sister Emma Weston would have to figure out what she wanted to do with the place, whether that was to sell it or continue renting it. "When we were inside, we were attacked by an intruder."

"Description?"

"Sorry, I don't really know," Rosemary replied, hoping she looked properly apologetic. "We were just about to turn on the lights in the hallway when he came at us, so it was pretty dark."

The detective scribbled something on his notepad. "But you're certain it was a man."

That seemed like a safe enough piece of information to pass along, so she nodded. "I think so. He was a little shorter than Will, but still tall. I couldn't see his face. His build seemed pretty athletic, though."

"Clothing?"

She shrugged. "Jeans. Some kind of dark shirt,

I think, but I don't know whether it was a T-shirt or a button-up."

"Collar?"

Again, all she could do was lift her shoulders.

"Did he say anything?"

Oh, Caleb had said a lot—most of it, things she really hadn't wanted to hear. However, since she couldn't repeat any of what the part-demon had said during that frightening encounter in the Las Flores Drive house, she replied, "No. He just came at us. I think that's why he got the drop on Will—we were both totally taken by surprise."

The detective made a few notes, although Rosemary saw the way his mouth tightened and guessed he wasn't very happy about the complete lack of any useful information in her report. "Anything missing?"

"What?" she asked, not sure what he meant.

"Anything stolen from the house?" Detective Phillips said, his tone so even that she knew he was probably starting to get annoyed with her and doing his best to keep the irritation out of his voice.

She shook her head. "No. That is, the house was empty—the previous tenants moved out a while ago. There wasn't really anything to take."

Nothing except a hard drive crammed full of footage that had incontrovertible evidence of demons really existing. Colin had hidden the hard drive in the crawlspace of the house, figuring it would be safe there. And it had been—until Caleb followed her to Las Flores Drive and realized the previously undiscovered house would have made the perfect hiding place for the footage. How he'd figured out the hard drive had been secreted in the crawlspace, she didn't know. Maybe, being part-demon, he'd been able to sniff it out. Or maybe he'd simply used his powers of deduction and realized there weren't a lot of places to hide something in an otherwise empty house.

"Any vandalism?"

"Not that I noticed. But we weren't in the house for very long before we were attacked."

A few more notes, and then Detective Phillips replaced his notepad in his inner breast pocket. "We'll want to take a look at the property."

"Sure," she said automatically, although she wasn't quite sure how to manage that. She assumed the police would want her there, but she wasn't leaving the hospital until she knew Will was all right. The nurse had made it sound as though he was doing okay, and yet, if they were performing an MRI, that must mean his injury was serious enough to warrant a thorough examination.

The detective must have noticed something stricken in her expression, because he said, "Sometime tomorrow is fine. We'll have a car go by the house a few times tonight, just to make sure everything is still quiet over there, but I think the assailant is long gone."

Oh, he was gone, all right. To where, Rosemary wasn't really sure. Probably not back to the rented house in Eagle Rock where he'd been staying, though. He'd told her he was from Indiana, but she figured that had to be a lie. Or maybe not. She tried to remember where the Underhill trust —set up by Belial in his disguise as Jeffrey Whitcomb all those years ago—and its demon trustees had been located. Somewhere in the Midwest, she thought, but she couldn't recall for sure. So maybe Caleb really had gone to Indiana.

If so, maybe she didn't have as much to worry about as she'd feared. On the other hand, if he really was hiding half a continent away, he could be up to all sorts of mischief.

Well, wherever he was and whatever he was doing, that would have to wait. "Tomorrow should be okay," she said.

"I'll give you a call in the morning," the detective said, and got a card out of his pocket and handed it to her. "I can meet you at the Las Flores house."

Rosemary glanced at the card before slipping it into her purse. The next day was Sunday, but she guessed that didn't make a difference. Detective Phillips was on duty on a Saturday night, which told her he wasn't working the regular nine-to-five, Monday-through-Friday shift. "Okay," she responded, since she really didn't know what else to say.

He offered her a reassuring smile, drained the last of his coffee, and then got up from the table, pausing to drop the empty cup in the trash before he left the cafeteria.

No more coffee for her, though. Rosemary had only drunk about half the cup, but the caffeine was already singing along her nerve endings, and she knew she'd hit her limit. A glance up at the clock on the far wall told her it was now almost nine o'clock, which meant Will had been admitted more than a half hour earlier. How long did an MRI test take? She had no idea because she'd never had any need to have one; her last physical injury had been a sprained ankle more than five years earlier, and that had only required simple X-rays to make sure she hadn't broken any bones.

Still, a half hour seemed enough time for something to have happened, so she went back down the hallway to the E.R. and approached the desk. "Any updates on Will Gordon?" she asked.

The woman checked the computer and nodded. "Yes, it looks like he's been transferred to a room on the fifth floor. Just go up and ask at the nurses' station there."

"Thank you," Rosemary replied, relief washing through her. Yes, he had been sent to a room instead of being released, but it must have been just a regular hospital room, since the nurse hadn't said anything about him being in the ICU.

After offering the woman a grateful smile, she went to the elevators and headed upstairs. A quick inquiry at the nurses' station provided the information that Will Gordon was in Room 522.

"I just checked on him a few minutes ago," the nurse offered with a smile. She was pretty and blonde and probably in her early thirties, closer to Will's age than Rosemary herself. No wedding ring, either.

And that was probably just about the most ridiculous thing to be thinking about right then. Maybe the nurse wasn't wearing a wedding ring because it got in the way while she worked. Allowing even the faintest feelings of jealousy to pop up when Will was lying in bed with a concussion was crazy.

"Thank you so much," Rosemary said, and hurried herself away from the nurses' station before she could do or say anything too foolish.

His room was down the hall to the left. She paused at the open doorway and made herself take a steadying breath. It scared her more than she wanted to admit how much she'd already come to care about this man, even though they'd only shared one kiss, even though she hardly knew anything about him. When she'd seen him lying on the floor at the Glendale house, barely breathing, the fear that had nearly overwhelmed her was unlike anything she'd experienced before.

She'd been so afraid of losing him, even though she had to acknowledge he wasn't *really* hers. Not yet, anyway. Maybe someday, if she was really lucky....

Another steadying breath, and then she entered the room. The lights were dim, and the TV had been turned on, although the sound was turned way, way down.

"Thank God," Will said, shifting slightly in his hospital bed as she approached.

"You're all right?" she asked, and took a few more steps toward him.

He looked all right. Of course, he had a bandage wrapped around his head and a gauze pad on the left side of his forehead, and he wore a hospital gown with some sort of old-fashioned foulard print on it, like something you might see on one of your grandfather's ties, but his color was good, and his extraordinary gray eyes focused on her easily enough. If he'd gotten bruised by his fall to the wood floor in the hallway at Colin's house, those bruises hadn't yet begun to surface.

"I'm fine," he said, and gave her a deprecating grin. "That is, my head hurts like hell, but I don't think I suffered any lasting damage." The smile faded, and he went on, "And you—you're all right? What happened?"

Rosemary reached over and took his hand. His fingers felt warm and strong. Surely if something was really wrong with him, they would have felt cool and clammy or otherwise not quite right?

A quick glance at the door told her that the nurses were out of earshot, and didn't seem inclined to interrupt their conversation…at least, not at that particular moment. Still, she thought it was probably better to be circumspect. "Maybe we should talk about that later."

He seemed to understand the reason for her reticence; although he didn't nod, his mouth compressed slightly. "But he didn't—"

"No, I'm good," she said, hoping he would get the point.

Will's mouth parted, but whatever he'd been about to say was interrupted by the arrival of the doctor, a man who looked to be in his middle or late fifties, balding and with a sharp beak of a nose. He glanced over at Rosemary, who wondered if she should excuse herself. After all, she and Will had kissed, but their relationship still was woefully undefined. Maybe he wouldn't want her around while the doctor discussed personal medical issues with him.

However, those doubts were immediately

dispelled by Will saying, "I hope you have good news, doctor."

Another of those glances, but then the man gave the slightest lift of his shoulders. "I do... mostly. I'm Doctor Littleton, and I've just been reviewing your MRI. You do have a concussion, but it's not a serious one, so it doesn't look as though any other tests are warranted for the moment."

"I can go home?" Will asked, face eager.

"We'd prefer that you stay in the hospital overnight for observation," Doctor Littleton replied.

For just the faintest moment, Will frowned. But then his expression smoothed itself, and he said, "But if you 'prefer' me to stay, that's just a recommendation, correct?"

The doctor hesitated. "Yes. I can discharge you, as long as you have someone to drive you home and that you also have someone who can watch you tonight and wake you up regularly."

"I can do that," Rosemary said, and then sent a quick, apologetic glance over at Will. "That is, if you want me to."

"I'd really appreciate it if you could," he told her, his eyes warming with gratitude. "You drove my car over here, didn't you?"

She nodded. "So, it really makes the most

sense. I can take you home and keep an eye on you all night."

"Well, then," Doctor Littleton said, then shifted, directing his next words to her. "I'll send you home with a list of instructions, but the most important is to make sure to wake him up every hour or so. Will, if you experience nausea or vomiting, or blurred vision or ringing in your ears, then call an ambulance right away."

"I will," he replied, although his expression had grown a little grimmer. Maybe he was mentally calculating whether his insurance would cover something like that, and whether it might not be better to just have Rosemary drive him back to the hospital. She couldn't begin to guess, since she had no idea what kind of health insurance a minister might have. It had always been a joke with Rosemary and her sisters that they'd either drive each other to the hospital or call an Uber if there was ever a problem, since their own modest health plans that they'd bought through the business were bare-bones at best.

Not that it mattered. If things went downhill fast with Will for whatever reason, Rosemary knew she'd pay for the damn ambulance out of her own pocket before she'd let anything happen to him.

"I'll start your discharge paperwork, then," the doctor said. "It'll be a half hour or so."

He left the room, and Rosemary and Will looked at each other.

"You're sure about this?" he asked.

"Of course," she responded, taking his hand once again. "You think I'd be able to sleep a wink if I had someone else looking after you?"

The corners of his mouth lifted slightly. "You wouldn't?"

"No, I wouldn't," she said severely. "Besides, it's partly my fault you got that concussion in the first place. It wouldn't feel right to have anyone but me keeping watch tonight."

His eyes held hers. "And that's the only reason?"

In answer, she bent down and kissed him lightly on the mouth. *Be brave,* she told herself.

Not looking away, making sure not to break their contact, she said, "You know it isn't."

And to her relief, he smiled.

Chapter 2

IN REALITY, IT WAS NEARLY AN HOUR BEFORE all the paperwork was managed and Will was able to climb back into his clothes and have a nurse push his wheelchair over to the hospital's main entrance. From there, Rosemary took over, rolling him out to the spot where she'd left the Challenger. He wanted to shake his head at what he viewed as overly cautious behavior, although he knew it was just hospital policy that prevented him from walking out to the car under his own power.

And honestly, even though he didn't want to admit such a thing to Rosemary, he could tell how shaky his legs felt as he climbed out of the wheelchair and into the car's passenger seat. In fact, as he sat down again and leaned over to buckle his seatbelt, he experienced a slight moment of dizziness, although he brushed it off and tried to tell himself that it wasn't so bad.

Rosemary told him she'd be back in a moment, and then rolled the wheelchair to the lobby before returning to the car. As she settled herself in the driver's seat, she looked over and sent him an encouraging smile.

"Still doing okay over there?"

"Okay" might have been stretching the truth a bit, but he didn't want to admit that maybe going home this evening rather than spending the night in the hospital might not have been the best idea. Still, they'd committed to this course of action, and Will told himself that he'd feel much better once he was back at his own house. He disliked hospitals, had spent far too many hours at the bedsides of ill and dying parishioners to ever feel comfortable in one.

"Great," he said, and although she lifted an eyebrow, she didn't question his assertion, only put the key in the ignition and cautiously backed the Challenger out of its parking space. From the way she drove—like the proverbial little old lady from Pasadena—he could tell she was intimidated by the vintage muscle car. Not so surprising, since her own Fiat compact probably didn't have even a third of the horses his '70 Dodge hid under its hood.

Once they were on the freeway and headed

east, Rosemary said, "You'll need to tell me where we're going. I've never been to your house."

Right. He should have realized that. His place actually wasn't all that far from Michael's big Craftsman house, where Rosemary had been housesitting for the past few months. "Get off at Lake," he told her. "Then you'll head north and turn right on Mountain. After that it's a left on Wilson."

She nodded. "Sounds like you and Michael were practically neighbors."

Will smiled. "Almost. It's about a half mile from his place to mine."

He almost added, *And his house is a lot more impressive,* but he didn't want to come off as overly deprecating. Michael's house was a show-place, true, but Will was proud of his own home, a small sanctuary he'd created for himself in a city thousands of miles from the town where he'd been born. It had also been a fixer-upper, or he would never have been able to afford the house on his modest salary.

"Well, that's convenient," Rosemary remarked. "At least I sort of know the area, although I haven't done as much exploring in Pasadena as I've wanted to. It seems like most of the time I'm just shuttling back and forth between Michael's place and the store in Glendora."

"I'd like to see your store sometime," Will said. "I always enjoy exploring a new bookstore."

Her mouth lifted in a faint smile. "Then you'll have to come over so I can give you the nickel tour. And that's all it would be—the shop isn't very big."

"I like small bookstores," he replied. "They're cozier."

She didn't quite shake her head, but he got the impression she thought he was only saying that so she would know he'd never judge her by how big or impressive her business was. He'd been telling her the truth, however; he found smaller bookstores to be more carefully curated, and he had a feeling that Rosemary and her sisters had done a very good job of choosing the selections offered in their shop.

Actually, though, what he really could tell was that they were both making small talk because neither one of them wanted to address what had happened between them in his office at All Saints, a kiss that had forever changed how they felt about each other. Or at least, Will knew that things between them had shifted, that there was a *then* forever separated from *now,* and they'd have to decide for themselves what they wanted to do from here on out. He knew what he wanted, but, despite what Rosemary said back in his hospital room, he still wasn't entirely sure how she regarded the current situation.

Or maybe he was misreading her utterly, and she was skating along the surface of things because she didn't want to address the other elephant in the room, the one involving the *Project Demon Hunters* footage, now in the hands of the enemy. It felt strange to think of matters in such stark black-and-white terms, since Will had always counseled trying to see the good in people, to do one's best to understand why a certain individual might believe or act in a certain way, and yet the enemy here wasn't simply someone whose political or spiritual beliefs were diametrically opposed to his, but a man who had the blood of demons running through his veins. The fallen angels who inhabited Hell had been adversaries of mankind from the very beginning, and were the real enemies of anyone who followed the path of the light.

Because they were enemies, and of a race utterly inimical to humankind, he didn't quite know what Caleb—and, by extension, his half-demon father—would even do with the footage now that it was in their possession. Possibly, it had already been destroyed. Or were they holding on to it because they thought it would in some way advance their cause? But that didn't seem very plausible, since the footage only documented that demons were real…therefore proving that Heaven and Hell were also real, and God as well. It was hard to see how confirming the existence of God could ever help the demons.

Will's head hurt too much to ponder that particular conundrum right then. Since Rosemary seemed content to let their conversation peter out, he sat quietly in the passenger seat and watched as she guided the Challenger off the 210 Freeway and onto Lake Avenue, then north toward the neighborhood of historic homes where his house was located.

After she turned left on Wilson, he said, "It's number 1102—up there on the right. The white house with the green trim. Just pull into the driveway."

She followed his instructions and parked in a location where he could open his door and emerge right next to the walkway that led to the front door. "Hang on," she said as she shut off the engine. "I'll come around and help you out."

Although he disliked the idea of being so incapacitated that he couldn't even get out of the car by himself, Will knew she was right to be careful. He'd already jarred his brain enough for one day —a single slip, and he could be right back in the hospital.

So, he sat and waited while she got out and locked the door behind her, then came over to the passenger side of the car and extended a hand so he could steady himself as he rose from his seat. Her fingers felt impossibly slender against his, but he found himself surprised by her strength as he leaned on her arm while she locked the passenger door as well before slowly guiding him up the path to the front of the house.

Never before had the stairs that led from the yard to the porch seemed so tall. Leaning heavily on Rosemary's arm, Will took each step with exaggerated care, until at last they'd reached the front door. Once there, he reached with his free hand to get the house keys out of his pocket. With some dismay, he realized how badly he was shaking—he couldn't seem to get the key in the lock.

"Let me," Rosemary offered, and she gently took the keys from his trembling fingers, making sure to keep the proper one extended, and inserted it in the lock. The door swung inward, and she helped him stumble across the threshold and into the cramped entryway.

Thank God his home had only the single story. When he'd bought it, he'd wished he could have afforded something bigger, but now he was glad that the small three-bedroom house didn't have any stairs. He doubted he would have been able to climb them in his current state.

"Your room?" she asked, her gaze not quite meeting his. Well, he could understand how she might feel a little awkward about taking him to his bedroom. It was a place he would have liked to end up with her at some point, although he couldn't have guessed that her first look at the room would involve her playing nursemaid.

He wouldn't sigh. Things happened, and he'd get past this.

"Down at the end of the hall."

She helped him through the living room along the hallway in question, and on into his bedroom. A brief pause as she reached for the light switch next to the door, and then they traversed the last few steps to the bed. Although he doubted she would have cared, not with much more important matters claiming her attention, Will was still glad that he'd performed his usual morning ritual of making the bed and putting away his dirty clothes, and that everything looked tidy enough. If you looked closely, you could see a faint layer of dust on the mismatched antique furniture, just because things had been crazy at All Saints lately and he hadn't had much time for cleaning, but at least the place wasn't a complete pigsty.

Another pause as she reached with her free hand to pull down the bedclothes, and then she turned to look up at him. "Do you need help getting your shoes off?"

While he hated to admit it, Will knew he probably did. Just the thought of having to bend over and undo the black lace-ups he wore made another stab of pain go through his head. "If you don't mind."

She shot him a dazzling—but brief—smile. "If I minded, I wouldn't have asked. Go ahead and sit down, and I'll take them off for you."

He went ahead and carefully lowered himself onto the bed, and then she knelt down and untied his shoes and set them on the rug. For a minute, he wondered if she was going to ask whether he needed help getting out of his clothes as well— and what he would do if she did—but apparently she'd decided that the shoes had been enough, because she straightened and reached over to fluff up his pillows.

"It's better if you stay sitting up," she told him. "How does that work?"

While he understood the wisdom of not having him lie on his back, he wasn't sure how comfortable the setup would be. However, once he'd gingerly scooted backward and leaned against the pile of pillows, he found it more relaxing than he'd thought. Also, his head didn't hurt as much in this position. "Seems comfortable enough."

"Good." She hesitated, then said, "How about some tea? Do you have any in the kitchen?"

He did, because he tended to switch over to tea after he'd had his morning cup of coffee. "Yes, there are some boxes in the pantry. That's where you'll find the coffee, too."

The mention of coffee made her appear a little more relaxed. "Thanks. I'll probably need it to stay awake."

She'd made the comment in the most neutral of tones, and yet he couldn't help but experience a small stab of guilt. Her day had been even more harrowing than his, and now she would have to stay up all night to make sure he didn't sleep for longer than an hour or so at a time.

"I'm sorry—" he began, and she shook her head.

"Don't," she said. To his surprise, she bent down and kissed him very gently on the forehead. "I'm doing this because I want to. It's the least I can do, after you put yourself in harm's way on my account. Just hang on for a few minutes—and I'll be back with some tea."

Another kiss, and then she was out of the room. A minute or two later, he heard her opening and closing a couple of cabinets, and then the sound of water running as she filled up the teakettle.

Even though his head hurt and he was starting to notice a whole host of other aches and pains, probably from taking such a hard fall on a wooden floor, Will couldn't help smiling a little at the mental image of Rosemary bustling around the kitchen, getting the kettle going. It wasn't so difficult to imagine the two of them in there together, making a meal or possibly cracking open a bottle of wine as they discussed what had happened to each of them that day at work. A certain warmth filled him at that pleasant daydream, a realization that he wanted such a scenario to be much more than just a fantasy.

He was getting way ahead of himself, he knew. That she'd kissed him again—even though those had both been very chaste, very delicate kisses—seemed to indicate she didn't think she'd made a mistake, that she wanted him to know she also welcomed this new closeness between them. Even so, it was a big leap from a few kisses to imagining a life shared together.

Still, he wanted his thoughts to settle there for a time. It comforted him to think they might have a future.

All they had to do was make sure the demons didn't get in the way of that future.

It was a little weird to be in Will's kitchen without him, to have to poke around in the cupboards without any guidance as she looked for some mugs for their respective cups of tea and coffee. But everything was laid out logically enough, and the kitchen seemed remarkably neat for a man who obviously lived on his own. The only thing out of place had been a plate and a mug sitting in the sink, probably set there when he'd left in the morning, so many hours ago now. The tidiness made her feel more comfortable poking around in the kitchen; if the place had been messy, she would have been jangly, even more on edge than she already was. Obviously, Will wasn't the kind of guy you'd have to nag to make sure he didn't throw his socks on the floor.

As she was waiting for the kettle to boil, she rinsed off the mug and its matching plate, and put them both in the dishwasher. The appliance seemed newish, as did the gas range and the refrigerator, as if Will had replaced all of them a few years ago. Actually, although she guessed the house had to be at least a hundred years old, it looked as if the kitchen had been updated in the recent past, with butcher-block countertops and the cupboards painted sage green with a friendly weathered faux finish. Despite her jangling nerves, something about the space felt soothing, and she could feel herself begin to relax.

Not too much, though. She wasn't sure they were safe here the way they would have been at Michael's house, since she had no idea whether Will had any demon-repelling wards in place like

Michael did. Or maybe the house was somehow sanctified because a minister lived here.

No, that was silly. This house wasn't holy ground the way a church would be. Even so, she knew the knot of tension at the back of her neck had begun to ease itself once she was here at Will's house and away from the hospital—although she jumped a little when the kettle began to boil, the noise startling her out of her reverie.

She'd decided to make Will some peppermint tea, since she wasn't sure whether caffeine would be a good idea. The fragrant aroma as the tea steeped made the room seem that much more homey, although it was soon overridden by the heavier scent of the brew she had going in the no-frills Mr. Coffee machine that sat on the counter.

Soon enough, both the coffee and the tea were ready, and she carried the mugs—Fiestaware in cheerful shades of tangerine for the coffee and turquoise for Will's tea—back with her to his bedroom. His eyes were closed as she entered the room, and she wondered if he'd fallen asleep already, but he opened them at the sound of her footsteps on the wooden floor.

"That smells good," he said. His voice seemed a little stronger now, possibly because he sat in his own bed and didn't have to expend any more energy than was strictly necessary.

Rosemary thought that must be a good sign.

Yes, they'd need to be careful for the next twenty-four hours, but Will was a strong man in good shape, and he clearly was already beginning to bounce back from Caleb's attack. "I made you peppermint tea. I hope that's okay."

"It's perfect. Thank you."

He took the mug from her and allowed himself a careful sip. Rosemary spied a coaster on the nightstand and set her coffee down on it, then went across the room to fetch a side chair that had been placed near the window. After bringing the chair over to Will's bedside, she sat down and lifted the mug of coffee. It was still almost too hot to drink, but she blew on it a few times and took a very small sip. Strong and black and bitter—and yet still better than that crap she'd gotten from the vending machine at the hospital.

"How do you feel?" she asked.

His mouth quirked a little. "Like someone backed my car over me a few times. But I'll live."

And thank God—or whoever was running things—for that. A few more inches to the left, and he would have cracked his head against the wall as he went down instead of merely slamming it into the floor. Just pure dumb luck; she had a feeling Caleb hadn't exactly been pulling his punches…or his glowing balls of fire, more to the point.

"Good," she said, trying her best to sound

casual. "I was kind of hoping you'd stick around for a while longer."

Will smiled and sipped again at his peppermint tea. "That's my plan." His expression sobered almost immediately, though, and he asked, "What happened back there?"

Rosemary knew he wasn't talking about the hospital. "We don't need to talk about that right now. You should rest."

"I am resting. But I want to know what happened. How did you manage to get us away from Caleb Lockwood?"

It was strange to hear Will using that last name, although it was the correct one. *Not as strange as having to remind myself that Caleb isn't even completely human,* she thought, and drank some more of her coffee. In a way, it was good that the brew was so bitter, because that was pretty much how she felt whenever she thought of the man who'd tried to insinuate himself into her life. What an idiot she'd been, falling for his facile charm.

But because Will was looking at her expectantly, she realized she needed to tell him something. Yes, he should be resting and not taxing his brain, but he'd probably be more agitated by a mystery he couldn't quite figure out than by hearing the actual truth. Problem was, she didn't know for sure exactly *what* had happened. She'd tapped into a power she didn't even know she possessed, but how she'd managed to do such a thing, she couldn't begin to guess. The whole situation still unnerved her, since she had absolutely no idea when those powers might decide to flare up out of nowhere. True, they'd only appeared when she and Will had been directly threatened, but....

One more swallow of over-caffeinated rocket fuel, and she set her mug of coffee back down on its coaster. "Caleb threw a ball of fire or something at you, and you were knocked out when you fell and hit your head against the floor. Do you remember any of that?"

Will shook his head. "The last thing I remember is Caleb dropping out of the crawlspace."

It wasn't terribly strange to lose a few of the minutes that immediately preceded a traumatic head injury. Still, Rosemary couldn't help feeling a little dismayed that he didn't recall how he'd confronted Caleb and asked him to hand over the hard drive, or the way he'd tried to take out the part-demon by using a slick *tae kwon do* maneuver on him. But none of that was terribly important. She hoped those memories would return in time, and if they didn't, well, she'd fill in the blanks at that point.

Instead, she told him how his fall had

knocked him out, how Caleb had wrested the hard drive away from her by using those same flames to torture her.

"I honestly think he was going to kill us both," she said. "Which I suppose would be the logical thing to do—for someone like him, anyway. But I...stopped him."

Will's brows pulled together in a frown, and then he seemed to wince, as if the movement pained him. He swallowed some tea and then said, "How? By appealing to his better nature?"

Her mouth twisted. "I don't think he has one. No, it was something I did—he tried to send those flames of his against us, and I—well, I don't know how I made it happen, exactly, only that I created some kind of shield that surrounded both of us, and Caleb's flames just bounced right off. After a second attempt, he realized he wasn't going to succeed, and so he disappeared."

"Into thin air?"

"Basically." Thinking about it now, Rosemary realized how surreal that moment had been. Yes, Caleb throwing fireballs had been weird enough, but there had been something even stranger about watching him vanish right before her eyes. That was the sort of thing you expected to see in a movie or a TV show, not with someone who occupied the same room as you. As she recalled, there had even been a weird little popping noise when he disappeared, as if the air itself had rushed in to fill the void he'd left behind. "And as soon as he was gone, I called 911."

A silence then as Will appeared to process what she'd just told him. He sipped from his mug of tea, then said, "You've never shown any sign of that kind of ability before?"

"No," she replied immediately. That was one thing she was sure about, even if the rest of her world currently felt as though it had begun to operate at right angles to reality. "I'm a psychic, but that just means I get feelings about things, or sometimes have dreams that come true." *Or talk to ghosts,* she added mentally, although she didn't know whether Colin's dead girlfriend had appeared to her because she was psychic, or simply because Madeline had known that Rosemary and Caleb were searching for Colin's footage. "I've never had any sign of telekinetic ability, or whatever you want to call what I did back at that house. It wasn't even conscious. It just sort of came from…nowhere."

"Not from nowhere," Will said, and she lifted an eyebrow. "It came from within you, because you were under duress and some part of you knew you had the means to protect me, to protect yourself. Sort of the psychic equivalent of a mother suddenly having the strength to lift a car off her young child."

Rosemary hadn't really thought of the strange manifestation in those terms, but she could see what he was saying. And in a way, she found herself comforted by the comparison. It was nothing freakish, only her innate abilities analyzing the situation and coming up with a way to make sure both she and Will survived Caleb's attack.

"Well, it definitely surprised Caleb," she said, keeping her tone deliberately light. "I'm sure he thought I was defenseless."

"His own fault for underestimating you," Will remarked, and a little flush of happiness went through her. Yes, he was lying there looking far too pale, and with shadows under his remarkable eyes that she didn't like at all, but she saw a warmth in his expression that was impossible to ignore. "I'm sure you gave him a nasty shock."

"I hope so." She reached over and took Will's hand, was glad to have him gently squeeze her fingers. It felt so good to have even this small bit of contact; it reassured her that he really was okay and that she hadn't lost him. "Serves him right for being such a jackass. But even though I surprised him, he still came out ahead in that encounter, since he has the hard drive and we don't."

A small breath escaped Will's lips. "I know. But losing one battle isn't the same thing as losing the war."

Her fingers tightened on his. Part of her didn't want to ask the question, but the words escaped her lips anyway. "Are you saying this is a war?"

Another breath, and his black lashes swept down against his cheeks as he shut his eyes. "Yes, Rosemary. The same war we've been fighting for millennia."

And since she honestly didn't know how to respond to that statement, she only clung to his hand and sat there in silence, wondering what in the world they were going to do now that the footage was in the hands of the demons.

They needed to save it…but she had absolutely no idea how.

Chapter 3

SOON AFTERWARD, ROSEMARY TOLD WILL HE needed to rest. His comment about being at war had disturbed her more than she wanted to admit, although she knew he'd only been trying to be truthful, had wanted to make sure she knew what they were up against. Which she supposed was the right thing to do, except that she had so little experience with this sort of thing. Michael and Will had been fighting the forces of darkness for years; she was late to the game and finding she didn't like it very much.

Once Will was asleep—she knew he slept because the rhythm of his breathing changed, and something very close to a snore escaped his nose —Rosemary got her purse, which she'd slung over the back of the chair where she'd been sitting, and retrieved her phone. By that time, it was past ten o'clock, both in California and Arizona, since the time zones wouldn't be out of sync until California went back on standard time in a few more weeks, and she knew Michael and Audrey had to be worried. Yes, she'd texted Michael to let him know she'd reached All Saints safely, but it had been crazy ever since then, and she hadn't had a chance to reach out and tell him what had happened.

A few more swallows of coffee to give her some much-needed energy, and then she composed an extremely long, detailed text message—so long, it got broken up into three separate texts as she wrote—explaining to Michael what had occurred earlier that evening, that Will was all right but Caleb had gotten away with the hard drive. She also let Michael know that she'd had to talk to the police but had managed to avoid giving away any information that might connect Caleb to Will's assault.

That project took around fifteen minutes, and the few swallows of coffee left in her mug were cold by the time she was done. She took a long look at Will, reassured herself that he was sleeping peacefully and should be okay for a few minutes, and then got up from her chair and headed into the kitchen to pour herself some more of that witch's brew. As she was taking another sip, her phone *binged*.

We're glad you're all right, Michael texted back. *Try to keep the police out of it as much as possible. If they start poking around, this could get a lot more complicated than it already is.*

Which was pretty much what Rosemary had already guessed, although she was glad that she and Michael were on the same page where the authorities were concerned. *I will,* she wrote. *I have to meet the detective tomorrow, and I know he's going to want to talk to Will, but by then we'll have had a chance to get our stories straight. It'll be fine.*

Good. I assume Caleb didn't leave much evidence behind.

As she recalled that horrible scene in the hallway of Colin Turner's Glendale house, Rosemary realized that the demonic flames Caleb had summoned only seemed to affect living tissue—they hadn't left any scorch marks behind on either the walls or the floor. That was a relief, because she knew otherwise she probably would have had a difficult time explaining to Detective Phillips how the walls in that particular section of the house looked as though someone had been shooting off a flamethrower in there.

I don't think so, she replied. *Maybe he left some fingerprints on the crawlspace access panel, but I don't see why they'd be checking up there.*

Did you leave it open?

She shut her eyes, envisioning the scene, and remembered that the rectangle of sheetrock had still been propped up against the wall when she'd called for an ambulance. Even if she'd been thinking clearly and had realized that the section of sheetrock needed to be replaced before someone noticed, there wasn't anything she could have done about it at the time, since she was far too short to reach the ceiling without a ladder.

Yes, I think it's still open, she texted Michael.

You need to make sure it's back in place before the police come by to look at the interior of the house, because they'll be sure to check the crawl-space panel for fingerprints or other physical evidence if they see that it's been tampered with. Do you know when they're planning to inspect the place?

Sometime tomorrow, she responded. *Detective Phillips said he'd be in contact, but he didn't give me a specific time.*

That gives you some flexibility. Take care of it before you contact him.

How nice of Michael to be giving orders from five hundred miles away. Rosemary scowled at her phone's screen in irritation, although she knew he was only trying to make sure the police wouldn't be able to find any trace of Caleb Lockwood in that house.

All right, she texted back. *I'll take care of it. No worries.*

Okay, Michael replied. *I'm worried enough for the both of us. Let me know how it goes tomorrow.*

I will.

That seemed to be that. Rosemary returned her phone to her purse and sent an anxious glance in Will's direction, but he seemed to have slept through her convo with Michael. Good. She'd need to wake him up at some point, but he'd only been asleep for about twenty minutes, so he had some ways to go.

In the meantime, she needed to figure out how in the world she could get herself over to the Glendale house so she could take care of that damn crawlspace. If Will had been in any better shape, she would have woken him up and brought him along with her, even if all he did was wait in the car while she worked. However, she knew he shouldn't be moved—he needed to rest and give his body time to heal from the trauma it had suffered.

She didn't dare leave him alone, however. Maybe there was someone at his church who would have come to his house to keep watch over him, no questions asked, but she knew absolutely nothing about his social circle there, whether he was particularly close with the staff at All Saints or possibly with certain members of his congregation.

No, she realized there was really only one person she could trust to come and look after Will during the hour or so she would be gone, someone who was utterly reliable and wouldn't ask too many awkward questions...she hoped.

In a situation like this, a girl needed to call her mother.

Will opened his eyes, thinking that he'd heard muffled female voices from somewhere within the shadowy depths of sleep. No dreams had haunted him, which was probably a good thing; he doubted he would be dreaming of anything good after the evening he'd had.

Then again, there had been that kiss with Rosemary...and the gentle kisses she'd given him right before he fell asleep.

In the next moment, though, he found himself blinking, because that was definitely not Rosemary sitting in the chair by his bedside. Oh, she looked a great deal like her, had the same curly chestnut hair and blue eyes, but the woman keeping watch over him now was definitely older, probably in her late fifties or early sixties, although the soft light from the lamp on the dresser across the room smoothed away some of the lines in her face.

"Good," the woman said. "I was just about to wake you, since it's been an hour."

"Who're you?" Will asked, although he thought he could already guess at the answer. However, the "who" in this equation didn't bother him as much as the "why."

"I'm Glynis McGuire, Rosemary's mother," the woman replied. "Rosemary had to run out for a bit and didn't want to leave you alone, so I said I'd come over and keep watch while she was gone. I live over in Sierra Madre," she added, as if she felt she needed to reassure him that it hadn't been any trouble for her to pop over to Pasadena and babysit a complete stranger.

He pushed himself upright and noticed that his head didn't hurt as much during that small exertion as he'd feared it would. Maybe he was bouncing back from the injury more quickly than he'd hoped. After reaching over for his now-cold peppermint tea and taking a sip, he said, "Where did Rosemary go?"

"To the house in Glendale," Glynis responded.

Worry stabbed through him, and he had to quell the impulse to push himself out of bed and chase after her. Even as the thought went through his head, he knew he was in no shape to go running off to Glendale—and besides, she'd probably taken his car, since her own little Fiat was presumably still parked in the structure near All Saints where she'd left it earlier that evening. "Why would she do that? It's not safe."

Glynis shook her head. If she was worried for her daughter, she didn't show any sign of it. However, her next words belied her calm appearance, because she said, "I tried to tell her that as well—at least, that's what I said after she explained to me what was going on, what had happened earlier tonight. But she said both she and Michael Covenant agreed that Caleb had already taken the thing he needed from the house, so there was no reason for him to be anywhere near the place."

"She talked to Michael?" Now Will's head felt as if it had begun to swim, although he guessed that was probably more because he had a sense of missing out on a great deal while he was asleep, despite being out of it for less than an hour.

"She texted him," Glynis said. "And they were both worried that the police might find some sign of your encounter with Caleb, so she went back to clean up the evidence."

"And you're all right with that?"

A rueful little smile tugged at Glynis's lips, still full and pretty, just like her daughter's. "Rosemary is an adult, Will. I can't exactly command her to stop doing something just because I don't approve of it. Besides, this is an extraordinary case. If Caleb is really who...*what*...Rosemary says he is, then I have to agree that it's probably a good idea to make sure the authorities don't get involved. At least, not any more than they already are."

"Oh, he's definitely what she says he is," Will said grimly. "I saw him use his powers. No human being could have done what he did back at that house."

"So, we're agreed."

He wouldn't go so far as to say that, but he had to admit Rosemary had done the right thing by reaching out to her mother. She would keep this secret, and any others as necessary, because she didn't want her daughter to get in trouble.

"You seem very calm about all this," he remarked, and Glynis gave an eloquent lift of her shoulders.

"Well, I'm psychic, just like my daughters, so I've seen more than my share of odd things. When dealing with the supernatural, it's often best to confront things squarely rather than try to run away from them, just because the more you try to avoid something, the more it makes sure to hunt you down and force you to acknowledge it."

Her voice and expression were still serene, and Will wondered what it was in her life that had brought her to this quiet acceptance of strange forces at work in the world. While he wanted to ask, he knew doing so wouldn't be appropriate. They were strangers to one another, almost as much as he was with Rosemary. Oh, they'd revealed a little of themselves, but there was still so much he didn't know about her…almost everything, if he wanted to admit it to himself. He knew she had two sisters and co-owned a bookstore with them, and that she had a house of her own in Glendora, one she'd happily moved out of on a temporary basis while the home next to hers was being renovated. But while he could guess that her parents were divorced—he didn't see a ring on Glynis's left hand, although he knew not all women wore wedding rings—the rest of her life before their orbits had intersected might as well be a complete blank.

Something he'd have to rectify in the very near future…if he was given the chance.

"Let me get you some more tea," Glynis said, now sounding much brisker. She got up from the chair and reached for the mug at his bedside. "Would you like anything else? Are you hungry?"

Maybe he should have been, since it had been hours and hours since the sandwich he'd hastily eaten before the Adult Children of Alcoholics meeting he'd hosted at All Saints earlier that evening, but his stomach turned over at the thought of putting anything solid in it. He shook his head. "No, thank you. Tea is fine."

She smiled at him and left the room, while he looked down at himself and reflected it was a good thing that he still wore his untucked shirt and trousers, rather than his usual bedtime attire of underwear and nothing else. Rosemary hadn't asked him if he wanted to change into something more comfortable, probably because she would have been embarrassed to help him out of his clothes at this early stage in their relationship.

Doing such a thing would have been just a little mortifying for him, too. He kept in shape, had a weight set in the spare bedroom and tried to run a few miles most mornings, but still, there was generally a point where he was comfortable getting undressed in front of a woman, and he knew he definitely wasn't there with Rosemary yet.

For a minute, Will lay in bed and did his best to gauge whether or not he was ready to get up and scrounge a T-shirt and a pair of sweatpants from the dresser. It wasn't that far, only a few steps, but…probably better to stay where he was. Since his shirt wasn't tucked in and his belt still resided in the little bag of personal belongings the hospital had sent home with him, he was comfortable enough for now. Besides, he had much more to be worried about than what he was wearing. He couldn't prevent his mind from dwelling on the image of Rosemary in Colin's former home, all by herself in a dark and empty house. True, the power was still on and the neighbors were close enough if anything went wrong, but really, what could neighbors do if Caleb Lockwood decided to swing back around and take another look at the place just to make sure there wasn't something he might have missed?

The mere thought of such a prospect made cold fear inch its way down Will's spine.

"It's fine," Glynis McGuire said, startling him as she reentered the room. She set a mug of fresh tea down on the nightstand and then resumed her seat in the chair at his bedside. "Rosemary just texted me to say she was at the house and everything is quiet over there. She'll be done soon enough and on her way back here."

"That's good news," Will replied, although he couldn't quite prevent himself from wondering exactly how long things would remain quiet over in Glendale. If it had even been Rosemary who'd sent the text in the first place. What if Caleb was there, had overpowered her and then taken her phone to send a reassuring text that all was well?

He must have been telegraphing his thoughts —or maybe she simply found his face easy to read —because Glynis leaned over and patted him on the arm. The gesture reminded him so much of something his own mother might have done in a similar situation, he couldn't quite prevent himself from giving her a rueful grin.

"Sorry," he said. "I should probably stop conjuring worst-case scenarios."

"I think that's understandable, given the situation," she said, blue eyes kind but troubled. "Have some tea, and then see if you can sleep again for a bit. If you're asleep, the time will go faster."

And he wouldn't be torturing himself with everything that might go wrong, although he supposed those fears might insinuate themselves into his dreams. Still, he thought Glynis had a point. He drank some tea—it was warm but not piping hot, leading him to believe she'd hadn't bothered to reheat the water in the kettle, had only poured out what was left over from when Rosemary had boiled it an hour or so earlier—and then made himself settle against the pillows and close his eyes. Maybe it was a little awkward to have Glynis there watching him, but she was a mother three times over; no doubt, she'd spent plenty of nights at bedsides before, watching over a sick child. He wasn't her son, of course, and yet he could tell she cared that he'd been injured and wanted to make sure he healed as quickly as possible.

He needed to do that. He needed to get himself back together as soon as he could...

because he had a feeling he was going to need all his strength in the very near future.

Rosemary turned on every light in the house. Ostensibly, this was so she wouldn't miss anything out of place, would make sure to erase every possible hint of Caleb's presence there, but she knew it was really so she wouldn't jump at every shadow, every faint noise.

Because it was creepy to be there. Maybe the prickly, crawling sensation along the back of her neck arose from the simple fact that both the people who'd once lived in this house and called it their home were now dead, or maybe it was the uncomfortable realization that Caleb Lockwood didn't need a key to come and go here, could just pop up right in front of her as she rounded a corner.

Part of her had been worried that Detective Phillips might have come by with a forensics team to check out the place despite agreeing to meet her at the property the next day, but the house looked undisturbed. Rosemary didn't know enough about police procedure to know whether that was normal or not; maybe the case didn't have super-high priority because Will had more or less walked out of the hospital under his own power, and nothing had been stolen from the house. It was still assault and battery, but could they really call it a robbery when she claimed the intruder hadn't taken anything?

She supposed the detective would illuminate some of those finer points when they met. For the moment, though, she had work to do.

As she'd told Michael, the piece of sheetrock that had covered the entry to the crawlspace was still propped up against the wall in the hallway. She looked all around, double-checking to make sure there really weren't any signs of the supernatural flames Caleb had summoned to attack her and Will, but the walls were smooth and bare, unmarked except for a few minor scuff marks that she guessed had been left behind by the tenants who'd recently vacated the place. It really did seem that the only thing she needed to do was get that sheetrock back in place and then hurry back to Pasadena.

She headed out to the garage, vaguely remembering that it hadn't been quite as empty as the rest of the house. There'd been a ladder, hadn't there, leaning against the garage wall next to the built-in storage cabinets?

Apparently, her mind had been playing tricks on her, though, because she didn't find anything as useful as a ladder, only some cans of paint and several boxes of unused floorboards, clearly left over from the time when Colin and Madeline had updated the house. Rosemary poked though the cupboards, hoping for maybe a folding chair or even a sturdy plastic box, something that would give her the extra boost she needed to reach the hallway ceiling.

Not a damn thing, though.

Scowling, she went back inside the house and inspected all the rooms, just to be sure she hadn't overlooked something. But the tenants who'd lived here last had done a good job of clearing out all their belongings, and the place was completely empty.

"Well, shit," Rosemary muttered, and stalked out to the hall, where she stared balefully up at the dark hole in the ceiling. It looked like a mouth to her, a gaping, hungry maw that would be all too happy to swallow her whole.

Which she knew was silly. It was just an opening to allow access to the home's ducting, no more, no less. And while she thought she could be excused for allowing her imagination to run away with her, she knew she was alone here. There hadn't been even the faintest hint of anyone else around, especially not the part-demon villain that Caleb had turned out to be.

She reached in her purse and got out her phone to check the time. A little after ten. Not even the local Walmart was probably open at that hour, and it wasn't exactly a good time to knock on a neighbor's door and ask if she could borrow a stepladder. If she'd been thinking a little more clearly, she would have gone out to Will's garage and poked around there to see if she could find a ladder to take with her, but she'd had that false memory of spying one here and hadn't thought such measures were necessary.

Well, the joke was on her.

If worse came to worst, she'd just drive back to Pasadena and get a ladder from Will's house—or from Michael's; she knew there was one tucked away in the far corner of the garage at the house where she'd been staying. However, she really hated the idea of wasting that much time and being away from Will for that long, although she knew he was perfectly safe with her mother watching over him.

Once again, her gaze settled on the rectangle of sheetrock leaning innocently up against the wall. Too bad she couldn't just snap her fingers and have it magically sail through the air and settle back in place.

Except....

The idea that flashed through her head was so ludicrous, she actually chuckled at herself for entertaining the notion at all. But for some reason, it refused to go away.

What if she *could?*

All right, maybe not snap her fingers, but only a few hours earlier in this very hallway, she'd somehow managed to summon a shield that had protected her and Will from the onslaught of Caleb's demonic magic. If she was able to do that, who knew what else she was capable of?

Besides, no one was here to see her fail. If this didn't work—and she was pretty sure it wouldn't —she could laugh at herself, get in the car, and see if there was a twenty-four-hour Home Depot somewhere nearby, or, failing that, go back to Michael's house and fetch the ladder there.

All right, then.

Rosemary planted her hands on her hips and stared at the piece of sheetrock, willing it to rise into the air and settle itself back in place. Of course, it just sat there.

"You're going to feel really stupid about this tomorrow," she muttered to herself, and then squinted and tried again.

Still nothing.

She knew she should probably just give up and get out of there before she wasted any more time. Then again, maybe she was taking the wrong approach.

Feeling more ridiculous than ever, she raised a hand, pointing it toward the sheetrock. "Use the Force, Luke," she murmured, and couldn't quite hold back a nervous chuckle.

Only…were her eyes deceiving her, or had the recalcitrant piece of plasterboard just moved ever so slightly?

She supposed it could have been a trick of the light, although the hallway was brightly illuminated by the overhead fixture and there wasn't much chance of her seeing something that wasn't there. The piece of sheetrock sure wasn't moving now, but maybe that was because she'd dropped her hand and wasn't focusing any longer.

Once again, she raised her hand. This time, though, she wasn't reminded so much of Luke Skywalker but a scene from a silly movie called *Mallrats* where one of the characters had basically imitated Luke in order to retrieve his own prop lightsaber. The joke there had been that the character reaching for the lightsaber in question was just an ordinary guy, and everyone in the audience had expected his efforts to be futile.

Except they hadn't been. He'd retrieved the damn lightsaber.

Move, damn you, she thought.

And there it was—much more than the brief shudder she thought she'd seen a few minutes earlier. This time, the piece of sheetrock shifted visibly and then began to slowly rise into the air.

Holy crap.

She couldn't lose focus now, though. Jaw clenched, Rosemary visualized the sheetrock drifting higher…higher…moving at just the perfect angle where it inserted itself into the opening in the ceiling and then settled in place.

Which was exactly what it did.

For a moment, she was so flabbergasted by what she'd done that she could only stand there and stare up at the opening to the crawlspace, no longer open at all. There was no sign that anyone had touched it, nothing that should make Detective Phillips believe it had been disturbed in any way.

Eventually, though, she realized she needed to get back to Will's house. There was no point in standing there and imitating a large-mouthed bass. Yes, this was the crazy cherry on top of a day that had been filled with craziness, but she could sort all that out later.

She walked through the house and shut off all the lights, and finally went out the front door and locked it behind her. Only when she was behind the wheel of Will's powerful car and back on the 134 Freeway headed east did the reaction really hit her. A shiver worked its way down her spine, and she clung to the steering wheel with tight, frightened fingers.

Because if she could make a piece of drywall float through the air and settle itself in position… what else was she capable of?

Chapter 4

HER MOTHER ANSWERED THE DOOR IN response to Rosemary's quiet knock, then quickly scanned her face. What she saw, Rosemary didn't know for sure. She'd done her best to compose herself on the drive home, but she had a feeling she hadn't been entirely successful. Her thoughts just didn't want to leave her alone, worrying at the problem of the strange way her powers kept increasing, stewing over what Caleb and his demon cohorts might be doing to the footage. Not knowing was always the worst.

To her relief, however, her mother only asked, "Everything went okay?"

"Just fine," Rosemary replied. On the drive back to Will's house, she'd decided not to mention the episode with the plasterboard to her mother. That would only open a whole other can of worms, and she was just too exhausted at that point to get into it. "No one was there. Like Michael said, Caleb got what he wanted and didn't have any reason to stick around."

A nod, but her mother's expression was still troubled. "Do you want to talk about that?"

"About what?" Rosemary said, although she knew exactly what her mother had meant with her question.

"About Caleb."

"Not really."

Her mother didn't respond, except for possibly the faintest lift of one eyebrow. "I made a fresh pot of coffee."

"Thanks." Rosemary headed toward the kitchen and set her purse down on the counter there. The space was filled with the warm scent of coffee, and she breathed it in as she went to fetch a mug for herself. Just the aroma was enough to make her feel a little more awake—or maybe she'd done that to herself, nerve endings thrilling from the strange new power she'd somehow awakened.

"I hope you don't blame yourself."

It figured that she wouldn't let it go. Rosemary knew her mother wasn't the type to nag or harp on topics that her daughters wanted to put behind them, but at the same time, she had a way of making damn sure you acknowledged a problem rather than simply sweeping it under a rug.

"I don't," Rosemary said. Well, that was a lie. She kept thinking there must have been some hint, some clue she'd overlooked, something that would have told her what she was dealing with in Caleb Lockwood. But no, she'd been so swept off her feet by his good looks and friendly, down-to-earth charm that she hadn't bothered to scrutinize him very closely. Also, some psychic she'd turned out to be—not even a ping of warning that Caleb wasn't all he seemed.

Then again, maybe he'd been using his own powers to make sure she wasn't able to pick up anything wrong about him.

Since her mother only sent her a very direct look, giving the lie right back to her, Rosemary knew she wasn't going to wriggle out of a discussion that easily. For a moment, she used pouring herself a cup of coffee as cover for her hesitation, but since Glynis knew her daughter hardly ever doctored her coffee, there was no point in fussing with cream and sugar—if Will even had any cream in the house.

"I was stupid," she said distinctly. "I shouldn't have taken Caleb at face value. I let myself get bowled over by him because I've been going through a bad patch lately."

Her mother folded her arms and kept gazing at her steadily. "I think you're being a little hard on yourself...especially since you seemed to realize early on that you also had an attraction to Will. When we talked the other day, you already appeared to have made up your mind which one of them you wanted to be with, even though you didn't want to admit it to yourself."

Well, that was true. Rosemary still didn't know whether it was an instinct deep within her that had recognized Caleb's "otherness" at some level she didn't quite want to acknowledge, or whether it was simply that she found herself far more attracted to Will physically, but when she'd left her mother's house on that Tuesday afternoon —a meeting that felt as though it had taken place a hundred years ago instead of only five days— she'd been in more mental turmoil than when she'd gotten there. She'd tried to act as though she was looking forward to seeing Caleb again, but she had been strangely ambivalent.

And now she knew why.

"How is Will?" she asked, deliberately changing the subject. No doubt she'd continue to beat herself up about her blindness regarding Caleb Lockwood, but she didn't see the point in continuing to hash it over with her mother.

"He's fine," Glynis replied. "I can tell he's in some pain, but honestly, he's doing extremely well, considering what he's been through. I made him some more peppermint tea, and he drank it and then went to sleep again."

That sounded reassuring, but Rosemary had to ask. "Not too long ago, I hope."

Her mother's mouth quirked a little. "Less than twenty minutes, so you don't need to worry about that." She paused before adding, "He seems like a very fine man. I like him."

"You do?" Not that any relationship she was in needed to be predicated on her mother's favor, but after screwing up so royally with Caleb, Rosemary figured it couldn't hurt to know that Will had Glynis's stamp of approval.

The twitch at the corners of her mother's lips turned into a full-blown smile. "Yes, I do. I can see why you were feeling so ambivalent about Caleb."

"And you don't think it's weird that he's an Episcopalian priest?"

"They don't take a vow of celibacy, do they?"

"*Mom!*"

Glynis chuckled. "Good to know I can still shock you occasionally. Why would I think it was weird?"

Rosemary swallowed some of the coffee her mother had made. It was better than Rosemary's batch; obviously, her mother knew her way around a Mr. Coffee a lot better than she did. "Well, we're not exactly what most people call Christian."

"Maybe not, but we've always believed in a

higher power of some sort, even if it isn't the one most Christians believe in." Her mother shrugged, and went over and poured some coffee for herself. "Honestly, I think it all goes back to the same place, when you get right down to it. The trappings don't matter."

Well, they mattered to a lot of people. Wars had been fought over those "trappings." However, Rosemary could see what her mother was driving at, and therefore didn't bother to argue. Besides, she'd been pretty blunt with Will about not being Christian, and he hadn't said a word about her lack of religion. If it didn't bother him, she supposed she shouldn't let it bother her.

"Point taken," she said. "But I should probably go check on Will." She glanced at the clock on the microwave: 10:55. It was going to be a very long night.

"You do that, sweetheart. I'll just finish my coffee and let myself out. Call me in the morning to let me know you're still both okay."

"I will." Rosemary set down her coffee, and went over and gave her mother a quick hug. "Thank you for looking after him. I didn't know who else to call."

Glynis returned the hug, squeezing her daughter for a few more seconds before she let go. "Oh, I'm sure Isabel would have come over and helped out if I wasn't available, but I'm glad I could do this for you. After all," she added with a small laugh, "this is probably the most excitement I've had on a Saturday night for a long time."

About all Rosemary could do was shake her head at her mother's self-deprecating comment. "Well, maybe that wouldn't be a problem if you signed up for one of those online dating services like Izzie and CeeCee and I have been bugging you about."

Glynis waved a hand. "Oh, I'm not that desperate. At this point, I'm set in my ways. I've got my house and my garden and the book club, and I don't need much more than that."

Rosemary wasn't so sure, but she knew better than to press the issue. Her mother had been alone for the greater part of seventeen years and had never shown any interest in remarrying or even dating, although Rosemary and her sisters had done their best to offer their own encouragement on the subject. On many occasions, she'd wondered if their mother was still so in love with their father—despite the way he'd walked out on his family—that she couldn't allow herself to think of being with anyone else.

Then again, maybe she was making the situation much more romantic than it actually was. Far more likely, Glynis had settled herself into a life that suited her and didn't see any need to complicate it with a man.

Well, Rosemary would be the first to admit that men could be complicated. On the other hand, she wasn't quite ready to give them up altogether. Speaking of which….

"I really should go and check on Will—"

"Go," her mother said, making a shooing gesture with her free hand. "Like I said, I'm going to finish my coffee and leave. I'll talk to you tomorrow."

Rosemary shot her a grateful smile and headed out of the kitchen, mug clutched in one hand. There would probably be many more to follow this one; it had been a long time since she'd pulled an all-nighter, and she knew she was going to need the caffeine. The last time she'd had to forego a night's sleep had probably been when she and her sisters were finishing up with preparations for the bookstore opening, and they'd stayed up all night stocking the shelves and doing the last little bits of prep because the painter they'd hired had flaked on them and they'd ended up having to do it all themselves. In an odd way, it had been fun, but she wouldn't have Isabel and Celeste here to help her stay awake. No, this time it was just her and Mr. Coffee.

When she entered Will's bedroom, she saw that he was asleep, head lolling to one side as he sat propped up against the pillows. Moving carefully, she went over to the chair and sat down, then took a sip of coffee. Before, it had felt awkward to sit here quietly and gaze at him, but now she was just glad she had the chance to do this for him, to be the person who would stand guard here during the dark watches of the night. There was something peaceful and quiet about this house, about the plain, mismatched antiques and the old wood floors and the faint scent of Murphy's oil soap that seemed to linger in the corners.

Or maybe she simply liked it because it was Will's house.

He moved then, eyelids fluttering, before his eyes opened fully and he focused on her. "You're back."

"Yes," she said. "Everything is fine. I'm sorry I left without saying anything, but you were asleep and I didn't want to wake you up."

That comment made him lift an eyebrow. "You're supposed to be waking me up."

"Not fifteen minutes after you've gone to sleep," she protested, although she knew she was probably being disingenuous. No, the truth was that she'd known if she told him what she needed to do, he would have done his best to dissuade her from going to the Glendale house. She hadn't wanted to get in an argument, and there was no one else who could have handled that particular little detail, not with Michael Covenant a whole state away from them. "Anyway, it was fine. The crawlspace is secured, and there isn't any other evidence of our confrontation with Caleb, so Detective Phillips is going to get a big ball of nothing when he comes over to take a look."

For some reason, Will didn't appear as relieved by this reassurance as she'd thought he would. His lips pressed together, and he said, "And you're sure there aren't any signs of forced entry?"

"Yes," she replied. At least that question had been easy enough to answer. Although she knew that Caleb must have entered the house the same way he exited it—i.e., by means of his inherited demonic powers—she'd still checked all the windows and doors, had made sure they were all still locked securely. Nothing had been disturbed. "I'm sure that will puzzle Detective Phillips, but since he won't be able to find any real evidence, he's going to probably realize pretty quickly that this is one case he won't be able to solve." At least, she hoped he would give it up once he realized he didn't have any leads to follow. Things were complicated enough with dragging the police into the whole mess.

"Let's hope." Will reached for his tea and sipped from the mug; Rosemary guessed the liquid inside must have been lukewarm by that point, even if her mother had made him a fresh cup. He didn't seem to mind, though. Expression thoughtful, he went on, "Did he say anything about interviewing me?"

Since she'd been expecting that question, it was easy enough to answer. "Yes, he wants to talk to you, but he said he was willing to wait until you felt up to it."

"I'd prefer to get it over with."

Rosemary could understand that. Much better to meet with the detective, offer a couple of not very helpful tidbits of information, and then get on with their lives. Still, a lot would depend on how Will felt in the morning. He seemed awake and aware now, even though he still looked far too pale, but she wasn't going to let him push himself too far.

"We'll see," she said, and drank some more of her coffee.

Apparently, he wasn't too thrilled with that non-answer, because he said, "I'm fine, Rosemary. I have a bump on my head and a good assortment of bruises forming, I'm sure, but there's no need to treat me like an invalid."

"That's not what the doctor told me," she returned. "He said I needed to keep a close eye on you."

"Which you are...except for your little jaunt over to Glendale." His eyes narrowed then, the distinctive crystalline gray almost obscured by his heavy dark lashes. "How did you manage to get the crawlspace sealed back up?"

There it was. She supposed she could have lied and told Will she'd found a ladder in the garage, but if they had any kind of chance of making this…whatever it was…between them work at all, she needed to be honest with him. Besides, what she'd done at the house frightened her, and she thought maybe she would feel better after she'd talked it over with him. Although she normally would have said she was doing just fine and didn't need anyone to hold her hand, she had to admit there was something infinitely reassuring about his presence, even when he wasn't operating at full strength, so to speak.

"I—" She hesitated and wrapped her fingers around her mug, taking a little comfort in the warmth that seeped through the heavy ceramic. For some reason, she suddenly felt cold, although Will's bedroom was certainly warm enough. "This is going to sound crazy."

His mouth lifted in a smile. "I think we've been through enough craziness lately that I'm pretty sure I can handle it."

Well, that was true enough. Ghosts…demons breathing green mist…the guy she'd been half-heartedly dating turning out to be not quite human…things had been sort of upside down this past week.

"There wasn't a ladder," she said quickly. "And I didn't know what to do, since the house was empty and there weren't any chairs or anything else I could stand on. So I…moved it myself. Like this."

She raised her hand in the same way she had back at the Glendale house, only without any intent behind the gesture. The last thing she wanted was to levitate his dresser or send the lamp on his bedside table flying through the air.

Will watched her, brow furrowed slightly. "You lifted it? Wasn't the ceiling too high?"

"It was. I lifted it with my mind."

His expression didn't change. "You're joking."

"No," she replied. She wished it was a joke. She wished things could go back to the way they'd been only an hour earlier, when she might have been psychic but didn't have crazy powers of telekinesis. "I've never done anything like that before. But somehow, I was able to do it tonight."

Will pushed himself a little more upright. A slight clenching of his jaw told her that the movement had probably hurt, but he didn't say anything, only continued to stare at her. At last, he said, "If you'd never done anything similar— never shown any signs of having powers like that —then why did you think you could do it?"

"Because—because I was feeling desperate!" Rosemary replied, guessing that she wasn't making a very good case for her story. "I guess I figured I could try, and then when it didn't work, I'd either try to find a hardware store open that late or just drive back to Pasadena and get the ladder out of Michael's garage. Only I didn't need to do that, because it *did* work. And I'm just a little freaked out about it."

"It's all right," he said quickly, as though realizing he needed to do his best to soothe her fears. "That is, you already knew you had powers beyond what most people possess, so it sounds as though you now have something a little extra in your toolkit. That's all."

He made it seem as though suddenly developing the ability to move things with her mind was no big deal. Then again, she'd been looking for some kind of reassurance from him, so it didn't make much sense to be angry with him for providing the comfort she needed.

"I'm not sure it's 'all,'" she said. "But…it does seem as if I have to really focus to make something happen. It's not like someone can make me angry and turn me into Carrie at the prom."

At that comment, he chuckled. "I have to say, that's a relief."

Was it strange that he should seem so unconcerned? Maybe that blow to the head had taken away his ability to be worried by strange phenomena. But no, Rosemary didn't think that was it.

Most likely, Will was doing his best to roll with the punches. And who knows—maybe he viewed her strange telekinetic ability as a gift from God, something that would help them prevail against the demons. She didn't quite see how, but she had to admit that was a much more reassuring way to look at the situation.

"For both of us," she agreed, then was quiet for a moment. A bracing sip of coffee, and another, and she realized she felt much better than she had when she'd come to Will's room a few moments earlier. Tone a little softer, she added, "You should probably try to go back to sleep."

His fingers played with the edge of the quilt that lay across his lap. "Easier said than done. My mind is going a mile a minute."

While she could understand why his thoughts might be racing, she knew he wasn't supposed to exert himself physically or mentally. "Well, try to tell your brain to take a breather. Do you meditate at all?"

"Actually, I do. And that's probably a good idea."

He shut his eyes then, and Rosemary saw how his breathing slowed slightly, how a certain tension appeared to leave his hands where he'd crossed them on top of his stomach. She didn't think he was asleep—not yet, anyway—but she thought he was allowing himself to slide down into slumber, quieting his mind and allowing the normal rhythms of his body to take over. Watching him, she experienced a brief stab of jealousy. Not that she wanted to be lying in bed with a concussion, but it would have been awfully nice to let herself go to sleep.

No such luck, however. A few more minutes passed, and then she was sure he slept. She realized she needed to text Michael to let him know how things had gone at the Glendale house, but she'd left her purse in the kitchen with her phone inside.

Once again, she got up with exaggerated care and tiptoed out of Will's bedroom, then headed down the hallway. Her mother must have left while Rosemary was talking to Will, because the kitchen was now empty, the mug Glynis had been using nowhere in sight, which meant it probably had been rinsed out and placed in the dishwasher.

Rosemary had already resolved not to say anything to Michael about her strange demonstration of telekinesis. She knew he would start asking her all sorts of questions, and she simply didn't have any answers for him at the moment. And for all she knew, both he and Audrey would pressure her to come to Tucson as soon as she was able so they could run tests on her or something. No, thanks.

Or maybe that was uncharitable of her. Right

then, she just felt tired, despite the coffee she'd already consumed that evening. Whether it would really be able to keep her awake might be a moot point.

But one way to stay awake was to keep busy. She retrieved her phone from her purse and was relieved to see that she hadn't missed any calls or texts. Not that she'd really expected to; her mother had just been here, and Celeste and Isabel probably didn't even know what was going on. Michael apparently was content to wait until she got back to him. And the call she'd been worried about the most—one from Detective Phillips asking to talk to Will now—hadn't materialized at all.

Hey, Michael, she texted, *the house is secured and Will is doing fine. With any luck, things will be quiet here for a while.*

She didn't get an immediate response, but she hadn't really expected one. After all, Michael couldn't have known exactly when she was going to be done with her errand, and he was most likely off doing something else. Maybe watching a movie with Audrey, or possibly getting ready for bed. Rosemary realized she didn't have a very clear idea of their daily schedule, although she'd gotten the impression that they weren't night owls. Well, that made sense, with Audrey working away on her Ph.D. She probably had to get up early most of the time.

Would Will mind if she rummaged around in the fridge or the cupboards? Rosemary realized she was hungry, although she couldn't help wondering if her sudden craving for a snack to nosh on stemmed more from a desire to do something to distract herself than because she really needed to eat.

She doubted he would care if she stole a few crackers or a carton of yogurt. At least, he didn't seem like the type of person to be selfish about such things.

Just as she was reaching for the handle on the refrigerator, however, her phone buzzed. She turned back to pick it up and saw a text from Michael.

That's good news. I'm glad everything went smoothly. No sign of C?

No, she replied. *It looks like he's gone for good…or bad, depending on how you look at it. Any ideas on where we can track him down?*

Working on it, Michael texted back. *All the Underhill trustees were in Indiana, so that could be where he went to ground. But you don't need to worry about that. You need to focus on Will's recovery.*

The subtext being that Michael didn't think she was up to the task of confronting the semi-demons in their lair, wherever that turned out to be. Of course, Audrey had made it sound as if the original trustees had set themselves up to appear like local pillars of society—bankers, lawyers, business owners—and so their "lair" might turn out to be the local country club.

To be honest, Rosemary didn't know whether she was up to that sort of thing, either. Besides, was there really any point in chasing after Caleb? From the way he'd been talking, he made it sound as though the demons didn't want that footage released, since proving the existence of demons meant also proving the existence of God, and that was something they'd really prefer to avoid. A populace strong in its belief in a Creator was a populace a lot more difficult to coerce or corrupt.

Then again, maybe the demons were going to hold off on destroying the evidence for the time being. Maybe they were trying to figure out if there was any benefit to releasing the footage, or at least certain portions of it, heavily doctored to have it work to their benefit rather than the reverse.

Hmm. Rosemary thought she might be on to something there. What if the Underhill demons—thanks to Caleb hanging around on indie film-maker Reddits or whatever—knew that there was a lot of interest in the *Project Demon Hunters* footage? Colin had been talking about it in places where he probably shouldn't, and maybe the plan was to re-edit the footage to make it look as though it was all obviously faked. That kind of maneuver would discredit Colin and also safely remove the threat of anyone thinking those demons were real.

All the more reason to get that footage before it was weaponized.

Her phone buzzed again. *You still there?*

Yes, she responded. *Sorry. I guess there isn't much else for me to do except wait to hear from the detective tomorrow.*

It'll be fine. I know you can't exactly rest, but try to take it easy. You've been through a lot.

"More than you know," she murmured to herself, but she only typed back, *Not as much as Will has. I'm good. I'll be in touch if anything changes.*

Have a good night.

Her phone went quiet after that, and she knew Michael had signed off for the evening. She went and slipped her cell into her purse, then slung the bag over her arm, intending to take it back with her to Will's room.

A blur of movement caught her eye, though, and she froze.

Madeline Nash's ghost stood at the far end of the kitchen, near the back door. She looked more transparent than Rosemary had ever seen her, was barely more than a wispy mist in the shape of a woman. The only solid thing about her was her eyes, which seemed like wells of darkness, impossibly deep.

For some reason, though, Rosemary wasn't afraid. She looked at the spirit and said quietly, "Colin's hard drive with the footage was in your house, but we were too late. The demons got it."

The ghost nodded. Her expression was too serene to be sad, although Rosemary got a sense of wistfulness from her. She spoke then, her voice a whisper so faint, Rosemary had to strain to hear it.

"You tried."

Yes, they had, and Will had ended up in the hospital because of their efforts. In this particular instance, though, she couldn't feel too great about telling herself that at least they'd done their best. This wasn't a football game.

Rosemary rubbed her brow and tried to convince herself that she really wasn't getting a headache. "Any words of wisdom?"

Madeline smiled. Or at least, her mouth curved upward, but she was so insubstantial that her expressions were getting almost impossible to read. "I did what I needed to. It's time for me to go."

"Do you have to?" Rosemary asked, worry stabbing through her. All right, the ghost of Madeline Nash hadn't exactly been the most reliable ally, but at least she'd done what she could to help. The thought of her being gone forever with so much still unresolved was not appealing at all.

"It's time." A pause, followed by a very faint whisper. "I'm not the only one who can help you."

And then she was gone. Rosemary took a step forward, hand outreached as though she thought she could somehow grab hold of the ghost and prevent her from leaving. But she was too late. Anyway, even if she had managed to get to Madeline in time, what was she supposed to hold on to? The other woman had been a ghost, no more substantial than the mist that sometimes hung around the foothills in the winter and early spring.

She stood there for a moment, staring at the spot where Madeline had disappeared.

I'm not the only one who can help you, she'd said. Maybe those words were supposed to be reassuring, but Rosemary had to wonder exactly what kind of "help" she meant.

Another ghost?

The ghost of whom?

There was no telling. Holding back a sigh, Rosemary took her purse and left the kitchen. Sudden fear made her hurry down the hallway to Will's room, but he was still sleeping peacefully, hands folded in his lap, eyes shut. She paused in the doorway and watched him for a long moment, a strange, unexpected tenderness stirring within her.

She had no idea what was going to happen next...but she knew she would do whatever she must in order to keep him safe.

Chapter 5

BIRDS SANG OUTSIDE THE WINDOW, AND A thin bar of sunlight slipped in between the heavy textured cotton of the drapes. Will cracked an eyelid and blinked at his surroundings, suddenly hit by the impression that he was late for something.

But then his gaze slid over to his left, and he saw Rosemary sitting on the chair by his bedside, head drooping over her chest so that her heavy, curly hair completely obscured her face. However, he could tell by her posture that she must be asleep.

And no wonder. She'd been up with him all night, dutifully waking him every hour or so to check and make sure he was still doing all right, wasn't having any odd headaches or bouts of nausea or double vision. The last time she'd woken him up had been a little before five, and the clock on the nightstand next to her said it was just past seven-thirty. Two and a half hours of sleep wasn't very much, and yet he had a feeling she would still berate herself for not managing to stay awake for the duration.

"Rosemary," he said quietly.

At once, her head jerked upward and her eyes flared open, and she looked at him in alarm. "Are you okay?" she asked, fingers gripping the edges of the wooden side chair where she sat.

"I'm fine," he said. To his relief, he realized that statement was nothing more than the truth. Yes, his head still ached, and as he shifted in bed, he realized he was bruised in places he hadn't imagined he'd been hurt, but those were superficial concerns. His vision was clear, and he knew where he was and what had happened the day before. No nausea at all—in fact, he found himself ravenously hungry, as if his body understood that it had gotten knocked around a bit and wanted some fuel to replenish his damaged tissues. "How are you?"

"Tired," she said, and reached up to rub the back of her neck. "But I'll live. I'm sorry I nodded off like that."

He made a dismissive gesture with one hand, awakening new aches in his arm. Still, they were manageable. "You made it most of the way through the night. I'd say that was more than good enough."

She didn't look too convinced, but she didn't argue. Quite possibly, she'd decided it wasn't worth the energy. For someone who'd spent the greater part of the night in a hard-backed chair, she appeared no worse for wear, except for some smudged mascara and a few shadows under her eyes.

"Do you need to get up?" she asked.

Which he realized was Rosemary's oblique way of inquiring whether he needed to go to the bathroom. And he did—quite urgently. He hadn't gotten out of bed at all the night before, and all that tea he'd drunk needed to go somewhere.

"Yes, I think I'd better."

She got up from her chair and extended a hand to him. He took it, again noting the strength in her slender fingers. And thank God for that strength, because he realized he was shakier than he'd first felt. No, he didn't think he was in any danger of stumbling and falling, but he knew it would have been a lot harder to make it out of bed and down the hall to the bathroom—the house was old and didn't have an *en suite* bath— without Rosemary's help.

At least she didn't offer to go in the bathroom with him. He shut the door and took care of business, then bent over the sink and splashed some cold water on his face. When he was done, he clung to the edge of the tiled counter to steady himself, then warily raised his eyes to the mirror.

Bad idea. Will supposed he should be glad that he'd hit the side of his head when Caleb attacked him and didn't do a face plant. No black eyes or bloody nose, but he still looked like crap —shadows under his eyes, dark stubble on his cheeks and chin only serving to emphasize how pale he was. He thought he looked every day of the ten years that separated him and Rosemary McGuire... and he didn't like that notion very much.

What the hell was he thinking?

That he was attracted to her, that he could probably be in love with her pretty easily if he allowed himself. Such a realization on its own told him he was already in deep trouble; he'd spent the past fifteen years doing whatever he could to avoid any romantic connections. Then she'd walked into his life, and it was as though every resolution he'd made about avoiding attachments had flown right out the window.

But he could worry about the emotional ramifications of this whole situation later. For the moment, he needed to focus on getting functional, and fast. Rosemary had done a great job of watching over him the night before, but he couldn't expect her to prop him up indefinitely. They needed to figure out what to do next, try to discover where Caleb had taken Colin's footage so they could come up with a plan to get it back. So much valuable time had been lost, although Will tried to tell himself that the part-demon hadn't triumphed absolutely.

If he had, Will would be dead, rather than simply stumbling around with a half-healed concussion.

He limped out of the bathroom and made his way back to his bedroom. Rosemary was at the window, peeking out past the curtains at the bright morning outside. She turned as he entered the room and said, "Are you sure you're okay with walking around so soon?"

"I'm fine," he reassured her. Well, halfway fine. Close enough. "I want to take a shower."

"I don't know—" she began, but he shook his head.

"A shower is the one thing that's guaranteed to make me feel better about life," he said. "If you want, you can take that chair out to the hallway and sit outside the bathroom while I'm in there. That way, if I fall over, you'll hear the thud and come in to rescue me."

Rosemary planted her hands on her hips and shot him a dubious glance. "Is that supposed to be a joke?"

"Maybe," Will said. "At least partly. I'll be okay."

She still didn't look convinced, but he was relieved to see she didn't offer any further protests, only picked up the chair and moved it out to the hall. Wisely, he decided not to comment, and instead fetched clean underwear and a pair of socks, along with some jeans and a button-down shirt. As he was stacking his clothes on top of the dresser, he realized with some dismay that it was Sunday morning...which meant he was supposed to be conducting a service in roughly an hour and a half.

That sure wasn't going to happen.

"I need to make a call," he told Rosemary as she peered around the corner of the doorjamb to see how he was doing. "Do you know where my phone is?"

"It's in that baggie of personal items the hospital sent home with you," she replied. "I think it's still in the car—I was so focused on getting you out of the passenger seat that I must have overlooked it. I'll go get it."

She disappeared before he could protest. And really, as much as he hated to stand there and have her go fetch the little bundle for him, he had a feeling that he really didn't have the strength to walk outside and get his belongings himself. Even if he did, the walk would have tired him out—and he knew he had a lot more he needed to get through today. As he'd reminded himself on more than one occasion, he needed to choose his battles.

Rosemary was back in just a minute, the baggie dangling from one hand. Seeing it, Will couldn't help but feel relieved; his neighborhood was generally safe enough, but even so, a cell phone sitting in an unattended car all night could have made a tempting target. Then again, although there had been a few burglaries in the area, none of them had ever touched his house. He'd always thought it was simply because he didn't have anything worth stealing, but maybe it was also that people knew a minister lived in this house, and any would-be thieves didn't want to risk the bad karma of stealing from him.

"Thank you," he said, and took the baggie from her and extracted the phone. "I need to call the church and let them know I can't make it in today," he added, and she gave a nod of comprehension. He supposed she hadn't stopped to think about what day it was, since he knew she didn't attend church.

This wasn't a call he'd take any pleasure in making, mostly because All Saints was already short-staffed, and having him out of commission would only make that much work for everyone else. However, since there was absolutely no chance that he'd be in decent enough shape to stand at a lectern for an hour and give a halfway coherent sermon, he knew he had no choice but to bow out and have Stan Ludlum, All Saints' senior pastor, take over that morning.

Luckily, he got Stan's voicemail. It always seemed easier to do this sort of thing when he didn't have to talk to an actual person. All too aware of Rosemary's clear blue gaze focused on him, Will left a brief message for his superior, saying that he'd suffered a fall and had a minor concussion, and so wouldn't be in for the next couple of days. That voicemail would give him some breathing room, and then he could reevaluate once those two days were up. At least he didn't have another support group meeting until Wednesday night, so he could let that slide for the time being.

He ended the call and set his phone down on the dresser. "All handled," he told her. "I'm going to get in the shower now."

"Okay. I'll wait out here in the hall."

Telling her she really didn't need to do that would be a waste of time, and so he only picked up his pile of clothes and went into the bathroom. It felt odd to think of Rosemary sitting on her chair just outside the door as he removed the rumpled garments he'd slept in, but he did his best to pretend this was just a normal morning, to turn on the hot water as though there was nothing particularly strange about this day.

Well, except for all the protests his abused muscles and bones gave him when he stepped into the shower and pulled the curtain shut. He gritted his teeth and turned up the water a little hotter, hoping the pulsing heat might help to soothe some of the worst aches and pains. It did seem to help a little, or maybe he was just getting used to how beat up he felt. At any rate, he found he could lose himself in the rituals of bathing, of washing his hair and soaping up and rinsing away some of the weariness of the day before. He even summoned enough energy to pick up his wet/dry shaver and get rid of the itchy scruff on his face, although he didn't worry too much about shaving as closely as he would have if he really were going in to conduct a service that morning.

Eventually, he was done, and he got out of the shower and dried off, then carefully pulled on his clothes and blotted his hair one last time. A little gel to keep it under control, and he was done. He opened the door to see Rosemary still sitting on her chair, although now she had her phone in one hand and appeared to have been checking her emails.

"You look better," she said as she looked up from her phone.

"I feel better. How about some coffee?"

She made a face. "I think I've had enough coffee to last me a lifetime. Do you have any Darjeeling or English Breakfast or something like that?"

"I have both," he replied, inwardly pleased that they seemed to have the same taste in tea. "Let's get some going."

He headed off toward the kitchen. While he made himself walk slowly, he found that he was beginning to feel steadier, that he didn't notice any dizziness or other signs that the concussion had worsened overnight. His stomach wasn't particularly happy with him, but he had a feeling that was more because he really needed to eat than because he was nauseated.

The teakettle still felt nearly full, so he only turned on the gas and got a couple of mugs out of the cupboard. Rosemary had paused near him and leaned up against the counter, although Will noticed how her gaze appeared to be focused on the back door.

"Do you see something?" he asked. It wasn't an idle question; it seemed that new powers were awakening within her, so he thought it was entirely possible Rosemary had caught a glimpse of something that eluded his own ordinary powers of perception.

She shook her head, looking slightly rueful.

"Not now. But I did see Madeline last night. She was standing right over there by the door."

Although he knew Madeline's ghost was entirely benign, Will still experienced a slight creepy crawly sensation on the back of his neck. It was one thing to imagine the woman's spirit haunting the house where Rosemary had been staying, and quite another to discover that she'd decided to make a visit here in his own home.

Still, he made sure to sound unconcerned by this revelation as he asked, "Did she say anything?"

Rosemary nodded. "Yes, she said it was time for her to go. I guess she'd appeared to me to tell me where to find the footage, and once she'd done that, she didn't have any reason to linger here."

While he found himself relieved that Madeline had decided to move on from this plane, Will didn't quite know if he understood her rationale. "Well, she told us where to find it, but since it's still missing…." He let the words trail off, but Rosemary seemed to understand.

"I know. It feels like unfinished business to me, too. But I wasn't going to argue with her." She played with the slender silver bracelet on her wrist, then added, "She also said I would get some other kind of help, but she didn't say from whom. I guess we'll just have to wait and see."

Should he be comforted by this promise of

amorphous assistance? He supposed so, but since they had no idea where this help would be coming from, it was probably better not to count on it.

The Lord helps those who help themselves, he thought with an inner smile.

The kettle started to burble away, indicating that the water within was about to boil, so Will turned off the gas and poured some water into their waiting mugs, then got the box of English Breakfast out of the cupboard and dropped a tea bag into each cup. "We can go sit in the dining room," he said.

Rosemary gave him a worried glance. "How do you feel?"

While he understood her concern, he hoped she wouldn't keep asking about the status of his health every five minutes. Honestly, as the aches and pains began to recede, he found he was more angry with himself than anything else. Maybe there wasn't anything he could have done to prevail against Caleb Lockwood in that particular confrontation, but he couldn't help thinking that if he'd only come up with the right strategy, the right maneuver, then maybe he wouldn't have gotten knocked out in the first place.

"I'm fine," he said. "But I usually sit at the dining room table while I have my morning tea or coffee, since this kitchen isn't big enough for a table and chairs."

Since that was only the truth—Rosemary could probably see for herself that the kitchen wasn't exactly the most spacious one ever designed —she didn't comment, only headed out to the dining room and sat down at the table there. It was in dire need of refinishing, and so he always kept it covered with a tablecloth, which meant they didn't need to bother with coasters.

After he'd sat down...and made sure not to let out a sigh of relief as he did so, even though he could tell that he needed to avoid being on his feet for extended periods...he cradled his mug in his hands and looked over at her. "Have you heard from the detective?"

"No," she replied. "But it's early. He's probably waiting for it to be a more decent hour." She picked up her mug and swirled the tea bag around in the water, then set the mug back down without taking a sip. "I need to get cleaned up before I meet with him, though. It might not make me feel any less tired, but I'll at least feel better about myself."

"We can head over to your place after we have our tea," Will said. "And probably we should pick up some breakfast along the way. I've got a couple of hardboiled eggs in the fridge, but I don't think that's going to cut it."

A tired smile touched her lips. "No, I think I need something a little more substantial than that.

There's a place down on Villa that does good breakfast takeout—"

"Louie's," he supplied, and she nodded.

"Right, that place. We can stop there and grab some stuff on our way to Michael's house."

Will noticed how she was careful to always refer to her temporary abode as "Michael's house" or "Michael's place," as though she wanted to make sure he knew she was well aware that it wasn't hers, that she was only caretaking the house for a finite amount of time. Did it feel odd to her, or was she simply glad that she'd found a convenient way to avoid the construction noise next door to her own house in Glendora?

Of course, she was now probably doubly glad to have an excuse to stay away from her Glendora home, considering the sigils of summoning they'd found carved into her hallway ceiling. Will had scratched them away, and he knew Rosemary had had her family come over and help her cleanse the place, but he knew if their situations had been reversed, he'd still be wary of staying there alone.

She could always stay here, he thought then, but immediately did his best to push that crazy notion aside. They barely knew each other, had only begun to tiptoe toward intimacy. It was a long ways from where they were now to the possibility of her spending the night at his house—or at least, spending the night in a way that didn't involve sitting in an uncomfortable chair and watching him while he slept.

The matter of breakfast settled, they drank their tea in a silence that felt strangely relaxed, given the situation. Once they were done, Rosemary took the mugs into the kitchen, overriding Will's protests that he could clean up. Instead, he sat and listened as she rinsed them out and placed them in the dishwasher. That task managed, she fetched her purse, and they went out to the car. Force of habit made him head toward the driver's side, and she shook her head.

"Not yet, hotshot," she said. "You're doing much better, but I don't think you should be driving."

He had to admit that she was probably right. While he felt halfway human at the moment, all it would take was a moment of dizziness or blurred vision behind the wheel to instigate an accident.

"Okay," he told her. "Although at some point, we're going to have to get your car from the parking structure over by the church."

"Oh, I know," she responded as she opened the passenger door for him. "But I'll see if my mother can drive me over there later today. Or if she's busy, maybe Isabel could do it."

Feeling resigned, he nodded. If he wasn't up to driving now, he doubted he would be later in the day, either. Tomorrow might be an entirely different story, but obviously, Rosemary's car shouldn't sit there and rack up fees any longer than was absolutely necessary.

They headed down to the little diner on Villa, which was a relic of the 1960s and still had a drive-through. That made ordering their breakfasts easy, and soon enough, they were headed east. A few minutes later, Rosemary pulled into the driveway and parked.

The kitchen at Michael's house definitely was big enough to accommodate a table and chairs, although it was a cozy little bistro set for two and nothing fancy. Still, it was good to sit there and look out at the backyard, still cheerful with its flowerbeds and expertly manicured lawn, even though the sunny weather from the previous week seemed to have taken a break, and heavy clouds had begun to move in overhead, blotting out what had begun as a bright morning.

He and Rosemary ate their breakfast sandwiches and hash browns, and Will had to admit it felt damn good to get some solid food in his stomach, even though in general he tried to avoid the greasy stuff. Then again, they weren't real hash browns if they didn't have a little grease.

"Much better," she remarked as she folded up the wrapper that had held her egg and cheese sandwich, then shoved it inside the bag that had contained their food. "I almost feel human now."

A pause, and then she went on, "I just wish I could get my mind wrapped around what I did last night. No matter what I do, it just keeps replaying in my head."

"You did an amazing thing," he told her. Did he dare reach out and touch her hand? He wanted to, very much. After all, they had kissed. It wasn't as though they hadn't shared any kind of physical intimacy. And he had the sudden intuition that Rosemary needed him to touch her right then, that she needed to know he wasn't put off by these powers of hers, no matter how strange they might seem to her.

In silence, he reached out and very gently laid his hand on top of hers. He saw how her big blue eyes widened in surprise...and also how she pulled in a little breath, as if acknowledging to herself how much she'd wanted that contact.

"It scares me," she said, her voice very quiet.

"There's no need for you to be scared," he replied. "You have a remarkable gift, one that helped you when you desperately needed a solution to a problem that confronted you. I don't see anything frightening in that...do you?"

A long silence. Her gaze moved toward the tabletop, to the sight of his large sun-browned hand covering her slender, pale one. When she spoke, her voice was troubled. "What are we doing, Will?"

"I don't know," he said honestly. "But I'm willing to find out if you are."

Again, she was still. However, she didn't move her hand, which he thought had to be an encouraging sign. At last, she looked up at him, worry clear in her eyes...but also a certain resolve, as though she'd decided that she wanted to move forward, even if she had no idea where exactly they were headed.

"I am," she said. Then, very carefully, she slid her hand out from beneath his and got up from her chair. She moved closer to him, then bent down and kissed him on the cheek. In a quite different tone of voice, she added, "I'm going to take a shower now," and turned away so she could head out of the kitchen and toward the stairs.

Will watched her walk away, a cautious joy rising somewhere in his heart. No, he didn't know where all this was going, but it seemed as though he and Rosemary had both determined that they were going to head there together.

For the moment, he'd allow himself to be content with that.

Chapter 6

LUCKILY, SHE'D WASHED HER HAIR ON Saturday morning, so Rosemary piled it on top of her head, secured it with a clip, and climbed into the shower in the guest bath, glad that she could get cleaned up quickly. Yes, letting the hot water beat down on her scalp probably would have felt good, might have helped with the dull headache currently pulsing behind her temples, but she didn't want to spend that much time on herself. Not today...not with Will waiting downstairs for her.

She thought she could still feel the pressure of his hand on hers, which she knew had to be her mind playing with her. Even so, she couldn't ignore how welcome his touch had been, how solid and strong and reassuring even that brief contact was. She needed that reassurance right then, when her own body felt somehow alien to her.

That reaction, while possibly understandable, was something she needed to get past, and quickly. As Will had tried to tell her, the only thing that had really happened was that the psychic powers she already possessed had decided to grow stronger, for whatever reason. Considering who they were up against, being more powerful had to be a good thing, didn't it?

Well, assuming she and Will ended up having a second confrontation with Caleb over the footage. Rosemary had to admit that scenario seemed like a long shot at the moment, since they didn't even know where the hell—no pun intended—he even was.

But Michael's "source" had managed to ferret out Caleb's true identity, and so that led her to believe it was probably only a matter of time before the mysterious hacker...or whoever he was...also discovered where her part-demon ex-boyfriend had gone to ground.

Caleb is not your ex-boyfriend, she scolded herself as she got out of the shower and toweled herself off. *A few dates does not a boyfriend make. He's just a guy you went out with a few times.*

A guy she'd kissed.

A shiver of revulsion went over her at that thought. It didn't seem to matter that at the time, she'd believed he was only an indie filmmaker from Indiana, nothing more, nothing less. She'd still touched lips to someone who wasn't completely human, who had the blood of demons flowing in his veins. And she'd almost done a lot more than merely kiss him, except that something within her had pulled back at the last moment, as though an instinct she didn't even know she possessed had reacted to his alien touch and drawn her away before things could progress any further.

Demonic radar or something…maybe. Just another hitherto undiscovered talent of hers?

If that's what it was, she wished it had gotten its act together a little sooner, like the moment Caleb Lockwood had set foot in Sisters We. Or maybe not. If he hadn't asked her to help him look for the missing footage, then maybe she would never have met Madeline's ghost, would never have had any reason to call Will Gordon and ask for his help.

So many dominoes, so many elements set in motion. Sometimes it was really hard to know what might have happened if that first domino had never gotten knocked down.

Rosemary did what she could to thrust Caleb out of her head. She should be thinking about Will now, not that lying part-demon jerk. It had been a relief to see how quickly Will bounced back from his concussion, but she knew he wasn't out of the woods yet. She got the impression he was pushing himself a little harder than he should, and yet there was only so much she could do to get him to slow down and give himself the time he needed to recover fully. And while she knew that was the prudent thing to do, she also couldn't help feeling that they didn't have the luxury of time at the moment, and Will was only being practical in trying to push himself as much as possible

When she went into the bedroom, she picked up her phone and checked it for any messages. Nothing so far, but the hour had just ticked past nine o'clock. Possibly, Detective Phillips was waiting until after ten to call her, or maybe he'd had something more urgent come up and was back-burnering Will's case for the time being. In a way, that would be a relief, although she doubted the detective would completely drop the matter, despite her wish for him to do that very thing. Dealing with the problem of the stolen footage was hard enough; she really didn't feel like having to dodge a police interrogation at the same time.

The cool, gray day seemed to call for a sweater, so Rosemary put on her favorite blue-gray embroidered cardigan, a white tank top, jeans, and some pewter-colored flats she'd bought on sale but hadn't had a chance to wear yet, since the weather had been so hot for most of October. A bit of makeup, a pair of silver hoops, and she figured she looked respectable enough to handle whatever she might encounter in the coming hours.

At least, she hoped she'd be up to the task. Considering that she'd had to deal with ghosts and demons and police detectives during the past week, she honestly didn't know what she might have to face next.

When she went downstairs, she saw that Will had moved into the library, where he sat in the big armchair by the bookcase, a hardback volume in his hands. She didn't know whether reading was the safest activity for someone with a recent concussion, but she decided it was probably better not to say anything. After all, she wasn't his mother.

Thank God.

"Still no word from Detective Phillips," she said, gesturing with her phone, which she'd brought downstairs with her.

Will closed the book and set it down on the table next to his chair. From where she stood, she couldn't see the title, although it looked like an older volume, dark leather with the dye rubbed off along the edges of the binding. "What about Michael?"

"Nothing from him, either." His current

silence didn't surprise her so much. After all, Michael had known she was going to be up most of the night looking after Will, and so he'd probably assumed she was tired and was leaving her alone. If he didn't have any new information to give her, then there really wasn't much point in making contact. "I guess we'll just need to hang tight until we hear from either one of them, even though I know that doesn't seem very productive."

"Maybe this would be a good time to get your car," Will suggested. "I can wait here while you go with your mother to get it out of hock."

She smiled a little at that description. "That's probably a good idea. It won't be too early for her —my mother is one of those people who's always up with the sun."

And because Glynis was already waiting to hear from Rosemary, calling before ten wouldn't be a big deal. She unlocked her phone and entered the number—it was faster than going to her contacts list, and since her mother had had the same phone number for the past six years, Rosemary had memorized it long ago. Acutely aware of Will's gaze on her—of how crystalline his gray eyes looked in the muted daylight that passed through the library windows—she waited for her mother to pick up, and then briefly explained how she needed to get her car out of the parking structure in downtown Pasadena.

Of course, her mother said that wouldn't be a problem at all, and that she'd be over in ten or fifteen minutes, depending on traffic. Good thing it was a Sunday and not a weekday, or even the few miles that separated Michael's house here in Pasadena from her mother's place in Sierra Madre could have turned into a major obstacle.

"She's on her way," Rosemary told Will after she ended the call. "So I should be able to get this wrapped up pretty quickly."

"That's good."

Because she didn't want to get into any kind of serious discussion during these few minutes while she was waiting for her mother to arrive, Rosemary instead asked Will what he wanted to do with the rest of the day—maybe take it easy and just hang out here at Michael's house and watch TV?

He said that sounded like a good idea, depending on what Detective Phillips needed from them. With any luck, he'd be willing to come here for the interview, but they needed to be prepared to drive to Glendale if necessary.

"Well, we'll deal with that when and if it happens," Rosemary said. "I mean, he knows you're supposed to be taking it easy. He might wonder why you're here instead of at your own house, though."

Will shrugged. "We can always ask him to

meet us there. He doesn't need to know you came back over here for a shower." His eyes met hers briefly, although she couldn't quite tell what was going through his mind. Voice level, he added, "I was also thinking that it might not be a good idea for either one of us to be alone tonight. Just in case."

In case of what? That he wasn't quite as recovered from his concussion as he wanted her to believe, or that he was worried the only reason Caleb hadn't come after them was because they'd been together?

Maybe a little of both. To be honest, Rosemary hadn't been looking forward to sleeping here by herself, even though she knew this house was perfectly safe.

But it wasn't, was it? After all, Caleb had walked into the place without any problem at all, had sat at the table over in the dining room and eaten pizza and drunk beer with her while they sorted through Colin's files from the cache in Michael's garage. So much for the anti-demon wards Michael had placed all over the property— they clearly couldn't keep out someone who was only a quarter-demon like Caleb.

Which meant he could waltz in here any time he damn pleased. A chill went over her at the mere thought of turning a corner and coming face to face with Caleb Lockwood.

"You're probably right," she told Will. "We might as well go back to your house, then—it's a more logical place for us to be. I can put together an overnight bag once I'm done getting my car."

And just like that, she'd committed to staying at Will's house. Rosemary wondered if she was slowly going crazy and just hadn't noticed. A distinct possibility, but she knew his home had a spare bedroom because she'd seen it when she'd taken a break during her vigil at his bedside to use the bathroom—the only bathroom, unfortunately. That arrangement might get a little awkward, although she supposed they'd manage.

"Good," Will said, and looked as though he was about to say more. However, the doorbell rang just then, and Rosemary went to answer it.

Her mother, of course. She told Will she was glad to see him doing so much better, and he smiled and thanked her. If Glynis hadn't been there, Rosemary might have kissed him before telling him she'd be as fast as she could, but such a public display of affection would only invite more questions. Better to get this over with.

She and her mother headed out on their errand—but not before Rosemary moved Will's car to a spot at the curb out front so it wouldn't be in the way when she returned. As they drove off, she had to hold back a sigh.

Just how many houses would those damn demons end up ruining for her?

Will had been in Michael's house several times before, but never alone like this. It felt awkward to sit there in the library and pretend the current situation was entirely normal, and yet he knew the best thing he could do for himself would be to remain in this chair and quietly wait for Rosemary to return.

His head hurt a little, and so he wasn't terribly eager to pick up the book he'd been inspecting. Instead, he shut his eyes and leaned against the back of the armchair where he sat, telling himself it was fine to do nothing for once, to let his mind be calm.

Naturally, that was when his phone buzzed in his pocket.

Frowning, he dug the cellphone out of his jeans and looked down at the screen.

Michael's number.

"Hi, Michael," he said, trying to sound rested and relaxed, and not as though he'd been knocked out cold by a demonspawn the night before.

"How are you doing?"

"Better," he replied. That was a safe enough answer, and nothing more than the truth—after all, he was feeling much better than he had the previous evening.

"Is Rosemary okay? I tried calling her first, but it went to her voicemail."

"She's fine. She went with her mother to get her car out of the parking structure by the church."

"Got it. Anything from the police?"

"Not yet."

A pause. Then Michael said, "Well, I guess they do things in their own time. Anyway, I know you and Rosemary will keep your stories straight. That's not what I'm calling about."

Will sat up a little straighter in his chair. There had been a note in Michael's voice he didn't quite like, something tense, worried. "What is it?"

"Have either of you experienced anything strange since your confrontation with Caleb Lockwood?"

Besides recovering from a concussion? Will thought, although he didn't say the words out loud. Instead, he replied, "Rosemary saw Madeline's ghost again, but otherwise, no."

"What did she want?"

Briefly, Will recounted what Rosemary had told him about the encounter, ending with, "I don't know who or what she was talking about in terms of 'help,' but I guess we'll just have to see what happens. But from the way Rosemary described it, it wasn't a frightening encounter or anything."

"Well, that's something." Michael released a breath, the sound a harsh rasp against the phone's tiny speaker. "No, something weird happened this morning. I was thinking about your confrontation with Caleb, how it really feels like you're getting in over your head—"

"Thanks for the vote of confidence," Will observed dryly. "I thought you asked me to keep an eye on Rosemary because you were worried that she might need some expert help."

"Well, true." Another pause, and he went on, "Look, if this was just a standard demonic infestation or oppression, then that's one thing. You know how to handle yourself in that kind of situation. But if we're dealing with cambions—half-demons—and their even more human offspring, then we're in uncharted territory. The usual methods aren't going to work."

Will knew that already from sad experience, recalling how he'd tried to use holy water on Caleb, only to have the part-demon basically laugh in his face. Anyway, the blessed liquid, which would normally make a demon recoil in pain and terror, hadn't done a damn thing to Rosemary's erstwhile boyfriend…or whatever he'd been to her. He related his experience to Michael, who made a grim sound.

"That's what I was afraid of. Anyway, I was talking to Audrey about it, and she agreed that maybe it would be a good idea for me to come to California and provide some assistance."

"You don't need to do that—" Will protested, and Michael cut him off.

"It's more like I *can't* do that," he said.

"What do you mean?"

"I mean that I went ahead and booked a flight on Southwest, and Audrey was going to drive me to the airport this morning. Only when we got in the car, it wouldn't start."

Annoying, to be sure, but car trouble was kind of a given in that it inevitably reared its ugly head at the most inconvenient time. He said as much, and Michael gave a humorless chuckle.

"Maybe so, but her CR-V is brand-new—it has less than five thousand miles on it."

"Still—"

"I know. I called Triple-A, and they came out and took a look. As far as they could tell, there was nothing wrong with the car."

"That's not the same as having a mechanic check it out," Will said, although he got the feeling that maybe he was protesting a little too much. It wasn't beyond the bounds of possibility to have a brand-new vehicle die on you...but it also wasn't very likely, either.

"I know, and Audrey said it was no big deal,

that I should just call a Lyft and that she'd have the car towed to the dealership when the service department opened the next morning. And so I called a Lyft…only to have the driver cancel on me."

That uncomfortable crawling sensation revisited the back of Will's neck, only this time, it had begun to inch its way down his spine. "Let me guess—car trouble?"

"Exactly. Which could also have been a coincidence, so I called another car—an Uber this time —only to have them cancel as well."

"More car trouble?"

"No," Michael replied, sounding more troubled than ever. "The driver got in a minor fender-bender on the way over to the house. I suppose some people would call that coincidence as well, but I didn't want to take any more risks, especially with innocent people's safety."

For a moment, Will could only sit there, phone pressed against his ear, as he did his best to process what his friend had just told him. "So, you're saying…what? That the demons are somehow trying to prevent you from leaving Tucson?"

"It sure looks that way. I don't know exactly what's going on, but as far as I can tell, they want to make sure that you and Rosemary are on your own."

Not the kind of news Will wanted to hear. Although he knew he would have done nothing less than his best to ensure Rosemary's safety, he supposed he'd always kept in the back of his mind the thought that if the situation got too bad, he could reach out to Michael for help. After all, he was only over in Arizona, not halfway around the world.

Now, though, it sounded as if that particular contingency plan wasn't something he could rely on. He pulled in a breath and said, "We'll manage."

"I'm not sure you realize what you're up against—"

"Well, you yourself just said that we were in uncharted territory, so it's not as if you know for sure, either," Will said reasonably. He was glad he sounded reasonable, that he was using what he liked to think of as his calm minister's voice, unruffled, certain that God would help him see a way through to a reasonable solution, even if he couldn't quite guess what that solution might be. "Besides, we just might have a secret weapon the demons don't even know about."

"What do you mean?"

Briefly, he described what had happened to Rosemary when she returned to the Glendale house, what she had done to ward off Caleb's attack. He ended with, "She honestly doesn't quite know how it happened, either, but she obviously has powers that none of us suspected. I don't know where Caleb is now or how he reacted to the way she defended herself, although I have a feeling he might be reevaluating whether it's wise to confront her openly again."

"I hope you're right," Michael said. "This definitely changes things, though. And it makes me feel a little better about the two of you being on your own."

While he certainly didn't expect Rosemary to bear the brunt of any demonic attack, Will privately agreed that the situation maybe wasn't quite as desperate as it appeared at first glance. Then again, he didn't know how reliable those magnified powers of hers even were. Maybe the next thing they needed to do was see how easily she could control them.

"We'll be fine," he said, and realized he truly did believe that assertion. "You and Audrey need to take care of yourselves. Besides, it's entirely possible that Caleb and the people behind him aren't going to do anything else. After all, on the surface, it looks as though they've won."

"For the time being," Michael said darkly. "I'm still working on tracking down where he might be. And actually, I think I'm going to have my research guy, Fred Peñasco, contact you directly with his findings, whatever those are. If the demons really are watching Audrey and me that closely, then it's probably better if I stay out of the loop."

On the surface, that sounded like a good idea, although Will thought they must be paying pretty close attention to him and Rosemary as well. He said as much, and Michael let out a breath of frustration.

"True, but they have more reason to be wary of Rosemary, I think. I was able to dispel Belial, even on his home turf at that estate in Connecticut, because he was still a pure demon and had to abide by the rules of possession and exorcism. These hybrids we're dealing with now—the cambions and their quarter-demon children—are an entirely different story. I mean, my house has all kinds of wards on it...the demons that went after Audrey's home never touched us at my place...but Caleb Lockwood apparently walked in there without any trouble at all. And that means my arsenal isn't going to be nearly as effective as I'd hoped."

Damn. Will supposed he should have thought of that, but more pressing matters had occupied his attention for the last day and a half. Yes, that disturbing piece of evidence definitely suggested that what had worked for them in the past wasn't going to help at all in their current situation.

"Right," he said slowly. "Then yes, have Fred

get in touch with me as soon as he has any information that he thinks might help."

"I will. Just…be careful."

Will didn't know how well he'd be able to follow that particular piece of advice, not when he and his friend seemed to have reached a tacit understanding that these demons—or cambions, or whatever you wanted to call them—needed to be confronted on their home turf. If they'd simply minded their own business, well, he might have been willing to live and let live, since he'd always believed that each individual should be judged by their own actions, their own merits. It wasn't Caleb's fault that his grandfather had been a demon, and if he'd done his best to repudiate that part of his heritage and live a good life, then Will would have lauded him for his actions.

But he'd lied to Rosemary, had launched a vicious attack at Will…had tried to hurt her as well. The only reason they'd both survived was that her own strange talents had managed to assert themselves to protect the two of them. Because of his actions, Caleb had forfeited any opportunity for leniency.

If this fight had to go to him…well, then, so be it.

Chapter 7

IT COST ROSEMARY NEARLY THIRTY BUCKS TO get her car out of the parking structure, but at least it hadn't been towed. A little adventure like that would have set her back hundreds of dollars and cost her an enormous amount of time—if she'd even been able to get the car out of the impound yard on a Sunday.

But that worst-case scenario hadn't materialized, so she gave her mother a relieved hug and thanked her again for driving her over to Pasadena, and said she'd give her a call when she had a chance.

"Things might be a little crazy for the next few days," Rosemary said. "I should probably call Izzy and CeeCee and let them know there's a good chance I'll have to take some time off. And I hate doing that, because I know Celeste needs as much spare time as possible to get Tyler's costume done for all the Halloween events coming up, but—"

"It's fine," her mother cut in, but gently; it seemed clear enough that the interruption was born from a desire to prevent her daughter from tying herself up in knots rather than because she had a habit of interrupting people in the middle of a sentence. "I can cover your shifts at the store if necessary. Don't worry about it."

"Mom, you don't have to do that," Rosemary protested. Yes, her mother had pitched in a few times in the past, like when both Rosemary and Isabel caught the flu in the same week, but she didn't want her mother to think she viewed her as an easy way to get out of work.

"I know I don't *have* to," Glynis said. "I offered. It's fine. Hopefully, I won't have to do much inventory, because my back isn't really up to hauling heavy boxes of books around, but otherwise, I'd be happy to help out."

A wave of relief washed over Rosemary. Smiling, she said, "No, we got our big shipment from Llewellyn Press last week, and we're not expecting anything like that again until closer to Christmas. And the small bits of inventory that do need to be handled, Izzy or CeeCee can take care of."

"Then it sounds like we're all settled. I'll just assume you won't be going in tomorrow, and then the rest of the week we can play by ear."

There was no way to truly express her gratitude, so Rosemary settled for hugging her mother once again. "I'll keep in touch," she promised. "Now, though, I should get back. Will seems okay, but—"

"But he got a nasty knock on the head yesterday," Glynis finished for her. "I completely understand. You go and look after him." She paused, a faint smile playing around her lips. "He seems like a very fine man."

"He is," Rosemary said, and decided she'd better leave it there. Oh, of course, she was happy to hear that her mother approved of Will, but she didn't want to risk waxing too rhapsodic for fear she might give away just how much space he now occupied in her heart and mind. Whatever this thing was between them, she could already tell it went far beyond physical attraction, although she knew that was a part of it as well. No, it was more that he accepted her for who she was, crazy psychic talents and everything else. So many of the men she'd dated in the past would have pulled a disappearing act the minute they heard about the crazy stunt she'd performed at Colin's house in Glendale.

Actually, she thought then, *if you want to be really honest, you know they would have bailed much earlier than that...like when you first mentioned seeing a ghost.*

No, paragons of courage those guys definitely were not.

Will was cut from different cloth—although she wanted to wince inwardly at that unintended pun. It said something that she didn't even care whether he was a member of the clergy, although if someone had asked her even a month ago if she'd ever consider dating a minister, her answer would have been an emphatic no.

Not that they were dating. They were…well, she didn't know for sure what they were doing. Being together, working together. That was certainly far more significant than sharing a few meals in restaurants or going to a movie or a concert together.

Then again, she thought it might be nice to do something so terribly mundane with him. A movie sounded like a wonderful change of pace.

She doubted there would be any movies in their near future, however.

To forestall any further discussion on the subject of William Gordon, Rosemary said goodbye to her mother and then climbed into her little green Fiat, which seemed almost like a toy car after Will's ferocious Challenger. However, she felt much safer in her own vehicle, since she knew exactly what it was capable of and didn't have to worry about an enormous 350-horsepower engine getting the better of her.

No, the Fiat carried her quietly back to Michael's house, where she pulled into the garage with a sense of relief. Maybe they wouldn't be staying here, but at least the place was familiar. There was something to be said for familiarity.

When she came into the kitchen, she saw Will hovering there, trying to appear as though he hadn't just been looking out the window to reassure himself that it really was her coming up the stairs on the back stoop. His expression was troubled.

"What the matter?" she asked, dropping her purse on the table by the window. "Does your head hurt? Are you feeling nauseated?"

"No to both of those questions," he replied, making an off-hand gesture, as if to brush away the minor concern of his physical health. "I just talked to Michael, and he has some pretty troubling evidence that the demons—or the part-demon cambions, to be more precise—have been interfering with him to prevent him from coming out here to California to lend a hand."

Rosemary wasn't sure which part of that comment she should unpack first. She stared up at Will and felt a frown crease her forehead, and decided to attack the easier bit first. "I wasn't aware he was even planning to come to California."

"I don't think he was…until you and I had

our little altercation with Caleb Lockwood." Will took a step toward her, then hesitated, as though unsure whether she would welcome any contact right then.

Well, she needed to put that particular worry to bed. She closed up the space between them and took his hands in hers. At once, his fingers tightened their grasp, showing her that he was very glad she'd reached out to him. "So, what happened?"

"It sounds like they somehow managed to tamper with Audrey's car—and also caused the Uber driver who was coming to take Michael to the airport to have an accident."

Could demons even do that? Well, obviously they could; Michael wouldn't have told Will he thought they were responsible unless he was pretty damn sure of that fact. She swallowed, a chill running through her that didn't have much to do with the gray skies which currently shrouded Southern California. "What did he do?"

"Well, he decided it was probably not a good idea to come out here." Will gave her fingers a squeeze and then let go, but only so he could stand a little farther away in order to get a good look at her face. "It means we're on our own."

"It's all right," she said immediately, without even stopping to think whether it was actually all right. But then, she couldn't feel frightened with Will standing next to her like this, even though she knew she probably should be. "We survived our encounter with Caleb, and now we know a lot more about the sorts of powers he controls. Not that I really think he's going to come after us. You yourself said he had what he wanted, so what would be the point?"

"I'd like to think that," Will said, but the worry in his clear gray eyes told her he wasn't precisely sanguine on the subject. "However, I also think it's probably a good idea to learn a little bit more about the powers *you* control. You saved us back at that house, but you still don't know exactly how."

No, she didn't. In fact, she'd done her best not to think about how she'd summoned that shield of glowing light, or the way she'd used her mind to lift that panel of drywall as if it was nothing, because to do otherwise was to admit to herself that there were hidden aspects to her brain that were pretty damn frightening.

"Do we have to talk about that now?" she asked, knowing how desperate she sounded.

"Not right this second," he said gently, and she allowed herself an inner sigh of relief. "It's probably better if you get your things together, now that your car has been taken care of. That way, we'll be over at my place whenever Detective

Phillips contacts you. He didn't call while you were out getting your car, did he?"

She shook her head. "No, I haven't heard from him yet. I'm not sure what that means. But you're right—give me a few minutes, and I'll pack my stuff."

"Take as long as you need."

That was generous of him, but Rosemary figured there wasn't much point in dilly-dallying. Already she was cataloging the items of clothing she would pack—mostly jeans and T-shirts and a few nice tops and sweaters, maybe a skirt just in case they decided to go out to eat or something. There wasn't much point in bringing along any of her wilder Stevie Nicks getups…not because she was worried about how Will would react to them, but mostly because they weren't exactly practical for anything that required much physical activity.

She sent him an encouraging smile and hurried upstairs, where she got out her overnight bag and a smaller matching tote, and filled them with enough clothing and toiletries to keep her going for at least three or four days. Anything more than that, and she'd have to come back here to restock, but she figured that was a safe amount to get her started. After all, she really didn't have any idea how long this whole mess with the demons was going to continue. For all she knew, they might never be able to resolve the matter.

Well, that may not be all bad, she thought as she shoved a third pair of flats into her bag and told herself she needed to stop there; she couldn't bring all the items she wanted, no matter how hard she tried to cram everything in. *Actually, it sounds like kind of a sneaky way to move in with Will without ever actually discussing it.*

And that, she realized, was absolutely crazy. Yes, she wanted matters to progress with Will, wanted to see where all this might end up, but a few kisses and some fairly intense shared experiences were not exactly a solid basis for deciding to move in with a person. In fact, she'd never been all that interested in living with someone, had always found it better when she and the guys she'd been seeing could go their separate ways at the end of the evening. Now, though…now she was fiercely glad that circumstances had forced her and Will together. She wanted to spend this time with him, even if she was a little afraid about what was going to come next.

Only one way to find out, she supposed.

Rosemary zipped both of her bags shut and then took them downstairs. Will had sat down in the family room, facing toward the television, although he hadn't turned it on. She couldn't tell for sure, since he'd turned toward her as soon as she paused in the doorway, but she had a feeling he'd had his eyes closed and was probably trying to rest while she packed.

However, she didn't see any signs of pain or fatigue in his face as he stood up and came over to her. "All set?" he asked.

"I think so," she responded. "And even if I've forgotten something, it's not as if it's a big deal to come back here and get it."

"True."

They went to the front door, where she paused to enter the "away" code for the alarm system. As it started beeping, they both headed outside, with Will waiting on the porch while she closed the door and locked it behind her. Since it was a chilly day, the windows were all shut anyway, and she'd locked the back door as she came in from the garage. The house was about as secure as she could make it, but Rosemary couldn't quite get rid of a little niggling doubt at the back of her mind. Was she doing the right thing by going over to Will's house? If something happened to Michael's place while she was gone, she knew she'd never forgive herself.

"It's all right," Will said quietly. "It was demons who burned down Audrey's house, not Caleb or any of the other cambions."

"Do you know that for sure?" she responded as she slipped the house keys into her purse.

His gaze shifted from her to the door and then

back again. "Maybe not for sure, because I wasn't there, but it really doesn't seem as if the cambions were involved in any of that mayhem."

In a way, that made sense. Demons could come and go without leaving any evidence. Caleb might have done much the same thing in the Glendale house, but he was still flesh and blood, was pretending to be a regular human being with a driver's license and—she assumed—a Social Security number and all the other trappings of a normal adult in the United States. Why risk leaving behind a fingerprint or a stray hair or a piece of lint or whatever it was that CSI units used to track down a perpetrator when you could have a nice incorporeal being do your dirty work for you?

"You have a point," she admitted. "And I suppose that doing anything to this house would draw way too much attention."

"Exactly."

Will sounded so confident, she didn't quite have the heart to point out that demons didn't always follow human rules of logic. And although she didn't want to sound callous, she thought privately that if demons or cambions or some sort of otherworldly vandals decided to torch Michael's beautiful house, better that they do so without her in it.

Of course, she couldn't know for sure whether

she'd be any safer at Will's house, but she tried to tell herself that they probably hated Michael more than they hated her or Will, just because Michael really had done them some damage by banishing Belial to Hell. Whereas she…well, she'd pretty much done everything she could do to help them, including leading Caleb right to Colin's former home in Glendale so he could scoop up the *Project Demon Hunters* footage.

Holding back a sigh, she went down the porch steps and over to where Will's car was parked at the curb. "I'm driving," she said.

He looked so resigned, she almost wanted to laugh. "I know."

They got in, and she guided the Challenger away from the curb and headed west. The two houses were so close together that there was no need to go back out on any main streets; she zigged and zagged her way over to Wilson, and in less than five minutes, she was pulling into the driveway of Will's modest Craftsman-style home. Just as she turned off the ignition, her phone rang from within her purse.

"I should get that," she said.

"Maybe it's the elusive Detective Phillips."

Rosemary didn't recognize the number when she glanced down at the screen, but she made herself answer anyway. If it was a robocall, she'd just hang up.

But no, that was the detective's no-nonsense voice coming from the speaker. "Ms. McGuire, I think you need to come out to the property in Glendale."

"Um…why?" she said, shooting a puzzled glance at Will. He lifted a brow but remained silent, probably realizing that it was better for him not to speak while she was on the phone with the authorities.

"I'd prefer not to discuss that on the phone. How soon can you be here?"

Shit, she thought, mentally casting around for excuses and realizing she really had none to give. *Shit, shit, shit.* "I don't know," she replied. "Maybe twenty minutes? I'm with Will Gordon right now and don't feel comfortable leaving him alone. Can he come with me?"

"If he's up to it," the detective said. "Maybe he can help shed some light on the situation. I'll see you soon."

The call ended there, and Rosemary lowered the phone from her ear, knowing her expression had to be a study in confusion. "He wants us to come to the Glendale house."

Will's dark brows drew together. "Did he say why?"

"No."

A pause, and then he shrugged. "Then I guess we'd better go and fight out."

Rosemary's slender fingers were tense on the steering wheel, but she drove calmly and competently enough as she pointed the Challenger west toward Glendale. Will remained silent, somehow realizing that to talk about what might be waiting for them in Colin's former house would only make her more anxious. His own thoughts raced as he wondered if the police had found some piece of evidence that might connect them to Caleb Lockwood, or whether they'd discovered that the crawlspace access had been tampered with.

The problem was, Will had been either unconscious or simply not present while all that was going on, and so he had absolutely no idea whether any damning evidence existed or not. All they could do was go to the house and hope that they'd been worried for no reason, that the detective simply wanted to meet Rosemary there so he could go over the crime scene with her in person.

If that was how these things even worked. He didn't watch crime television shows, and he'd never been the victim of a crime—well, except for someone breaking into his car years and years ago when he was a student at Boston University—and so he honestly had no idea what to expect.

When they turned the corner onto Las Flores Drive, Rosemary made a shocked sound. Instead of the single unmarked car they'd been expecting, there were several black and white squad cars and an ambulance parked in the driveway and on the street in front of the house, in addition to a black Ford Taurus that Will guessed was the detective's vehicle. The perimeter of the property was blocked off with yellow crime scene tape, and a group of people—neighbors, probably—stood off to one side, gawking at the hubbub.

"What's going on?" she asked in a low voice, and he shook his head.

"I don't know. We just need to stay calm and see what Detective Phillips has to say to us."

White-faced, she parked the Challenger in the nearest available space and then took the keys out of the ignition. They got out and began to walk toward the house, only to have the detective meet them at the bottom of the driveway.

"Ms. McGuire, Mr. Gordon," he said, his expression blank and unsmiling.

"Did something else happen here?" Rosemary inquired. Her expression was one of curiosity and not concern, but Will could see how tense her delicate jaw was—and he guessed Detective Phillips could, too. "Was there another break-in?"

"Not exactly," the detective replied. His glance moved toward Will. "How are you feeling, Mr. Gordon?"

"All right if I don't move too fast," he said

easily, not sure whether his casual demeanor would fool anyone. But he didn't want to act as though he was overly worried by the activity on the property. After all, he hadn't done anything, so why behave as though he had?

"Then I'll try to walk slowly." The detective gestured for them to follow him down the driveway and through the front door. "I got permission from the owner's sister to enter the property and begin the investigation, so I came by as soon as I was able to get a spare set of keys from the man who was acting as Colin Turner's property manager."

Rosemary sent Will a quick sideways glance. About all he could do was manage a very small lift of his shoulders, worried that Detective Phillips would see even that small gesture. How the detective had managed to track down Emma Weston, Colin's sister, so quickly, Will didn't know. The house had technically been owned by a trust, and it had taken Michael Covenant's researcher Fred days to find out who was actually behind that trust.

But the "how" of it all probably didn't matter too much at the moment. The far more pressing question was, why all this commotion over a simple break-in at a house that didn't have anything to steal? True, there had been an assault, but it wasn't as though anyone had been killed or even seriously injured.

"I came in and took a look around," Detective Phillips said as he led them through the empty living room and toward a sliding glass door that looked out on the backyard. When Will had come here with Rosemary, they hadn't gone outside, and so he didn't even know what the yard looked like. Now he saw that it was small and neat, like the house, with an oval pool taking up most of the space. "Then I went outside."

The sliding glass door stood open, letting in a cool, damp breeze. Increasingly mystified, Will and Rosemary followed the detective out to the patio.

His blood seemed to freeze. Off to one side, looking incongruous next to a lounge chair with a blue and white striped seat, was a gurney. A cloth covered it, but you could tell there was a body underneath.

Cold fingers gripped his, and Will looked down to see Rosemary clutching his hand. He gave her fingers a reassuring squeeze, but since his own heart had begun to beat a little faster and a chill was working its way down his spine, he really wasn't sure how much reassurance he'd actually provided.

Detective Phillips walked over to the gurney,

then reached down and pulled back the sheet, revealing a man's pale face. His dark eyes stared sightlessly at the gray sky, and his dark blond hair was still damp and pasted against his skull. He must have been in the water for some time, because his face looked gray and pinched, and yet somehow bloated.

Rosemary let out a shocked cry and raised her hands to her face. The drowned man on the gurney was a stranger to Will, and yet he thought he could guess who it must be.

"You know this man, don't you, Ms. McGuire?"

For a few seconds, she was silent—not out of reluctance to reply, Will thought, but because she still hadn't quite come to terms with what she was seeing.

At last, she nodded. "Yes," she said, her voice so faint, it was hardly more than a whisper. "That's Caleb Dixon."

Chapter 8

WAS THIS REALLY HAPPENING? THE WORLD
seemed to spin around her, but she made herself
gulp in a deep breath of cool, damp air and focus
on the horrible sight of Caleb Dixon—no, *Lockwood,* she reminded herself, a little proud that at
least she'd had enough of a grip on herself to give
Detective Phillips the fake name Caleb had been
using—lying on that gurney, obviously dead.

No, it couldn't be possible, though. She'd seen
him disappear right before her eyes, mocking her
as he vanished with Colin's hard drive in his hand.
How on earth could he have ended up dead in a
swimming pool?

Besides, could quarter-demons even drown?
She had absolutely no idea how strong Caleb had
been, so she didn't know whether he had his own
particular set of vulnerabilities like any other

mortal, or whether there was something else going on here that she just couldn't figure out.

In silence, Detective Phillips handed over a sodden, crumpled piece of paper encased in a clear plastic bag. Staring down at it, Rosemary realized it was a picture of her with Caleb. A moment passed before she could gather her racing thoughts to realize the photo was a selfie he'd taken with her when they'd gone to the street fair in Monrovia. At the time, she hadn't thought much of it, mostly because she figured that, as a film-maker, Caleb liked to document places he'd gone and people he'd seen. He'd obviously printed out the photo, although she couldn't quite guess why.

"We found this in Caleb Dixon's wallet," the detective said. "Can you tell me where this was taken?"

She blinked, and tried to keep her voice from shaking as she replied, "At—at the street fair in Monrovia. Caleb and I went there about a week and a half ago."

"And how do you know Caleb Dixon, Ms. McGuire?" The detective's tone was gentle enough, as though he was doing his best to respect her obvious shock, but she could tell that he wanted answers and wasn't going to let her leave until she provided them.

"I—" She reached up to push a wayward curl back off her forehead. The headache that had disappeared a few hours earlier had now returned with a vengeance. Probably the shock of seeing Caleb's body, along with her lack of sleep, but the combination was painful. She had to think fast, though. She'd only told the detective that she'd surprised an intruder here and hadn't gotten a good look at his face, so she figured it was probably safe enough to provide a little truth...with a lot of fiction mixed in. "We dated a little."

"When was the last time you saw him?"

The image of Caleb's dark eyes dancing with devilish delight as he held the hard drive flickered through her mind, but Rosemary thrust it away and forced herself to focus on her last public inter-action with him. "Um...almost a week ago now. We had dinner at Eden Garden in Glendora on Monday night. But we had an argument and, well, we broke up."

"I see." Detective Phillips had his notebook out again and was making some rapid notes. "Did anyone at the restaurant see you fighting?"

"No," she said quickly. "We actually argued after, when he took me back to the house."

"What was the argument about?"

Her gaze flickered to Will. She hated to drag him into this, but the story she was concocting would at least explain why he'd come with her to the house on Saturday night. "Mr. Gordon, actu-ally. We'd met at a church function and started to get friendly, and Caleb got jealous. I tried to tell him that he and I had only gone out a couple of times and our relationship definitely wasn't exclusive or anything, but he didn't want to hear it. I had to tell him to leave."

The detective's cool dark gaze moved over to Will. "Did you know anything about any of this, Mr. Gordon?"

Will shook his head, his gaze nearly as impassive as that of the man who faced him. "No. But Ms. McGuire and I had just started seeing each other, and so I really hadn't asked her much about her private life."

"Caleb must have been jealous," she said, praying her story would sound plausible to the stony-faced detective. "He must have followed me here on Saturday night to see what I was doing, who I was with."

Detective Phillips' head tilted to the side the barest fraction of an inch as he appeared to consider what she'd just said. "Could he have been the one who assaulted you?"

Rosemary made a helpless gesture with her hands. Had that looked too dramatic? She didn't know; she'd never had to lie to the police before. "Maybe. I don't know. It seems really out of character for him, though. I mean, he wanted to make movies. He didn't seem like the violent type."

"Are there any injuries to his fists?" Will asked

then, his eyes narrowing slightly. "That is, I was hit pretty hard. Wouldn't there be some sign of that on his hands?"

"Possibly," Detective Phillips allowed. "The body was in the water for at least twelve hours, although we'll have to wait for an autopsy to get a more accurate duration. We'll look for wounds on his hands, though."

"Or maybe," Rosemary suggested, figuring it couldn't hurt to muddy the waters a bit, "maybe he came back to poke around and surprised the same guy who attacked us."

"Another possibility." The detective made a few notes on his pad.

"You don't think we're suspects, do you?" Will said. He still looked very calm, but Rosemary could see the way his hands clenched into fists for a second and then relaxed.

"Oh, probably not you, Mr. Gordon," Detective Phillips said, his tone unconcerned. "You were suffering from a concussion and in the hospital."

"And I was there with him," Rosemary cut in, although she realized she should probably stop there before she got herself in trouble. At least, any more trouble than she was already in. "In fact, I was talking to you, detective, at about the time Caleb probably drowned."

He raised an eyebrow. "We don't know for

sure when he fell—or was pushed—into the pool. Yes, I spoke with you at the hospital, but I don't know what you did after that."

"I went back up to see what was going on with Will," she said. "The nurses on the floor will tell you that—and so will Dr. Littleton, the doctor who was handling Will's case."

"Well, then," the detective said as he returned his notepad to his pocket, "I suppose you don't have anything to worry about…unless the autopsy shows that Caleb went in the pool some time after you discharged Mr. Gordon from the hospital."

Rosemary wasn't sure what to say in response to that comment. Yes, she could protest that she'd been at Will's bedside all night, except that wasn't the precise truth. She'd come back to this very house and sealed up the crawlspace. Had Caleb been floating in the pool the entire time she was here? The very idea made gooseflesh creep along her arms, but she supposed it was possible. She hadn't looked out into the backyard at all, had only gone back and forth between the hallway where the entrance to the crawlspace was located and the kitchen and the garage. There hadn't been any reason to go near the sliding glass window in the living room; in fact, she'd actively avoided it, since there weren't any window coverings installed, thanks to the house being between tenants, and she hadn't wanted to risk someone catching a glimpse of her as she moved around the place.

Will shot a troubled glance at her before turning his attention to Detective Phillips. "You honestly don't think Rosemary had anything to do with this? For one thing, I don't even see how she could have overpowered someone like Caleb Dixon. He looks like he's at least ten inches taller and seventy pounds heavier."

This reasoned argument didn't seem to make much of an impression. The detective shrugged and shoved his hands in his trouser pockets, then said, "You'd think that, but I've seen a lot of strange things on this job." His gaze flicked to Rosemary and he added, "You're not under arrest, Ms. McGuire. We're done here. But make sure you're reachable in case I have any further questions once I get the autopsy results."

About all she could do was give him a very small nod. She guessed that any further protestations of innocence wouldn't go over too well with him, so the best thing to do was to get the hell out of there.

Apparently guessing at the reason for her silence, Will said, "We'll just see ourselves out."

He put a hand on Rosemary's arm, and she allowed him to guide her through the house and past the ambulance blocking the driveway. As they walked, she reached into her purse to put her sunglasses on her nose. It wasn't really that bright out, thanks to the cloud cover overhead, but that same group of neighbors was still standing on the sidewalk and gawking at the house, and she figured she might as well hide something of her face so they couldn't get a good look.

At least Will didn't try to get behind the wheel. Yes, she was shaken up, but she knew he wasn't ready to be driving yet. They both got in their seats, and she started up the Challenger and drove a little ways down the street so she could use a convenient driveway to turn the car around. With as rattled as she was feeling right then, she knew she probably couldn't pull off a three-point turn in an unfamiliar vehicle.

He waited until she was back on the freeway and heading toward Pasadena before he spoke. "How are you doing?"

"I don't know," she replied, making sure she kept her gaze fixed on the road ahead of her. For some reason, she felt as if she wanted to cry, which was silly, wasn't it? After all, Caleb Lockwood hadn't been a great guy. In fact, he'd been a lying part-demon. Why should she be crying over him?

She didn't want to admit to herself that the odd rush of grief she was currently experiencing could be nothing more than her way of distracting herself from the frightening possibility that she might be a murder suspect.

The freeway blurred, and she tried to blink back the tears. It would really be the cherry on the cake of her day if she managed to get them both into an accident because she'd lost it behind the wheel.

"Rosemary."

No way would she look over at Will. She had to stay focused on the freeway, on the cars around them, although the traffic was pretty light, thanks to it being in the middle of the day on a Sunday.

His hand descended on her leg. Somehow, she could feel the warmth of his touch even through the heavy fabric of her jeans. "It's okay to be upset," he said quietly. "You felt something for Caleb, even if it didn't last. Don't beat yourself up for wanting to grieve."

"You don't have to be all ministerial," she returned, knowing even as she spoke how snotty her comment sounded. "I'm not a member of your congregation."

Will withdrew his hand. She risked a very quick glance over at him from the corner of her eye and saw that he didn't look upset. In fact, he appeared more contemplative than anything else.

"I know that," he said. His tone was very gentle. "I wasn't talking to you as a member of my congregation. I was talking to you as a friend."

For some reason, that comment didn't reassure her very much. "Is that all I am—a friend?"

"You know you're much more than that to me."

Did she know that? Rosemary wanted to believe his words, but she didn't have much to base them on. One real kiss and a few little pecks that might as well have been between friends. Since she didn't know exactly the best way to respond, she lifted her shoulders but remained silent.

Will was also quiet for a moment. When he spoke, he didn't sound upset with her, but rather puzzled. "Have I misread you? Or do you think this isn't the right time for us to be getting involved, considering everything else that's going on?"

She found her voice, knowing she needed to speak now or risk losing the little they'd already shared. "No, you didn't misread me. As for it being the right time…." The words trailed off, and she pursed her lips, trying to think of a way to phrase what she wanted to say without it sounding horribly awkward. It wasn't that she worried about how Will might react to a declaration of her feelings—she knew he wasn't the sort of man who would turn tail and run at the faintest hint of actual emotions. No, mostly she just didn't want to sound like an idiot.

He didn't say anything, only waited for her to continue.

The Lake Avenue exit was coming up, so she pulled over to the right and got off the freeway. As they waited for the light at the top of the off-ramp, she gave a humorless little chuckle. "I'm not sure having this discussion right now is exactly 'the right time.' Can we continue this when we get back to your place?"

"Sure," he replied easily.

Well, there was a little bit of a reprieve. She knew the way well enough that she didn't need him to guide her in, and pointed the car north on Lake before turning right on the side street that would lead them to Wilson Avenue and his house. Just as she pulled into the driveway, a few drops of rain pattered onto the windshield.

Pretty good timing, although it might have been nice if the weather had held off until they were safely inside. Rosemary got out of the car and hurried around to the passenger side, but Will had already climbed out and shut the door behind him. He held one hand up to shield his head as he fished in his pocket for his house keys with the other.

By unspoken agreement, they both half-walked, half-ran to the porch. Just in time, too, because the rain began to fall in earnest almost as soon as they reached shelter.

"Was it supposed to rain?" Will asked as he unlocked the door and they went inside.

"I don't know," Rosemary replied. "I haven't been paying much attention to the weather reports—I've been kind of occupied with other stuff the past few days."

He chuckled, then shut the door and engaged the deadbolt. It was only a few steps from the front door to the living room, and he sat down on the couch and leaned against the cushions, then let out a small sigh. Immediately, she went over to him and sat down as well, studying his face for any obvious signs of pain.

Nothing there, except maybe a slightly taut look to his mouth. Nevertheless, she asked, "How are you doing?"

"I'm fine," he said. "A little bit of a headache, nothing serious. I think all this was a bit more exertion than I'd planned for. That's all."

Rosemary could well believe that. No doubt Dr. Littleton over at Glendale Adventist would have had a few choice words to say about all the running around she and Will had done that day. He probably shouldn't have even left the house, should have spent the afternoon on the couch with his feet up and his favorite movies streaming on Netflix or Amazon Prime.

"Let me make you some tea," she offered, and he gave her a grateful smile—albeit one with a bit of regret mixed in.

"I'd rather have a glass of wine."

So would she, but even she knew that alcohol was a no-no for someone who'd just suffered a concussion the day before. "Maybe tomorrow," she said lightly. "We'll just have to wait and see how you're doing."

He gave a resigned nod. "All right."

Rosemary got up from the couch and went into the kitchen, then put the kettle on to boil. The rain had begun to come down even harder, and she frowned. While Southern California sometimes got storms in October, it was far more common to get the hot, dry Santa Ana winds than this kind of weather. Where had it come from?

The demons sent it, she mocked herself, and went to fetch a couple of mugs from the cupboard.

Then again, thinking about demons probably wasn't a very good idea. Her mind went immediately to the horrible sight of Caleb's pale, bloated body on that gurney, the face she'd once thought so handsome almost distorted beyond recognition...but not entirely. She could tell it was him, not some lookalike he'd used as a decoy to mess with her head.

Because that would be convenient, wouldn't it? To believe he somehow wasn't dead, had planned all this as some sort of a trick? Rosemary wasn't quite sure why he'd bother with such an elaborate ruse, but she'd be the first to admit that demonic thought processes were not her area of expertise.

She supposed an autopsy and its accompanying check of dental records would confirm beyond a doubt that he was in fact Caleb Dixon. Lockwood. Whatever. Or maybe not. Maybe Caleb and the rest of his kind were very careful to not let that sort of information be readily available. But surely he'd gone to the dentist—his teeth had been perfect.

Just like the rest of him.

Not his heart, though, she thought fiercely. *Not his soul. Those were both as shriveled and black as those of a true demon.*

Once again, incongruous tears stung her eyes, and she gulped in a deep breath and made herself get the box of English Breakfast out of the cupboard. She realized she probably should have gone to sit with Will while the water was boiling, but she found she didn't want to do that. Because if she was in there with him, he'd want to continue their conversation, and she still didn't know for sure what to say to him.

I think I'm falling in love with you and I know it's crazy because we don't even know each other.

Yes, that would probably go over really well.

She sniffled and reached up with her ring fingers to carefully press at the outer corner of each eye, blotting the tears that threatened to gather there. Why that particular trick worked, she didn't know for sure, but it was a good way to preserve her makeup and not turn into a soggy mess.

The water in the kettle began to boil, and she turned off the heat and poured a measure into each mug, then took a deep breath and made herself go back out to the living room. Will hadn't moved from where he sat, although his head was angled toward the front window, the one that looked out over the street. That was a good sign, wasn't it? If he had really overdone things, he probably would have had his head against the cushions and his eyes shut.

At least, that was what she hoped.

She went over to the sofa and handed Will his mug of tea. He murmured a thank-you as she sat down next to him, then lifted the mug to his lips and blew on the liquid inside.

"So…." he said, and let the syllable trail off.

"So," Rosemary repeated. Her fingers tightened on the mug she held, the ceramic almost too warm against her skin. Still, she was glad of the heat, because the day had turned a lot colder than she'd expected, and the interior of the house was a little chillier than she would have liked. "I'm not even sure what to say to you."

"Well, the truth, hopefully."

Yes, she supposed that was exactly what Will would want. He wasn't the sort of person to shy away from the truth, no matter how uncomfortable it might be.

"I…." She stared down into her mug, but even if psychics in the past might have been able to read a person's fortunes from the patterns formed by tea leaves at the bottom of a cup, all she had was a bag of Republic of Tea to work with, so that wasn't going to happen. "I honestly didn't plan for any of this to happen."

"Neither did I." His tone was a little amused, and she risked a sidelong glance at him to try to get a read on his expression. The corners of his mouth had lifted slightly, but his eyes looked serious enough. "I told Michael I'd be happy to help you out if the occasion arose, but I didn't imagine I'd find in you something I've been missing."

Yes, that was exactly how she felt about Will. Like there was some part of her that had gotten lost along the way, and she hadn't even realized it was gone until she met him and looked into his eyes. She surprised herself by asking, "Have you ever been married?"

He lifted his mug of tea and took a sip before replying, "No. I was engaged once."

Rosemary studied his expression. Once again, he looked more thoughtful than anything else, not as though he was harboring regrets over that one-time engagement. "What happened?"

"It was a long time ago. I was just finishing up my undergraduate degree in archaeology."

Well, there was something new she'd just learned about him. She supposed she'd never really thought about what a minister might have majored in, had thought that he must have studied comparative religion or philosophy or something along those lines. "And...?"

He sipped his tea again and then set the mug down on a coaster on the coffee table in front of them. Not that the table in question really required that level of protection; its surface was scratched and already marred by several rings left by careless cups and mugs in the past. Rosemary wasn't an expert on antiques by any stretch of the imagination, but she had a feeling the table was nearly as old as the house itself.

"I realized I had a different calling, that I wanted to go to divinity school. I applied a few places, not sure whether I would get in. Then I was accepted at Fuller Seminary here in Pasadena, and I had to break the news to Lois."

"She was your fiancée?"

Will nodded. "Of course, I'd told her what I was doing, but I don't think she really took me seriously. She thought I would stay at Boston University and get my master's degree there, just as she planned to do. When I told her I wanted to come to California and have her come with me, well, she wasn't very happy."

Pride in her home state made Rosemary wonder why Will's former fiancée hadn't jumped at the chance to get out of Boston. As far as she was concerned, Southern California was pretty much perfect in every way. All right, the traffic sucked and housing costs were insanely high, but the weather was great.

Rain dripped off the eaves outside, and she mentally added, *Most of the time.*

"Couldn't Lois have gotten her master's degree here?" she asked, deciding to leave the benefits of Southern California living out of the conversation for the time being.

"Yes, but she didn't want to. All her family was in Boston, and she loved it and didn't want to leave." Will shrugged. "I can understand that. I grew up in the area as well, and it was the only thing I knew, but I also knew I needed to go where my heart told me to go. I suggested that we try keeping things going long distance while we pursued our graduate degrees, that I'd come back to Boston after I was done here at Fuller Seminary, but she wasn't interested in doing that. So… we broke up."

He spoke casually, but Rosemary thought she could detect the underlying hurt in his voice, that

Lois hadn't cared enough to try to hold their relationship together for the couple of years they'd have to be apart. Well, if this Lois person couldn't tell how amazing Will was and how he was totally worth making some sacrifices for, then she didn't deserve him.

"And there wasn't anyone after her?" Rosemary wasn't sure she could believe that. He seemed pretty much perfect to her—handsome and smart and strong and kind—and so she thought there must have been plenty of single women in the congregation at All Saints who would have been all too eager to snap him up.

"A few relationships. Nothing important." He shifted on the couch so his gaze could meet hers, and a little thrill went through her body as she looked into the crystalline depths of his extraordinary eyes. "Nothing that lasted. I didn't want anything to last. I told myself that my life, my service to my church, was enough. Now, though...."

"Now?" Rosemary whispered.

"Now I know I want this," Will said, his tone low, earnest. "I think I realized it from the moment I met you, even if I didn't want to acknowledge the way you made me feel. That probably sounds crazy, but—"

She didn't let him finish. No, something inside told her to lean forward, to press her lips against his, to truly seal the connection between them in a physical way rather than simply talk about it. For the barest second, he didn't respond, as if he was startled by the kiss, but then his mouth opened and she tasted the aromatic savor of tea on his tongue, felt the warmth of his fingers against her cheeks as he cupped her face in his hands.

The room was so quiet that she could hear the pounding of her heart, the throb of blood in her veins. Never before had she felt so close to someone else, even though she'd been far more physically intimate with other men. There was something extraordinary in Will's touch, in the way his quiet strength answered the need in her soul. She drank it in, until at last she realized she needed to come up for air, if for no other reason than to process what had just happened between them.

Her lips lifted from his, but she reached over and took his hand, wanting to make sure he knew she still wanted to feel his closeness, to sense the connection between the two of them. He squeezed her fingers and smiled.

"You're sure?" he asked. That was all, but she understood.

"Yes," she replied.

Whatever happened, there would be no going back.

Chapter 9

FOR A LONG MOMENT, THEY SAT IN SILENCE on the couch and listened to the rain pour down outside. Will was happy for the weather, if only because it made him feel safe and sheltered in the house that had been his home for the past nine years. Maybe his was a spurious sense of safety at best, since the place wasn't warded against demons and he had absolutely no idea what was going to come next, but for the moment, he only wanted to savor this sensation of closeness, of how wonderful it was that this amazing woman had come into his life and somehow, miraculously, wanted to share hers with him.

Her next words, however, broke the spell. "You're sure you want to get tangled up with someone who's a possible murder suspect?"

She'd spoken lightly, almost as if she was

trying to make a joke, but he'd seen the fear far back in her sky-colored eyes. "I think Detective Phillips was just trying to scare you. We both know you're innocent, and there's absolutely no way he can prove otherwise."

"You say that," she returned, "but we don't know for sure. What if the demons killed Caleb just so they could frame me? They could have planted evidence or something—a hair, or whatever."

"Rosemary." Will put his hand on hers, doing his best to somehow make her feel the reassurance flowing from him into her. "Even if they find a hair that belongs to you somewhere in the house, so what? We both already told Detective Phillips we were there checking the place for Emma, so a piece of evidence like that won't prove anything, other than we really had been there, just as we said we were. Besides, as evil as the demons are, I'm not sure they would kill one of their own simply to complicate your life."

Her expression was dubious, but after a moment, she shrugged. "Maybe. I mean, they're demons. It's not as if they think the same way we do."

Well, that was true. By their very nature, demons were alien, completely hostile to humankind and all its endeavors. Possibly, they'd decided that Caleb was of no further use to them once he'd located Colin Turner's hard drive, and so had decided to use him to get some kind of revenge on Rosemary.

Will wasn't sure whether that particular theory held any water, though. For one thing, he didn't believe they were even dealing with actual demons here, but rather the half-demon cambions and their offspring. Their human blood might have made them less likely to do anything that would hurt one of their own, and would allow them some sense of familial loyalty. Or at least, he could hope that was the case.

"I think we just have to accept that there are things going on right now we don't completely understand," he went on. "But we should be glad that we're safe, and we're together."

Rosemary's expression brightened at those words. "Those are definitely two things to be happy about. And you're right—I know I'm innocent, but…." The words faded away, and she hugged her arms against herself, as though she'd taken a sudden chill. "What if Caleb was dead when I went back to close up the crawlspace? Or worse, what if the attack happened while I was messing around in the house and I just didn't hear anything? Maybe I could have saved him."

Will knew he needed to keep her from beating herself up any more than she already had. He laid a hand on her leg and said, "I'm sure you would have heard him fall in the pool, even with the windows shut. It's admirable that you'd want to help him even after what he did to you—"

"And to you," she interjected, as though she wanted to make sure he hadn't forgotten the concussion and other bumps and bruises he'd suffered the night before.

"Yes, and me," he amended. "But none of that was your fault. I'm willing to bet that the medical examiner will find the time of death to be much later in the evening, long after you left the house. I'm sure it won't come to that, but if necessary, I'll swear before a judge that you were with me all evening."

"Except you weren't."

"If Caleb Lockwood died after midnight, then yes, you were here. I distinctly remember you waking me up pretty much every hour on the hour."

That remark made her smile a little, and Will was glad of that, because the lightening of her expression erased some of the weariness from her delicate features and made her look much less worried. "Doctor's orders, remember?"

"Yes, I remember. But you were with me, and that's our story. More than that, it's the simple truth."

"They might say you were lying to protect me."

"I doubt it." He squeezed her leg again, and then lifted his hand and reached for his tea. It was getting to be just lukewarm, but it still tasted good. "Remember, I'm a minister at a very prominent church. No one's going to accuse a pillar of the community of lying to the police."

One of her eyebrows quirked upward at an amused angle. "Oh, so you're a pillar?"

"I am," he said with a grin. "A paragon and all that."

"Okay, now you're just teasing me."

"Maybe."

He reached for her and kissed her again, marveling a little at how perfectly their lips seemed to fit together, how wonderful she felt in his arms, almost impossibly slim but with a core of inner strength for all that. A curl brushed against his cheek, and even that soft touch was enough to awaken a heat within him. It had been a very long time, and he wanted her.

Badly.

But he'd long ago learned how to push his physical needs aside when necessary, and he knew this wasn't the time. Not yet. They cared for each other, had acknowledged their feelings even if they hadn't formally said the words, but it was all so new for them nonetheless. And even if he thought Rosemary was ready to share his bed, he couldn't quite ignore the injury Caleb Lockwood had inflicted on him just the day before. He was all right to walk around and do a few simple things, but that kind of exertion couldn't be good for him.

Oh, those reasons sounded so logical, so noble. Maybe they were even true, on some level. But Will also had to acknowledge that he didn't want to push things between him and Rosemary now because he feared he might suffer a relapse that would delay his recovery. The last thing he wanted was to hurt himself or impair himself in any way so he wouldn't be up to a confrontation when it mattered the most.

"Anyway," Will went on, "enough about that. The good detective knows where to find us if he has any other questions, and there's no point in worrying about something that isn't even going to happen."

"Fine," Rosemary said, sounding somewhat resigned. "So, what do you want to do now?"

"Why don't you tell me a little more about yourself? I just told you all my deep, dark secrets, so it's only fair that you should return the favor."

Her eyes glinted with amusement. "I wouldn't call getting dumped by an inconsiderate ex a 'deep, dark secret.' Anyway, you already know pretty much everything there is to know about me —you know about my sisters and the store, and you've seen my house and met my mother. What else is there?"

"What about your father?" Will asked, and realized right away that he'd misstepped. The twinkle left Rosemary's eyes, and she looked away from him and fidgeted with the cuff of the embroidered sweater she wore.

To her credit, though, she didn't sidestep the question. She took a breath, as if to give herself the courage to answer, and then said, "He walked out when I was ten years old. I don't really know what the whole story was behind my parents' split —I was only a kid, and my mother didn't like to talk about what really happened."

"I'm sorry," Will said, and he genuinely was. In his work, he'd seen plenty of families torn apart by divorce, and it was almost always the children who suffered the most. Her sisters would have been just enough older that they might have had some mechanisms in place for dealing with the breakup of their family, while ten-year-old Rosemary would have possessed the fewest resources to manage such a disruption in her life.

A weary lift of her shoulders, as though she'd had other people offer the same expressions of sympathy in the past and had learned long ago that they really didn't do any good. "It's a thing that happened. And it wasn't too long afterward that we went to live with my grandmother, and she had a way of making everything fun. Honestly, after the first six months or so, I hardly missed my father. He'd always worked such long hours and traveled for business so much that he was hardly ever around for us anyway."

Something about the brittle, too-casual tone Rosemary used to make that claim told Will she wasn't telling the truth about her feelings. Or rather, she was telling the truth she'd created for herself to cover up the reality of the pain she carried with herself to this day.

Rather than point any of that out to her, however, he only nodded and reached for his luke-warm tea. "What did your father do?"

"Something in finance. I don't really know. The company he worked for was downtown, in one of the high-rises there. I remember thinking that was cool because it seemed as if you had an office in one of those buildings, you'd be able to see forever." Her mouth turned down and seemed to tighten as she added, "Not that I would know from personal experience, since he never took me to see where he worked. I suppose he figured that because he traveled so much, there wasn't much point."

And if her father had had a high-powered job of some sort in the finance sector, then he most likely wouldn't have wanted to use up any of his valuable office time by taking his daughter to his place of business. Rather than make a remark along those lines, since Will doubted Rosemary would appreciate such a comment, he asked, "Where is he now?"

"Dead," she said briefly, and he could feel his brows lift in surprise.

"What happened?"

She pulled in a breath. "I don't know all the details. A car accident of some kind. I was seventeen when it happened—I guess my father had kept my mother as his emergency contact, so she was the person the local authorities called."

Saying "I'm sorry" again didn't seem as though it would meet with a favorable response, so Will settled for sending her a sympathetic glance as he said, "That had to be tough."

"I don't know." Rosemary picked up her mug of tea and tapped her fingers against the side, although she didn't appear as though she actually planned to drink any of it. "By that point, he'd been gone for seven years, so he was already out of my life. It was more like closure than anything else." She paused there and looked up at Will, her expression rueful. "That probably sounds terrible."

"No," he told her, hoping she would see that he didn't condemn her for her reaction. "I think that's a completely understandable response."

"Maybe. Anyway, I remember thinking it was kind of ironic, just because a car accident is how my father lost his parents. My mother said he was orphaned when he was only a toddler and didn't have any other family, and so he ended up in the foster care system. I suppose it says something about him that he ended up being so successful despite having the deck stacked against him like that." Another lift of her shoulders. "But that's why I don't have any contact with anyone from his side of the family—there really isn't anyone to be in contact with."

It sounded like a lonely existence. Will wondered what could make a man walk out on what—on the surface, at least—must have looked like a picture-perfect family, especially when he had no support system of his own. From what he'd seen of Glynis McGuire, she certainly didn't seem like the kind of woman who would be anything except a supportive partner. "Was he living in L.A. when the accident occurred?"

A brief shake of her head, her eyes fixed on an indefinite point somewhere past where Will sat. "No. I guess he'd gotten a transfer to Chicago. My mother actually went to Illinois so he wouldn't be buried completely alone, but we kids stayed here in California with our grandmother."

Rosemary's expression was almost preternaturally calm as she relayed this information, as if she'd relived the tragedy so many times before this moment that it no longer had the power to hurt her. Will wanted to take her in his arms and comfort her, but he had the impression that she didn't want to be soothed, only wanted him to know what had happened so he'd have some context for the current makeup of her immediate family.

"That was good of your mother," he said. Already, he'd formed a very favorable impression of Glynis McGuire, but knowing that she'd traveled halfway across the country to help lay her former husband to rest made him think he might have underestimated her.

"She said it was because she needed her own closure," Rosemary replied. "Which I can understand. But anyway, he's buried in Chicago, and that's why it's just my mother and my sisters and me. My grandmother was an only child, so I don't have any cousins."

Perhaps she had some distant relations out there in the world, but it seemed clear to him that Rosemary didn't have any desire to seek them out, for whatever reason. Maybe she was so used to depending on her sisters and her mother for her family connections that she didn't see any reason to reach out beyond them.

Knowing how limited her circle truly was made him feel protective of her—which Will guessed she wouldn't much appreciate. He knew better than to say anything along those lines, although he vowed to himself that he would do whatever was necessary to make sure she was safe, and remained that way.

Then again, in that encounter with Caleb Lockwood, she was the one who'd saved him, rather than vice versa.

"What about you?" she asked, clearly ready to change the subject.

"What about me?" he returned, and she grinned.

"Divorced parents?"

"No," he replied. "My parents are still together —my father was a civil engineer with the city of Boston. He retired just last year. My mother is a real estate agent and loves it and doesn't want to retire, although my father keeps nagging her about it. He wants to buy an RV and travel the country with her."

Rosemary looked almost wistful. Was she imagining what it would be like to be with someone who still enjoyed her company so much that even after almost forty years of marriage, he still wanted to spend all his time with her?

It was early days yet, but Will had a feeling he could see himself in that same position with her— if she really was willing to let things continue to develop between them.

"That sounds like fun," she said. "Brothers and sisters?"

"One of each. I'm the oldest."

That revelation made her crack a smile. "Then we're a walking cliché, aren't we?"

He tilted his head at her, not sure what she'd meant by that remark.

"Isn't that the usual pairing?" she inquired. "Youngest child and oldest child? The oldest is the responsible one, and the youngest is the one who keeps their partner from being too serious and encourages them to take risks and have fun."

Well, he had read articles along those lines, and he supposed he could see how such relationships would make sense. Opposites attracting, and all that. And he thought such a theory might help to explain why things with Lois hadn't worked out. She was also an oldest child, and they'd butted heads on more than one occasion, both of them firmly convinced they were in the right and the other person didn't know what they were talking about. Someone with the flexibility of a youngest child might have been more willing to reach a happy medium.

Right then, though, Will couldn't even feel regretful about the way things had turned out with him and Lois. After all, if they'd stayed together, his life would have taken a very different path—a path he was sure would never have crossed Rosemary McGuire's. Most of the time, the universe knew what it was doing, even if mere mortals didn't always want to acknowledge the fact.

He felt his mouth lift in a lopsided smile. "Well, I've definitely taken some risks since meeting you. I'm not sure whether getting attacked by a man who's part demon exactly classifies as 'fun,' though."

Obviously, she didn't take any offense at his remark, because her blue eyes glinted with amusement. "Oh, that's nothing. Just wait until someone tries to accuse you of murder—that's when the fun really starts."

However, Will didn't see anything funny about the situation. "Detective Phillips hasn't accused you of murder."

"Yet."

So they were back to that. While he could see why that terrible possibility was preying on her mind, he knew Rosemary needed to set it aside for now. "It's his job to consider possibilities, no matter how far-fetched they might be. There's no evidence, though. You know that."

She didn't look convinced, but she didn't protest, either. Instead, she snuggled up closer to him and laid her head on his shoulder. It was good to feel her weight against his body, to breathe in some of the shampoo sweetness of her hair, which had almost a vanilla scent. She pulled in a breath and released it, but didn't speak.

Will sat quietly, somehow knowing she needed this moment of closeness and silence, needed to go within herself to regroup and find a way to keep her panic at bay. He could understand why she was frightened; unfortunately, innocence wasn't a silver bullet, wasn't always enough to keep a guiltless person from ending up on the wrong side of the law. However, they needed to get past this. Neither of them knew what Detective Phillips had planned, or whether he possessed some kind of damning evidence against Rosemary—or even any evidence at all.

No, the more pressing worry that haunted Will's own thoughts was how Caleb Lockwood's death benefited the demons at all. He supposed it was remotely possible that a regular human could have overpowered the part-demon man, even if such a feat didn't seem all that plausible, considering the supernatural powers he controlled. But it appeared far more likely that another demon—or part-demon—was responsible for pushing Caleb into that pool and making sure he drowned.

But why?

Rosemary stirred and sat up straight, then pushed her heavy curls so they fell down her back rather than into her face. "I'm hungry," she announced abruptly. "What about you?"

To tell the truth, Will hadn't really thought about eating something, even though noon had come and gone more than an hour earlier, and his breakfast had been pretty meager. He suspected that Rosemary was thinking about food because she wanted something to distract herself from Caleb's unexpected death, but he couldn't really blame her for that.

"I could eat something," he said. "Whatever you like—I think most of the same places that would deliver to Michael's house would deliver here as well."

She seemed to perk up a little at the realization that she could order her favorite comfort food and not have to try something new. "Perfect," she replied. "Do you like barbecue? There's a great place up on Mountain that delivers."

"Love it," he said. "And mac and cheese and coleslaw on the side?"

"Absolutely."

Maybe Dr. Littleton would have prescribed something a little healthier for someone recovering from a concussion, but Will wasn't going to worry about it. After all, he needed to get his strength up, and some warm, hearty food on a cold day like this seemed like just what he needed.

As he watched Rosemary make the call, he found himself smiling a little, despite the worry that weighed on his mind. It felt good to have her sitting there on his couch, to have her doing something that showed she was already starting to feel a little more at home here. He didn't know how this day was going to end, but he knew he would have her with him, and that was the important thing.

The rest of it? Well, they'd confront whatever the world tried to throw at them—demons, murder investigations, or various other assorted catastrophes—and know that neither of them would have to face those challenges alone.

Chapter 10

AMAZING HOW FOOD COULD MAKE YOU FEEL so much better about life. Rosemary had never been into ribs—and was even less so now that she had cut most red meat out of her diet—but the barbecue chicken she was currently devouring was divine, and the mac and cheese that had come along with it was pretty darn near sublime. Coleslaw she could take or leave, but she could tell Will was enjoying it, and that worked for her.

No phone calls, either. While they were waiting for the food to arrive, her phone had rung and she'd found herself immediately tensing, but it was only Isabel calling to let her know that she would be the one taking Rosemary's shift at the store on Monday and possibly beyond that day if necessary, since their mother had gotten in touch to let her know what was going on, and Isabel had decided she'd rather cover those hours herself. Actually, Izzie had sounded almost bubbly—for her, anyway—although that was most likely because she'd realized Caleb was the "darkness" she'd seen surrounding her sister the week before, and now he'd been exposed for what he was, he didn't pose as much of a threat.

Rosemary almost told her sister that Caleb was dead and therefore not any kind of threat at all, but something stopped her. Maybe it was only that the investigation was ongoing, and therefore blabbing about his murder when the details hadn't even been released to the public yet probably wasn't a good idea. Also, revealing any of the facts about his death most likely would have also let slip that her own sister might be implicated in that death, even though she honestly had nothing to do with it. Isabel had sounded relieved, and Rosemary figured it was better to let her enjoy that feeling of relief while she could. In the very near future, the situation might change dramatically.

For the moment, though, she could only be glad that she didn't have to worry about working at the store. Most of the time, she truly did enjoy her job, but she knew she would have been distracted if she'd had to work the next day, and wouldn't have been able to keep her mind off Will and how he was doing.

Although, she thought as she watched him make short work of a drumstick, he seemed to have bounced back pretty damn quickly. From time to time, she noticed a hesitancy in the way he walked, as if he might have suffered a very brief bout of dizziness, but those moments didn't occur very often. His speech wasn't slurred, and his energy levels seemed very good. Not bad for someone who'd slammed their head basically full force into a wood floor just the night before.

The rain had slowed down but hadn't yet let up, which made her doubly glad that they had nowhere they needed to be except right here. Of course, she and Will could also be sitting ducks here in this house, but....

She set down her fork and gazed across the dining room table at him. Seeming to notice her regard, he lowered his mostly eaten drumstick and lifted an inquiring eyebrow.

"Do I have barbecue sauce all over my face?"

"No," she replied with a grin. However, she continued to look at him, mostly because she enjoyed doing that, liked taking in the contrast between his sooty hair and brows and those extraordinary gray eyes of his, the well-defined contours of his cheekbones and jaw and nose. Still smiling, she added, "Well, you do have a little smear in the left corner of your mouth."

He lifted his napkin to dab at the spot. "So, if

it's not barbecue sauce, what's the matter? You look as if you have something on your mind."

"I was just thinking," she replied. "We don't really have any idea what kind of powers I can control—"

"True," he cut in. "I was actually thinking we should try testing them to see if we can get any more information."

Good idea, although she'd had something a little more concrete in mind. "Yes, we should probably do that," Rosemary said. "But I wanted to try something else first. How hard is it to set up those demon-repelling wards Michael has all over his house?"

The half-amused glint in Will's gray eyes vanished, replaced by a frown. "I'm not sure how useful they are," he told her. "They didn't keep Caleb out."

"True," she said. "But they would do something, right? Against real demons, I mean."

"Yes. If properly set up, of course."

"Do you know how to do that?"

He shook his head. "Not exactly. I've blessed this house, which means it has its own low level of protection. What Michael did—that's basically advanced spell-casting, and my studies never took me in that direction."

"But you've worked with him," Rosemary said. At least, she seemed to recall Will telling her that Michael had used him as backup on several occasions.

"Yes, on a couple of cases where he needed assistance. But I mostly just provided moral support—and prayers." Will paused there, his brows drawing together. "What were you thinking, Rosemary?"

It had just been a flicker of an idea, and yet she figured it couldn't hurt to try...unless she was inviting disastrous consequences by even attempting to create protective wards without proper training. Still, she thought, nothing ventured....

"I suppose I was thinking that maybe if I warded this house, those wards might be stronger than the ones protecting Michael's place because my own powers are, well, stronger." Oh, that sounded awful, partly because such a proposition made it seem as if she thought the strange talents she'd exhibited ever since their confrontation with Caleb somehow made her more qualified and capable to cast protective spells than Michael Covenant himself, who'd been studying those sorts of arcane practices for more than a decade.

However, Will didn't seem put off by her suggestion. Instead, he leaned back in his chair and clasped his hands in his lap, obviously thinking it over. Then he said, "I suppose it's worth a try. Because if you are able to cast better, stronger wards, then they very well may be able to keep out part-demons like Caleb, and not just your regular garden-variety demons."

"Caleb is dead," she pointed out.

"True," Will allowed. "But we don't know how many others like him are out there."

Way to make a girl feel better about life, Rosemary thought. But, to be fair, one of the things she liked most about Will was his utter honesty. Better for him to tell her the truth of how he viewed a situation than sugarcoat it and leave her unprepared to face whatever harsh reality might present itself later on.

"All the more reason why we should give this a try," she said. "So…how does it work, exactly? Do you have any books with warding spells in them?"

"A few," he replied. "There are probably more in Michael's library."

"Assuming he didn't take those books with him to Tucson," Rosemary said, beginning to wonder whether this was such a good idea after all. She knew that Michael had packed up the most valuable volumes in his library and brought them along with him when he and Audrey left for Arizona. Unfortunately, what she didn't know was whether the books that contained the warding spells were the ones he considered valuable, or whether they were something he could easily replace.

Will pushed his plate out of the way and clasped his hands on the table. "That I don't know. I could call and ask him."

"Better not," Rosemary said quickly, then paused as he sent an inquiring glance in her direction.

"Why not?"

"I don't know," she replied, wondering what it was that had made her blurt out those words in the first place. A feeling, an odd little spurt of alarm that had flared up when she imagined picking up the phone and calling Michael to ask him about his spell books. Whatever had prompted it, she knew better than to ignore those feelings…psychic flashes…bursts of intuition. They'd saved her ass on more than one occasion. "But if the demons somehow knew he intended to come to California to help us, then it seems reasonable to expect they might have a way of listening to his phone conversations. The last thing we want to do is telegraph to them anything we might be planning."

Will didn't appear overly surprised by this leap of logic. A slow nod, and then he said, "You're right, of course. Let me get the books I was thinking of, and we can get started with those. After that…we'll see."

"Okay."

He got up from the table and disappeared

down the hallway. While Rosemary hadn't done much exploring of the house—she'd thought it would be rude to stick her nose in every corner of the place while the man who owned it was sleeping off a concussion—she'd seen enough to know that it had three bedrooms: the master, a guest room, and a third space that Will seemed to use for a combination office/library, since she'd glimpsed a cluttered desk and a series of antique bookcases jammed into a room that seemed far too small for all that furniture.

Rather than sit idly and wait for him to come back, she rose as well and stacked their dirty plates, then took them out to the kitchen. After she set them down on the counter, she returned to the dining room to retrieve the leftover food, thinking she could put it in the refrigerator in its take-out containers, since she didn't know where Will kept his Tupperware.

"The storage stuff is in the lower cupboard next to the refrigerator," he said helpfully as he appeared in the kitchen doorway.

"Thanks."

Sure enough, there was a nice matching set of glass storage containers with plastic lids in the cupboard he'd mentioned. There weren't a lot of leftovers, so it didn't take very long for her to package everything up and put it away in the fridge.

"You've got them?" she asked as she turned back toward him, noticing for the first time the two small leather-bound books he had tucked under one arm.

"Yes. Like I said, these are sort of beginner-level stuff, but they're all I have."

Rosemary went over and kissed him on the cheek, and his eyes lit up immediately. Smiling, she said, "Well, since I'm a beginner, I guess it's good that those books are for people like me. No point in attempting calculus when you haven't passed Algebra 1, right?"

"You have a point." He glanced back toward the living room. "We might as well try this in there. You'll have more room to move around."

She couldn't quite see why that mattered. "Do I need room?"

The corners of his mouth quirked—just a little, not so he was actually laughing at her ignorance. However, she knew she was ignorant about this sort of thing. She'd never cast a spell in her life.

All right, technically, she had murmured a teeny little spell to summon Madeline Nash's ghost back when she and Caleb had been trying to figure out where Colin had hidden the footage, but that very small bit of magic hardly counted.

Still looking amused, Will said, "You'll need

to draw the spell circles, and sometimes they can be fairly large."

Dismayed, she looked past him to the living room, to the polished oak floor and the friendly mismatch of antique furniture. "I don't want to mess up your house—" she began, thinking of the patterns Audrey and Michael had erased from the floor of the Whitcomb mansion in Glendora, how Audrey's description had made them seem very large and very complicated.

"You won't," Will interrupted. "You're not summoning demons—there's no paint or blood involved. No, these spell circles are the kind you draw with holy water."

"I'm supposed to write symbols with water?" Rosemary asked, knowing how dubious she sounded. "How will I know if I screw something up?"

"You won't. Or rather, you'll know if we have a horde of demons appear in the middle of the room."

She crossed her arms and gave him what she hoped was a convincing stink-eye. "That's supposed to be reassuring?"

"No," he answered easily. "It's just the truth. Come on."

Wondering if she'd made a terrible decision in attempting to ward the house, Rosemary followed Will into the living room. He took the books from under his arm and set them on the coffee table, then went over to the antique cupboard placed up against one wall and extracted a small plastic bottle from one of the shelves inside. Silently, he handed it to her, and she took it from him.

"Holy water?" she asked, and he nodded.

"It never hurts to have a decent supply around."

No, she supposed it didn't. The bottle looked completely prosaic, but she had to trust that the liquid it contained was the thing she needed to create some viable demon-repelling wards.

Without waiting for her to comment, he went on, "Before you start creating the actual wards, though, you'll need to prepare yourself. Do you meditate?"

"Yes," Rosemary said, glad that she practiced that ancient art on a regular basis. She didn't pretend to be a master, but she had become pretty good at maintaining focus, on working her way through the visualizations that allowed her to exercise some control over the racing thoughts that all people had to deal with.

Will looked pleased. "Good. Then this should come naturally to you. The most important thing is to do what you can to remove all negative thoughts, anything that might lead you to believe you won't be successful in casting these spells. In your case, you might also want to think of what it was you did to protect me—and yourself—from Caleb's demonic magic. Obviously, you were very effective, so you'll want to invoke some of that power now."

What *had* she done, exactly? She'd been driven by fear and worry and desperation, but something within her had risen to the occasion and had allowed powers she didn't even know she possessed to come alive and do their work. She thought of the white light of protection, and how it had somehow coalesced within her and became something tangible, something that made Caleb's evil demon-fire bounce off its surface as though a glass bubble had encased her and Will.

That brilliant white light, absolutely pure, absolutely good. It had helped her before, and would help her again.

"I think I have it," she whispered, eyes half shut as she imagined that white light flowing through her body, filling her so that her skin shimmered with its energy.

"My God," Will said.

His voice was also hushed, and Rosemary's eyelids popped open. She looked down at herself, saw the way she seemed to be glowing from within, hands encased in glimmering white light. Because she was wearing a sweater and jeans, she couldn't see much more of her skin, and yet she somehow knew all of her glowed in the same way.

Like she was radioactive.

She gasped, and the glow disappeared immediately. Heart pounding, she touched a finger to the back of her hand. It felt completely normal—if anything, a little cool to the touch, since the house wasn't overly warm.

"It can't hurt you," Will said. He came over to her and took her hand in his. "It's part of you, Rosemary. Do you understand?"

Did she want to understand? Part of her didn't, not really, because these powers surfacing from nowhere frightened her. On the other hand, it would be stupid to ignore them just because she didn't fully understand them yet. Her strange gifts were what had beaten Caleb, and so she knew she had to accept them now. Otherwise, there was a very great chance she wouldn't be so lucky the next time she had to confront someone of demon-kind.

"I understand," she murmured. "Or at least, I understand if I don't think too hard about it."

A sudden, swift smile, and he bent and kissed her. Gently, but the touch of his lips against hers awoke a hungry heat within her, one she wanted to succumb to. It would be so much easier to keep kissing Will and then move matters down the hall into the bedroom. However, she knew that doing such a thing wouldn't help her at all. Oh, she wanted to be with Will, but sex wouldn't be anything except a distraction at this point. Once the house was safely warded…well, then they would talk.

"Try it again."

She nodded, then pulled in a breath and made herself focus again, closed her eyes and imagined the beauty and strength of her power as it grew within her, light pulsing like a star gone nova, only healing instead of hurtful. This time when she opened her eyes, she knew what to expect, and the pale shimmering glow that surrounded her hands didn't surprise her, but instead only awoke a sense of wonder.

"What do I do now?" she whispered.

Will bent and lifted the book from where it had been waiting on the coffee table, then opened it to a page toward the beginning. "We'll start with a simple charm of protection. Considering the power you seem to possess, you may not need to do anything more than that."

Should he be that confident in her ability to create the wards? Rosemary didn't know for sure. Yes, that glow had been extraordinary, but just because something looked spectacular didn't necessarily mean it possessed any real substance.

However, she supposed she'd find out soon enough.

She glanced down at the page Will had selected. The book was either quite old or a facsimile of a much older edition, since it had been printed in an old-fashioned font, the kind that had the funny lower-case "s" shaped like an "f"—like you'd see on the Declaration of Independence or something. Because of the typography, it was a little difficult to read, and she made herself go over the charm several times so she wouldn't trip over her tongue while reciting it out loud.

"All right," she said, looking up from the book to see Will watching her intently. As soon as their eyes met, however, he gave her an encouraging smile.

"Then go ahead."

One brief pause to pull in a breath and steady herself, and then she said in a firm, clear voice, "All within is good. Circle of air and spirit, surround this place. Let no harm come to those who dwell here or remain within these walls. Light against dark, bright against black, so let it be."

As she spoke, she raised her hands and saw again the pulsing white glow of her power—or talent, or gift—emanating from beneath her skin. More than that, though, it seemed to spread out from her body to encompass the entire room first, and then move beyond that, going to include every square foot of Will's house.

This time, she thought she could actually feel it as well, like the soothing warmth of the sun against her skin, bright and pure and utterly welcome. As Will had said, she suddenly understood there was no reason to be frightened of it, because as strange as this might seem to her at the moment, she was only summoning an energy that had lived within her for her entire life. Now at last she was able to use it as it had been meant to be utilized.

Once she was done speaking the words of the charm, she lowered her hands and glanced around again. Nothing seemed materially different—well, except for Will staring at her with something like awe in his expression.

"Don't you dare look at me like that," she said, the edge to her voice effectively dispelling whatever effects of the invocation might have still lingered in the space. "I'm still me."

At once, he nodded and came over to her. She didn't notice any hesitation as he took her in his arms, held her close. Yes, that was better. In Will's embrace, she still felt like Rosemary, not some strange creature who'd emerged to take her place.

"Of course, you're still you," he told her. One hand moved over her curls, tender but not hesitant at all. "But you're also amazing."

Since he held her close, she couldn't exactly shrug. That was all right, though; she couldn't think of anywhere she'd rather be than in his arms. "Well, I'll admit that looked kind of impressive. But I don't know whether it actually *did* anything."

He pressed his lips against the top of her head, then pulled away so he could gaze down into her face. However, he held on to her hands, as if he understood that she needed him to maintain some kind of physical contact in order to reassure her that his feelings hadn't changed...despite the way she'd displayed her powers just a moment earlier.

Mouth quirking a little, he said, "I suppose if we're not attacked by demons, then we'll know the wards are working."

"We weren't attacked by demons before," she pointed out, and he chuckled.

"True. But still—"

He was interrupted by a loud ring from his back pocket.

"Your butt's ringing," Rosemary said, grinning despite herself.

"I can let it go to voicemail."

The thought was tempting, but with everything that was going on, she guessed it probably wasn't a good idea to ignore what might be an important phone call. "No, you'd better answer it. Maybe it's Michael."

That argument seemed to convince him, because Will let go of one of her hands so he could reach into his pocket and extract the phone. He frowned as he looked down at the screen. "It's not Michael—I don't recognize the number."

In which case it might be a better idea to allow the call to slide over to voicemail. Rosemary's own phone got spammed so often that she never answered it unless the call was coming from a number in her contacts list.

However, apparently Will wasn't quite as cautious, because he shrugged and swiped the screen to accept the incoming call. "Will Gordon." He was quiet for a few seconds, and then an expression of surprise passed over his face. "Oh, hello, Fred. Yes, Michael told me he planned to get in touch with you and set it up so we could communicate directly." Another pause, during which Will's brows drew together in a frown, although he remained silent as he appeared to listen to what the other man was saying.

Rosemary didn't know who "Fred" was, although clearly, he had to be a friend of Michael's…maybe his mysterious "source," the person who was so skilled at digging up information other people wanted to remain buried. She went ahead and let go of Will's other hand, since it seemed as though he might be on the phone for a while, and sat down on the couch. Now that she was sitting, she could sense how rubbery her legs felt, as if she'd gone for a hard run. It seemed that summoning the white light and casting a protection charm took more energy than she'd imagined.

Will continued to stand where he was, his frown deepening as he listened to Fred talk. Whatever the call was about, clearly, it had to be important. At last, though, he said, "I understand. You can text the information to this number, and Rosemary and I will discuss it and get back to you. Thank you for letting me know."

As she watched, he touched his finger to the screen to end the call, and then slid the phone back into his pocket. His frown didn't go away, though; if anything, it only intensified.

"What was that about?" she asked, since it didn't seem as if he was about to volunteer any information.

"That was Fred Peñasco—Michael's data guy," Will replied, thus confirming her theory as to the caller's identity. "Strange thing, though."

"What was strange?"

He came over and sat down next to her, then laid a hand on top of hers. Rosemary could feel warmth flow through her at his touch, at the casual way he'd reached over to her, no hesitation, just a desire to reaffirm their closeness. If he was at all put off by the power she'd displayed a few moments earlier, she never would have been able to guess by looking at him.

"Well," he said, "I knew Michael was going to

pass my contact info along to Fred, so I wasn't that surprised by the call. No, what's strange is that Fred said he'd tried to call me three times today before this, and the calls kept getting dropped."

"Maybe he lives somewhere with bad reception," she suggested, but Will shook his head.

"No, he specifically mentioned that he's in a suburban area where he routinely gets at least four bars, so the problem wasn't on his end. He said he was about to give up and go through Michael again, only he thought he'd give it one last try. This time, the call came through."

"And…?" she prompted, wondering what was so significant about that. After all, cell phones and cell service could be extremely unreliable, no matter where you were or which carrier you used.

"It came through only a minute or so after you warded this house," Will said. "Maybe it's just coincidence, but I somehow doubt that."

For a second or two, she could only stare at him. The numbers began to add up, and she ventured, "So, you think the demons were somehow blocking Fred's call from coming through, and then when the wards went up, they couldn't interfere anymore?"

"Yes," he said simply.

As theories went, she didn't quite know what to make of that one. All right, the timing was a little suspicious, but she honestly thought it had to be a coincidence. Could demons even interfere with cell phone transmissions?

She would have liked to reassure herself that no, of course they couldn't, but then she recalled how they'd also reportedly messed with Audrey's car—and had somehow caused an accident so the Uber driver who was going to take Michael to the airport had to cancel the booking. If all that was true, then she realized there was an awful lot they could interfere with…if that interference suited their purposes.

"Why wouldn't they want Fred to contact you?" she asked at last.

Will gave her a weary smile. "Because he had information to pass along that they wouldn't want us to have."

"What information?"

His hand tightened on hers. "He thinks he's located where the cambions and their children have been living. If Colin Turner's footage hasn't been destroyed yet, that's where it has to be."

Rosemary stared at him, her mouth dry. Deep inside, she'd hoped this might all be over, that with the footage gone and Caleb dead, there wasn't anything either she or Will could do.

Now, though, she realized they still had a long ways to go.

Chapter 11

INDIANA. OF COURSE. CALEB HAD TOLD HER he was from Indiana. Rosemary had assumed that statement was a lie, along with pretty much everything else that had come out of his mouth, but apparently, he'd been telling her the truth about his origins. Most likely, he hadn't seen the harm, since he'd never been specific about the exact town. Indiana was much, much smaller than California, but even so, it would have been difficult to track down his origins without a little more information.

But Fred had done it, because that was what Fred did. Rosemary realized Will was staring at her, clearly expecting some sort of a response, and so she cleared her throat and said, "How did he figure that out?"

Will's shoulders lifted slightly. "He didn't go

into the details. I suppose it doesn't really matter. The important thing is that he says the Lockwoods—and the six other families descended from the original trustees—are still there. Prominent members of the community, from the way Fred was talking."

Of course, they were. They'd been put in place as doctors and lawyers and bankers and other members of the top tier in the area. No doubt their wealth had increased through the years, just as Belial's own fortune had. Rosemary didn't know much about small Midwest towns, but she knew enough from living and running a business in Glendora—a smallish place with families who'd been there for several generations—that it could be pretty hard to insinuate yourself into that sort of milieu. She and Will would stick out like sore thumbs.

That thought made her pause. Crazy how she'd immediately leapt to the idea of them going there to find the footage, even though he hadn't even suggested such a thing. And yet…that was the logical next step, wasn't it? Michael wasn't about to leave Audrey alone in Tucson, not with the demons clearly waiting to pounce.

"When do we leave?" she asked.

Will's eyes widened. "I didn't say we were going to Indiana."

"You didn't have to." Her fingers tightened on

his. "Who else is going to go after the footage, especially with the demons working to keep Michael in Tucson?"

Will didn't answer right away. His mouth was tight, and she wondered if his head was hurting him again. "No one, I suppose."

The last thing she wanted was to push him into an adventure he didn't want. Hell, she didn't know whether she was terribly keen to go chasing off to Greencastle, Indiana, of all places, to run right smack into a den of demons. All right, half- and quarter-demons, but still.

"If you're not feeling well enough, then maybe Michael—" she ventured, but Will wouldn't let her get any farther than that.

"Michael has his own problems to deal with," he cut in. "In their own way, he and Audrey are under siege just as much as we are. Or possibly worse, since it seems you have greater powers that can be brought to bear against our enemies."

"Maybe," Rosemary returned, not caring how dubious she sounded. Yes, it was clear enough she had talents that most people didn't, but those powers didn't make her invincible. She hadn't even been able to prevent Caleb from getting away with the hard drive. If she was that ineffective against even a single quarter-demon, how in the world was she supposed to prevail when surrounded by a whole town full of them?

All right, that was probably a bit of an exaggeration. Even if the original demons had been pretty fruitful and had multiplied at rates greater than the general population, she didn't think they could have taken over a whole town in just a couple of generations. Still, they were probably pretty thick on the ground, all of them with their own powers. Caleb on his own had been scary enough; she really didn't want to think about what it would be like to take on forty or fifty or even a hundred part-demons just like him.

"Anyway," Will went on, "I feel much improved, and I'm sure I'll only be that much better tomorrow."

"That's when you want to go?" In a way, heading out to Indiana would be easy enough, since she'd already packed her things to come here to Will's. It wasn't as though she'd have to go back to Michael's house and get a bunch of personal items for the trip.

"If at all possible. It's already getting late in the day, so I don't think trying to leave now would give us much of an advantage." He hesitated there, and then gave her another one of those tired but charming smiles. "Besides, I'm not going to lie—I could definitely use a real night's sleep in my own bed before we go off to vanquish demons."

Whereas she wouldn't be sleeping in her own bed, but the one in Will's guest room. Actually, it wasn't really "her" bed at Michael's place, either, and so she figured she could handle the guest room bed here without too much trouble. Anyway, she was tired enough after getting barely two hours' worth of sleep the night before that she figured she could probably fall asleep on a rock.

"We'll do that, then," she said. "I'll let Isabel know that I may not be in to work this whole week, and we'll just see how it goes from there."

As Rosemary spoke, though, she experienced a small twinge of regret mixed with worry. It was one thing to take off a day, or maybe two. But being away for a week would be placing an undue burden on her sisters, even if their mother came in to lend a hand and carry some of the load. Unfortunately, there didn't seem to be much of an alternative. There was no one else who could take on the task of going to Greencastle and handling its attendant demons.

Despite those misgivings, she also knew she couldn't let worries like that prevent her from doing what needed to be done. If it turned out that the footage had been destroyed, well, she and Will would figure out what to do next. Something inside her told her it still existed, though. Just a small certainty, enough to let her know they wouldn't be embarking on a fool's errand. This wasn't about helping Caleb—that ship had sailed as soon as his true identity had been revealed—

but about making sure the world knew the truth about the demons. Michael and Audrey wanted that, and Rosemary had to believe Colin had wanted it as well, or Madeline Nash wouldn't have worked so hard to get her message across to the one person she'd thought could help.

No, if she walked away now, Rosemary would be letting all of them down. Whether or not her strange talents would be up to such a confrontation, she had no idea, but she had to try.

"That sounds like a good idea," Will said. He'd probably noticed the way she'd sat there and stewed over their plan of action, but had decided not to comment on it. "Why don't you go ahead and call your sister about covering for you at the store, and I'll go online and see about booking us a flight and a hotel."

Those practical considerations made her give him a very straight look. "Do you need any help with that? Last-minute airfare can be expensive, and—"

"It's all right, Rosemary," he interrupted, but gently, as though he wanted to make sure she knew he appreciated her concern. "I have some reserves I can tap into for this sort of thing. If it ends up being a problem, I'll let you know."

She supposed she'd have to be content with that. Arguing the point would only make it sound as if she didn't trust him to accurately represent his finances to her. However, she also vowed silently that she would find a way to reimburse him for at least her half of the expenses, if not more. That was only fair; her savings account was pretty plump, since her day-to-day cost of living tended to be pretty minimal.

"All right," she said. "I'll go ahead and call Isabel."

"And I'll see what I can find for airfare and accommodations."

He got up from the couch and headed down the hallway to his office, while she also left the living room and went into the kitchen, which was where she'd left her purse. When she activated her phone, she was glad to see she hadn't missed any calls or texts. Not that she'd been expecting any, but she still had the fear lurking at the back of her mind that Detective Phillips might contact her at any moment to haul her in for questioning.

If that was his plan, he didn't appear ready to execute it late on a Sunday afternoon. Rosemary was able to get in touch with Isabel and let her know that she had to go out of town unexpectedly. Of course, her sister started to ask questions, but Rosemary only said that she hoped it would only take a day or so and that she should be back in California by the end of the week—and definitely in time for all the Halloween celebrations the week after that.

"But you're not coming to dinner tonight?" Isabel inquired, and Rosemary couldn't help giving an inner wince. With everything that had been going on, she'd completely forgotten about the McGuire Sunday dinner. Then again, she guessed her mother already knew she wouldn't be attending, or she might have reminded her daughter about it when they went to retrieve her Fiat from the parking garage.

"No, I'll have to skip this week," Rosemary said. "But I think Mom already knew I wouldn't be going, so it shouldn't be too big a deal."

"Sure," Isabel responded. She hesitated before adding, "Maybe next week you can bring Will to meet everyone."

That seemed a little early to be introducing him to the family...but was it? After all, he'd already met her mother. And while Isabel seemed to have been glad that Rosemary had been taking things slowly with Caleb, she didn't appear to exhibit that same reluctance when it came to Will Gordon.

"I'll see," Rosemary replied, figuring that was about the best she could do, given the circumstances. "But I think he'd like that."

"All right," Isabel said. "Wherever you're going...be careful."

That was all she said, but Rosemary understood. Maybe she wasn't seeing darkness on the horizon as she had when Caleb was in the picture, but her sister still seemed to sense that Rosemary wasn't jetting off for some pleasure trip to Tahiti.

"I will," she promised. "And I'll be in touch just as soon as I know when I'll be back at work."

"It's not a problem. Mom already said she was willing to pitch in if necessary. But you take care."

"I will."

They ended the call there, and Rosemary put her phone back in her purse. She left the kitchen and went into the office, where Will sat in the desk chair with his laptop open in front of him as he scrolled through a couple of travel sites. He looked up as she entered and pointed at a chair placed over by one of the bookcases.

"Go ahead and have a seat," he told her. "Sorry about the books."

Because of course there was a stack of books sitting on the chair, as though they'd ended up there because he'd run out of room on the book-shelves. Rosemary suppressed a grin and gathered up the stack, then set it down on the floor in a spot that appeared to be relatively out of the way.

"It's fine," she said. Actually, it was nice to be with someone who appeared to love books as much as she did. So many of the men she met didn't seem interested in reading at all. "Have you found anything?"

He nodded. "I think so. The best flight I've

found is one from Ontario—I figured we wouldn't want to fly out of LAX—that only has an hour layover in Dallas Fort Worth. It leaves a little before one in the afternoon and gets us in to Indianapolis at eleven."

"So we'll lose a whole day traveling?"

"It looks that way." He leaned back in his chair and ran a hand through his hair, ruffling it slightly. The resulting disheveled style made him look so gorgeous in a rumpled way that Rosemary didn't sit down, but instead went over to him and pressed a kiss against the top of his head. He lifted a hand from the keyboard and reached out to her, their fingers clasping so he could pull her closer and give her a real kiss. When it ended, he remarked, "You're quite distracting, you know that?"

She grinned. "I try to be. Anyway, if you think that flight is the best one, then you might as well book it."

"Okay." He was silent for a few minutes as he made his selections and then entered his credit card information. Rosemary tried not to wince at the price, although she realized that a little over five hundred dollars for last-minute airfare across the country really wasn't that bad. She couldn't help noticing that he didn't book round-trip tickets, probably because they had no idea how long this crazy mission was even going to take. Once that was done, he navigated over to the hotel booking site. "It looks like there's only one real hotel in Greencastle itself," he told her. "Luckily, it's pretty highly rated."

"Would it matter if it wasn't?"

His mouth quirked. "Probably not." A minute or so passed as he went through the process of entering his information there, and then he closed the laptop. "We're all set. Now all we have to do is rest until it's time to leave."

Rosemary could have thought of a few things they should do to occupy themselves…but she also knew that their upcoming trip would be tiring enough for him. Maybe once they were in Greencastle they could make full use of their hotel room, although she knew she'd have to wait and see how Will was feeling. This wasn't a pleasure trip, after all. Honestly, she didn't know exactly what it was.

More like a suicide mission, she thought grimly, although she pushed that horrible notion away almost as soon as it entered her head. Neither one of them exactly knew what they'd be facing once they reached Indiana.

Which was probably a good thing.

She managed a smile and touched Will on the shoulder. "Well, now that's taken care of, why don't we relax for a bit? I doubt a doctor would recommend reading, but it should probably be okay for you to put your feet up and watch TV for a while."

He didn't respond at first, and for a moment, Rosemary was worried he might protest, might tell her that no, they couldn't waste time watching television and instead needed to have her work on flexing her psychic muscles, just so they could see what her powers could and couldn't do. That probably was a good idea, and yet she knew she was dead tired, and if she was feeling that way, she could only imagine how Will must feel. Practice was good, but rest was better.

His mouth lifted in response, and he nodded. "Yes, let's take it easy for a bit."

Odd how they could have such a lovely, easy evening when they had so much hanging over their heads. Just as Rosemary had suggested, they watched TV—or rather, they binged old *Quantum Leap* episodes from a DVD boxed set he owned—ordered in dinner, and then watched one more episode before they both started nodding off a little after eight.

"We might as well try to sleep," he told her, and she made a face like a five-year-old being told she was staying up past her bedtime, mouth pursed and nose screwed up. She looked so adorable, he wanted to lean in and kiss her, kiss her hard—but he knew that probably wasn't a very good idea. They'd both been keeping things as casual as they could, although Will could feel the sexual tension simmering just under the surface. Tired as they were, they might not be able to hold back if he initiated anything that seemed like intimate contact.

But then Rosemary had chuckled and said, "I feel like a loser going to bed this early, but I see your point. We're already close to passing out."

"Exactly."

So they'd gotten up from the couch, and he'd told her to go ahead and use the bathroom first. While he was waiting for her, he sat on the bed with his feet up, noting how exhausted he really was, praying that his strength would return the next day. At least he would be able to sleep normally tonight rather than being woken up every hour on the hour, but he still worried that he was pushing things. Unfortunately, he didn't have much of a choice. The only other person he knew who could have managed this trip to Greencastle was a state away in Tucson…and apparently was under siege by demons doing everything they could to make sure he stayed put.

Will did his best to reassure himself that Rosemary's remarkable powers were their ace in the hole, the one thing the demons couldn't see coming. At least, he had to hope that Caleb hadn't reported back to his father or someone else in authority how his would-be girlfriend had turned out to have some fairly spectacular demon-fighting tricks up her sleeve. It was hard to know for certain, since he had no idea when Caleb had actually died.

Only part of the mystery, however. More important was who had killed him...and why. The only thing they knew now was that it hadn't been Rosemary.

"I'm out!" she called down the hallway.

"Thanks!" Will called back, and pushed himself up off the bed. He caught a glimpse of her going down the hall in an oversized T-shirt and a pair of black leggings, her wild hair caught up in a scrunchie. From the back, she looked about fifteen years old, and he had to suppress a smile. A woman of contradictions, Rosemary McGuire.

And he liked her that way. She was so utterly different from anyone else he'd known, so strong and smart and beautiful, but vulnerable, too, doing her best to hide the hurts she'd carried with her through the years. He felt honored that she'd allowed him into her heart, and vowed he would do whatever he could to make sure she remained safe through any ordeals they might face in Greencastle.

There was barely any sign that she'd used the

bathroom before him, except for a damp towel and a few splashes in the sink. Obviously, she'd tried to be careful to leave things as clean as she'd found them, and he smiled a little at her thoughtfulness.

No point in studying his reflection—he already knew he looked like hell. No, he splashed some water on his face, brushed and flossed and took care of other business, then went down the hall back to his bedroom. The room felt very dark when he turned out his bedside lamp, although he somehow knew there was nothing to fear in that darkness. Why should there be? Rosemary had used the glowing power of light within her to cast wards stronger than those which protected Michael Covenant's house, and Will felt sure nothing that meant them any ill could make its way in here.

Even so, despite knowing the house was protected, and despite knowing he was probably more tired than he'd been since the days when he pulled all-nighters in college, he found himself restless, as though they had overlooked something vital, a clue that had been right under their noses the entire time. Was it merely that they should have guessed the cambions and their families still lived somewhere in Indiana?

He didn't think so. After all, there hadn't been much time to put two and two together.

But something....

Problem was, he hadn't been trained for this sort of thing. He wasn't a detective or private investigator. Hell, he didn't even read mystery novels.

Still....

He sat up in bed, frowning. Maybe it was simply the thought of the demon/humans who lived in Greencastle, Indiana, but Will realized the one thing they hadn't done was check Caleb's house here in Southern California. At least, he assumed the man must have had some sort of home base here, although Rosemary hadn't mentioned it. Not terribly surprising—he could tell she was embarrassed by her relationship with Caleb, was still giving herself grief over that even though there was no way in the world she could have known who—or what—he really was.

A quick glance at the digital clock on his nightstand told Will it really wasn't that late, not quite eight-thirty. Not so strange a time of night to go visit a house, even on a Sunday evening.

Suddenly determined, he pushed himself out of bed, paused to throw on a T-shirt so he wouldn't walk into the guest room bare-chested, and then headed down the hallway. Rosemary had pulled the door shut, so he paused and knocked.

"Rosemary?" he said. "Are you awake? I just thought of something."

A few seconds passed, and then the door opened and she stared out at him, expression confused but not sleepy. Apparently, she'd been having as hard a time falling asleep as he had. "What is it?"

"Where was Caleb living?"

She blinked. "What?"

"Did you ever go to the house where he was living here in Southern California?"

Almost at once, the bewilderment left her features, and her eyes narrowed slightly. "Yes," she replied. "It's in Eagle Rock."

"Could you find it again?"

"I think so." She tilted her head up at him and asked, "What are you thinking, Will?"

"I'm not sure," he said. "A hunch, nothing more. But maybe—just maybe—Caleb left the footage there before he went back to the Glendale house and got ambushed."

"Which means we might not have to go to Indiana after all?"

"Maybe not," Will replied. "We'll have to see what we can find."

"Sounds like a plan," Rosemary said, and then flashed him a smile. "I hope those plane tickets are refundable…."

Chapter 12

THEY'D GOTTEN DRESSED AGAIN IN HASTE, and Will handed Rosemary the keys to his car as they exited the house. At least by that point, the rain had stopped, although the roads were still slick and she knew she'd have to be careful. Good thing that the freeways were never all that busy on Sunday nights.

She slid behind the wheel of the Challenger, then backed out of the driveway and guided the car down Lake Avenue so they could jump on the westbound 210 Freeway. Will didn't speak, but she could sense the tension in him. Was he keyed up because he didn't like the idea of her driving his car, or was it simply that the thing they sought might soon be within reach?

Or they could be going on a wild goose chase, just as she had with Caleb when he was tricking her into helping him find the damn footage the first time. Also, just because she knew where he'd been living while maintaining the false person of Caleb Dixon, would-be indie filmmaker, that didn't mean they'd be able to gain access to the property to do a search.

"Caleb has a roommate," she blurted, and Will looked over at her in some surprise.

"Have you met him?"

"No," she admitted as she guided the car over into the fast lane. "Caleb said he was off on a location shoot."

"Which might or might not have been the truth."

That was the problem, wasn't it? It seemed Caleb had pretty much lied to her every time he opened his mouth, but he might have mixed some truth in with the lies. Well, if it turned out the mythical roommate actually was home, she'd make up some kind of story—that she'd left something there the last time she'd visited, and she'd tried to call Caleb and never got an answer, and oh, no, something terrible had happened to him? She had no idea….

Rosemary felt her mouth curl in a grim little smile. Seemed like she was getting pretty good at this lying thing as well, considering the story she'd just cooked up in her head, not to mention the whoppers she'd told Detective Phillips.

Because Will was staring out the car window at the rain-slick freeway, he apparently couldn't see her expression. He went on, "I think it's far more likely he lived alone. He wouldn't have wanted a regular human to know anything about his comings and goings."

"Unless his roommate was another part-demon, just like him."

They did seem to pop up with alarming regularity, after all.

"Possibly."

They drove in silence after that, until Rosemary eased the car off the freeway at the Eagle Rock Boulevard exit and then turned off into the hills. Thank God she'd driven this way on her own, and not just as a passenger in Caleb's car, because generally once she'd driven to a place, she could remember pretty well how to get there.

And that was the case now, as she allowed her bump of direction or whatever it was to guide her up to the street where Caleb's house was located. As they drove, however, she noticed right away that a small group of people were standing at the base of the driveway, apparently having some sort of a discussion, although the street wasn't very well lit and she couldn't quite make out their expressions.

"What's going on?" she murmured, and Will shook his head.

"I don't know," he said. "But we're here now, so I think we need to still try."

"It's okay," Rosemary told him. "I already have a story ready to go."

The corner of his mouth that she could see lifted slightly. "Well, that should help."

She pulled up to the curb and parked, and then the two of them got out of the car. As the little group of people in the driveway turned to look at them, Rosemary was glad that she'd finger-fluffed her hair and put on some lip gloss before leaving Will's house, just in case they ended up having to actually interact with anyone.

Putting what she hoped was an appropriately concerned expression on her face, she approached the closest member of the group, a woman around her mother's age, with dishwater-blonde hair and skin that looked deeply tanned even in the dim illumination from the streetlight half a block away. "Excuse me...what's going on?"

The woman stared at her for a second or two, and then, improbably, recognition seemed to dawn on her sharp features. "You came and visited Caleb, didn't you?"

"Yes," Rosemary replied. "We dated for a little bit. Actually, I left my earrings here a while back and was trying to get in touch so I could come get them, but Caleb never returned my calls. He—"

"Oh," the woman said, her hand going to her mouth. "You didn't hear?"

"Hear what?" Rosemary returned, although of course she knew exactly what the woman was talking about.

"I'm Linda," the woman said. "I own the house Caleb was renting—I live up the street." She gestured vaguely up the hill. "I'm so sorry for you to find out this way, but the police called me earlier and told me he'd been found dead of an apparent drowning."

Next to Rosemary, Will shifted and stared at Linda. "He what?"

"Who're you?" she asked.

A natural enough question, considering that, as far as Linda knew, Rosemary was still dating Caleb. "He's, um…he's my big brother Will," she said hastily. "I had him come with me as moral support."

This bald-faced lie made Will lift an eyebrow —but only for a second, his incredulous expression come and gone so quickly, Rosemary doubted Linda had even noticed it.

"Oh, well…I'm sorry you both had to find out like this," she said. "I guess the police called me because mine was the only local contact number he had in his wallet."

Rosemary nodded, doing her best to look shocked and surprised and sad. Actually, she was a little surprised by the revelation that the house was owned by someone up the street and not some mythical roommate's parents in Tempe, Arizona. Not too much, because Caleb hadn't told the truth about much of anything, but she did find it interesting that he'd taken the risk of renting a place where the landlord lived so close by. Had he been enamored of the view, or had he simply taken it because he needed a home base and maybe Linda was an easygoing landlord, someone who didn't ask for a lot of references, or possibly just offered a month-to-month agreement instead of the sort of ironclad leases that most homeowners these days required?

There was no way to ask without sounding completely intrusive, and so Rosemary shrugged the question aside. What she really needed to do was get inside the house and see if that damn hard drive was somewhere in there.

"It's all right," she said slowly, knowing that Linda was still watching her, obviously expecting an answer. "We, um…we actually had kind of a spat. It was stupid, but…." She let the words trail off, then gathered a breath and said, "I thought that was why he wasn't calling me back. And I know this sounds terrible, but is there any way you could let me inside to see if I could find my earrings? Normally, I would never ask, but they belonged to my grandmother and—"

"Oh, no, it's fine," Linda broke in, her expression sympathetic. "The police have come and gone, and they cleared me to enter the property. Let me take you inside and see if we can find those earrings."

Relief surged through Rosemary, and she allowed herself a quick glance at Will. He nodded almost imperceptibly, and followed a few paces behind as the two women walked up the driveway and then went inside the house. Linda reached over to touch the switch on the wall just inside the front door, and recessed lighting in the living room turned on, illuminating the space.

Everything looked pretty much as it had when Rosemary was here almost two weeks earlier—the same mishmash of hand-me-down furniture, the same flat-weave rug on the wooden floor. For some reason, she'd been expecting to see the house turned inside out by the police, but she realized they had no real reason to do a thorough inspection here, since his death had happened miles away. No, they'd probably come in and looked for anything that might have provided a reason for his presence at the house on Las Flores Drive, but there certainly was no reason to tear the place apart.

But if the police had been here, there was always the chance they'd found the hard drive and taken it with them, especially if Caleb had just dropped it on the kitchen table or something before he headed back to Glendale. Which begged the question as to why he would have gone back to the house in the first place, but Rosemary feared he'd taken that particular bit of information with him to the grave.

Since Linda was looking at her, obviously expecting her to say something, Rosemary said quickly, "Um, I think I left my earrings in Caleb's bedroom. Let me just go and check."

She hurried off, leaving Linda and Will standing in the entry. The landlord said, "It was so nice of you to come with your sister over here," to which Will murmured something Rosemary couldn't quite hear, although she guessed his response would be noncommittal and not anything that would rouse the woman's suspicions.

If it had felt strange to walk into the house at all, it was stranger still to enter Caleb's bedroom. Nothing here had changed, as far as she could tell —the same black and white classic monster movie posters hung on the wall, and the same mismatched furniture stood where it had been when Caleb had brought her here to…well, to have sex with her. Thank God her instincts had finally kicked in and allowed her to get away before anything had actually happened.

Which made her wonder why it had taken her

so long to realize—subconsciously, if nothing else —that something wasn't quite right about Caleb Dixon. Usually, she had much better instincts about people than that. For all she knew, he'd been using his demonic powers to subtly coerce her, to make her think she was attracted to him. It seemed a plausible enough explanation, one that neatly let her off the hook for her lapse in judgment.

Anyway, she didn't have time to waste wondering about such things. Since the police had already come and gone—and since they already knew that she and Caleb had been seeing each other—she didn't worry too much about leaving fingerprints behind on anything, only opened the nightstand drawers and the drawers in the banged-up highboy in the corner, and then opened the closet door so she could go on her tiptoes and peek at the shelf inside, in case he'd deposited the hard drive in the closet.

However, there was absolutely no sign of the damn thing in any of those places, and it wasn't under the bed or hidden between the sagging mattress and the worn box spring. Frustrated, she let go of the mattress and smoothed the bedclothes—a gesture born of habit more than anything else, since the bed hadn't been neatly made when she came in, and she doubted anyone would have noticed her snooping.

A frown creased her brow as she paused at the doorway to listen. It sounded as though Will and Linda were still talking quietly, and therefore providing an opportunity for Rosemary to look through the rest of this part of the house. There was a second bedroom furnished with more hand-me-downs and some Marvel movie posters on the wall, but something about it felt contrived, as if Caleb had only set it up that way so the room would look as though his mythical roommate actually did live there.

That bedroom didn't yield anything; the drawers were all empty, and the closet only had a few men's shirts in it, shirts she suspected had been purchased at the local Goodwill or some other thrift store. That left only the bathroom, and while it seemed to have been used—Caleb's razor was still lying on the counter, and the medicine cabinet had deodorant and aftershave and a half-used bottle of ibuprofen in it—there definitely was no hard drive to be found in that room, either.

Something about seeing the razor there on the tile countertop made a hard little lump form in Rosemary's throat. Just as she'd done when Detective Phillips asked her to identify Caleb's body, she tried to tell herself that the world wouldn't miss Caleb Lockwood, that he wasn't even completely human, and yet it still seemed horrible and tragic that he'd left his razor in the bathroom, thinking he'd use it again the next day, and now he was dead, erased from this world.

Don't lose it, she told herself, and did her best to blink away the hot tears from her eyes. True, Linda probably wouldn't be all that surprised to see her return to the entryway looking upset and weepy, but Rosemary knew Will would wonder what was going on with her, and she honestly didn't know if she could completely explain her reaction. After all, Caleb had tried to kill the both of them. He wasn't the sort of person she should be crying over.

She forced herself to take a couple of deep breaths, then went back out to where Will and Linda were waiting for her. As Linda sent a questioning look in her direction, she shook her head.

"No, I couldn't find them," she said. "I know I left them on the nightstand, but they're gone."

"Oh, I'm so sorry," Linda replied. "Why don't you give me your phone number, and if they turn up when I'm clearing out the house, I'll give you a call."

Rosemary manufactured a smile, although she really didn't want to give the other woman her contact information. Then again, she could give Linda a wrong number, one with a digit incorrect. That was the sort of thing that could be explained away as a simple mistake.

234 • CHRISTINE POPE

"Sure," she said, and waited as Linda got her phone out of her pocket, then rattled off the number, purposely replacing the 8 in the last four digits with a 5. "Oh, and they're little gold earrings with amethyst drops, just in case you do find them."

The other woman nodded. "I'll keep an eye out."

"Well…." Rosemary let out what sounded to her like an exaggerated sigh, although Linda appeared sympathetic. "Thank you for letting me look. We'll head home now."

"It's no problem," Linda assured her. "And I really am sorry about what happened to Caleb. He seemed like such a nice young man."

There really wasn't any way Rosemary could respond to that comment without uttering another bare-faced lie, and she didn't think she was up to the task right then. Instead, she nodded and went out the front door, Will a couple of paces behind her. Wisely, he remained silent until they were safely back inside the Challenger and headed back down the hill.

When he spoke, it was with an amused lilt to his voice. "You know, I've been trying, but I don't see much of a family resemblance between us."

"Oh, stop," she said, not bothering to temper the rebuke in her tone. "I had to come up with some kind of lie to explain you. I doubt Linda would have been quite so sympathetic if I'd showed up at Caleb's house with my new boyfriend in tow."

"Am I your boyfriend?"

Rosemary risked a quick look over at him. He now appeared quite serious, head tilted slightly to one side as he awaited her reply.

"I don't know," she responded honestly. Before he could begin to speak, she went on, "I mean, there's obviously something going on between us. But calling you my 'boyfriend' sounds a little…trite."

"You have a point." Will was quiet for a moment, waiting until she had safely merged back on to the freeway before continuing. "I'm glad you think there's something going on between us. I suppose there's no real need to codify it."

"Well, thank goodness for that," she said, and he chuckled.

However, his expression sobered quickly enough. "I wish we could have searched the entire house."

"I know." Rosemary had been thinking pretty much the same thing, but she knew they'd pushed their luck as it was. Linda probably would have wondered exactly what was going on if Rosemary had started tearing the kitchen apart in the search for her missing earrings, whereas it had been logical enough for her to look for them in the bedroom. There really hadn't been any place to hide the hard drive in the living room; the coffee table there didn't have any drawers, and the entertainment unit was actually just a table with a TV sitting on it. No real storage, which meant the kitchen seemed to be the only other place where the hard drive might have been stashed away.

Except the garage, or maybe his truck. She tried not to sigh in exasperation and told herself they'd done their best.

Will reached over and touched her knee. "It's all right. We tried."

"And what if we end up going all the way to Indiana, only to find out all we've accomplished is to 'try'?"

He didn't answer right away, although out of the corner of her eye, she could see his shoulders move in what might have been a shrug. "Then at least we tried. We've both already acknowledged that there's a chance Caleb or one of his associates has already destroyed the drive and the files it contained. But until we have proof one way or another, we shouldn't give up."

"You're right, of course." Rosemary let out a gust of a breath and wished she wasn't so tired. Then she would have suggested that they have a glass of wine together once they got home and talk it over some more. Now, though, she knew the best thing to do was to go straight to sleep.

Thank goodness their flight didn't leave until the afternoon; at least they wouldn't have to be up at the crack of dawn.

"I don't know about 'of course.'" He gave her arm a squeeze and then let go so he could lean against the back of the seat. "But we both know that information is too valuable to be lost, so we forge ahead."

"Together," she said, and he nodded.

"Yes, together." His left hand reached toward her, and she let go of the steering wheel with her right so she could clasp fingers with him, feel the strength of his touch and the welcome warmth of his skin.

Whatever happened, she wouldn't be doing this alone.

Chapter 13

A LOUD KNOCK AT THE FRONT DOOR WOKE Will. He sat up in bed and cast a bleary eye at the clock next to his bed. The alarm had been set for eight, just in case he somehow managed to actually sleep in, but it was only a little past seven now.

Who the hell would be knocking on his front door at this hour?

He pushed back the covers and got up, stopping for a moment to pull on his sweat pants. The night before, he'd been so tired that he'd collapsed in bed still wearing a T-shirt, although he'd planned to take it off before he slept. Now, though, he supposed it was a good thing he hadn't gotten that far.

When he opened the front door, he saw Detective Phillips standing there, flanked by a pair of uniformed officers. At once, a cold thrill of fear worked its way down his spine, but Will managed to keep his voice level as he asked, "What can I do for you, detective?"

"Rosemary McGuire is staying here, correct?"

"Yes," Will replied. "What do you want with her?"

Detective Phillips didn't blink. "That's between me and Ms. McGuire. Go wake her up, please."

"I'm already awake," came Rosemary's voice.

Will glanced back over his shoulder and saw her standing a few feet away from him, wild curls sticking out every which way and her face pale. She came closer and peered past him. Despite her obvious worry, she sounded calm enough when she spoke again.

"What's going on?"

"I might ask you the same thing, Ms. McGuire," the detective replied. "Do you want to tell me what you were doing at Caleb Dixon's home last night at approximately 8:50 p.m.?"

She couldn't really go any paler, but Will watched the muscles in her throat tighten as she swallowed. "Looking for my earrings, just like I told his landlord," she said evenly.

"And why was that errand so urgent that you had to go running out at almost nine o'clock on a Sunday night to take care of it?"

"Because," she began, then paused. One hand reached up to push a tangle of curls behind her ear. Watching her, Will wished he could step in and do whatever might be necessary in order to offer a defense for her actions, but he knew the best thing to do was remain silent. Any interference from him would only antagonize the man who stood before them now. "Because I got to thinking about it, and I realized if I didn't go over there and try to find them as soon as I could, then whoever ended up clearing out Caleb's things would probably take them for themselves or sell them or whatever. I didn't want that to happen."

"These earrings are that important," Detective Phillips said, both his dubious tone and the lift of his left eyebrow seeming to indicate he didn't believe a word of her story.

"Yes," Rosemary replied, her chin lifting. "They belonged to my grandmother."

"And yet you left them behind at Caleb Dixon's house."

"Because we had a fight, as I told you before, and I left in a hurry."

This explanation didn't seem to move the detective. He stood there, watching her with narrowed flint-gray eyes, and another chill moved down Will's back. "You and Mr. Dixon seem to have quarreled a lot for a couple who was only dating casually—to use your words. Over at Colin

Turner's house in Glendale, you told me that you'd had an argument at the Eden Garden Café, and that was when you broke up."

Oh, hell. Will could excuse Rosemary for not keeping her stories straight—she'd just been woken up abruptly and had been through hell over the last forty-eight hours—but he knew Detective Phillips would use her gaffe as more ammunition to prove her guilt.

Voice still calm, she said, "Actually, yes, we did fight a lot. That's part of the reason why we broke up. The argument at the restaurant was just the last straw for me. But we'd quarreled at his house before then."

"Do you have anyone to corroborate your statement?"

"No," Rosemary replied, an edge to her tone that hadn't been there a moment earlier. "Because the only other person who was there was Caleb, and obviously, he's not around to tell you anything."

She stopped there, tears beginning to well up in her eyes. Will had seen her give in to that strange sorrow over the part-demon twice before, and so he wasn't too startled by the display. The detective, however, stared at her for a moment, as if he wasn't quite sure what to make of a suspected murderer who wept over the death of her supposed victim.

Figuring he'd better step in, Will said quietly, "The earrings were very important to her. Maybe she had a lapse in judgment, but that's not a crime, is it?"

"No," Detective Phillips responded. "But it is suspicious behavior."

Rosemary crossed her arms and glared up at him. Her eyes still looked full of tears, but none of them had fallen. "What did the autopsy tell you?"

"That Caleb Dixon probably died sometime between eight-thirty and ten-thirty that night," he replied.

Relief rushed through Will. If the estimated time of death had occurred during that period, then Rosemary couldn't possibly be charged with Caleb's murder, since she'd been at the hospital that whole time. The detective seemed to understand the situation as well, because he continued.

"Which means you're cleared...for the moment. But something very strange is going on here."

Well, that was only the truth. Unfortunately, there was no way either Will or Rosemary could tell the detective what they were really looking for, or why Caleb had been at the house on Las Flores Drive at all. Eventually, his murder would end up in a cold case file, since Will had a feeling the Glendale P.D. would never be able to discover who had really pushed him into that pool...or why.

To her credit, Rosemary didn't use the detective's revelation about Caleb's probable time of death as a chance to crow about her newly established innocence. Instead, she said politely, "Do you have any other questions? Because I was about to get in the shower."

"Not at the moment," Detective Phillips said, looking irritated. "But make sure you're available if something else comes up."

"I will," she replied. "Have a good day."

The expression on the detective's face seemed to indicate that he definitely was not having a good day, but Will wasn't going to worry about that. He gave the other man a nod and shut the door, then reached out and pulled Rosemary into his arms. She burrowed into him, holding on for dear life, as though she was afraid the police would return and tear her from his embrace.

A minute or so later, she shifted and looked up at him. "I thought for sure they were going to haul me away and place me under arrest."

Those same fears had passed through Will's mind, but he gave her what he hoped was a reassuring smile. "I have a feeling Phillips showed up in person to try to throw you off balance, to see if he could get you to confess to something incriminating."

She let out a breath. "Well, that strategy might have worked, except I had you here with me. That gave me some extra strength."

"You didn't have anything to confess," he pointed out, and she shook her head.

"I did, too. I searched Caleb's house under false pretenses."

"I'd consider that a minor infraction at best."

"Still."

Despite having the shadow of a murder investigation lifted from her, Rosemary's expression remained worried. Will clasped her hands in his and gave them a gentle squeeze. "The detective doesn't need to know why we were there. Our reasons for looking in his house have absolutely nothing to do with Caleb's death."

Rosemary didn't respond right away. Her brow furrowed slightly, and then she said, "But...what if they do?"

He sent her a questioning look. "I don't follow."

"What if...?" The words trailed off, as though she was trying to pick apart the train of thought that had led her to this point before she went any further. "What if someone else wants that footage, too? Someone who was willing to murder Caleb to get it?"

That was an angle Will hadn't even thought of. He said, "Maybe. But if we're going to tackle a thorny question like that, I think we need some coffee."

Something in the tense set of her shoulders seemed to relax slightly, and she even managed a small smile. "Coffee would be great."

They went into the kitchen, and he got out the bag of French roast from the cupboard and started a pot brewing, while Rosemary leaned up against the counter and watched him. Some rosiness had returned to her cheeks, and she looked somehow simultaneously beautiful and simply adorable, with the clean, perfect lines of her delicate features surrounded by that halo of wild hair. Will thought of how he would love to have her like this with him every morning, starting off their day with coffee and some shared time together.

Of course, it would be preferable if their morning conversation didn't have to involve a murder investigation, but he figured they would just take it one step at a time.

While they were waiting for the coffee, he got some water for the two of them. Rosemary accepted the glass he handed her with a look of gratitude on her face, and she drank almost a third of it before she put the tumbler down on the counter. "Thanks," she said. "I guess I didn't realize how thirsty I was."

"Well, we did a lot of running around last night and then didn't stop to hydrate before we went to sleep." Her comment prompted Will to take a few healthy swallows of water from his own glass. "So...who else do you think would be looking for the footage?"

"I have no idea," she confessed. "It's just that someone killed Caleb, and it sure as hell wasn't either one of us. What motive would they have for murdering him if it wasn't that damn footage?"

"There could be a lot of reasons," Will replied, turning over possibilities in his mind. "Maybe he interrupted an intruder—"

She lifted an eyebrow at that suggestion, and he had to admit to himself that it sounded fairly weak. No ordinary human could have overpowered Caleb, so anyone intent on casual burglary would have had a nasty surprise if they tried to take him on. Which seemed to indicate his killer had to be another demon—or part-demon. Were they quarreling amongst themselves? Maybe there was one faction that wanted to save the footage but then doctor it somehow, while yet another simply wanted it destroyed outright. He said as much to Rosemary as he went over to fetch them a couple of mugs, and she was silent for a moment as she mulled over that particular possibility.

"I can see how that might make sense," she said at length. "After all, we don't know anything about these part-demons except that they all have human blood mixed in, to varying degrees. But, judging by the way Caleb acted when we surprised him at the house, I think we can safely say that none of them are probably very nice people."

"No, probably not," Will observed. Maybe there were one or two whose demon blood hadn't bred true, but he guessed that was probably a long shot, and certainly nothing they should count on. "Which possibly means they're already prone to quarreling amongst themselves. But that mystery is something the police can figure out on their own."

"Do you think they even will?" Rosemary asked. She took the mug of coffee he handed her and gave him a smile, one that sent a certain heat to several portions of his anatomy he probably should have been ignoring for at least another day or so. "Track down Caleb's killer, I mean."

About all he could do was shrug. "I have no idea. Honestly, I'm not even sure if they'll be able to positively identify the body."

"I thought I already did that."

"Well, you confirmed his identity to a point, but I think they'd still need to check dental records or DNA or something along those lines."

Her expression turned thoughtful. "Right. Well, if the demons in Greencastle are doing their best to blend in with their neighbors, then I assume they'd go to the dentist occasionally, if only to keep up appearances. There probably are records somewhere."

"That might or might not be accessible. For all we know, the local dentist is also a demon."

Rosemary sipped her coffee, then grinned. "Considering some of the experiences I've had at the dentist, I could totally believe that."

Will chuckled, and went over so he could stand next to her. Almost at once, she leaned her head against his shoulder, and again a warm flush went through him. Not so much of desire this time, but of what he realized was pure happiness. It felt so good to have her this close to him, to be able to breathe in the soft scent of her hair and know that she wanted to be here with him just as much as he wanted her here. He honestly had never thought he would be this comfortable with a woman again. Yes, his head still ached slightly and they were about to fly two thousand miles to drop into a town infested with part-demon adversaries, and yet he still didn't think he would have traded places with anyone in the world.

She spoke then, her voice not much more than a murmur. "I wish we didn't have to go. I wish we could just be here together and do something fun."

"Like what?" he asked, thinking it might be enjoyable to indulge the fantasy for a little while.

Besides, he really did want to know what she considered a fun pastime.

"Mmm...." She trailed off there as she seemed to consider his question. "I don't know. Go to a pumpkin patch and pick out some pumpkins for your front porch. This house really needs some Halloween decorations."

Will couldn't help smiling a little at her criticism. "Oh, it does?"

"Yes. Didn't you know it's a crime to have a house with a front porch this nice and not have Halloween decorations on it?"

"Well, tell you what." He shifted his position slightly so he could face her, and she shot him an inquiring look, obviously wondering why he would move away when they were being so cozy. That was an easy question to answer, though.

He wanted to see her lovely face.

After taking a quick sip of coffee, he went on, "When we get back from Indiana, we'll decorate the front porch. Just nothing too gruesome—this neighborhood has some fairly small children."

"Yes, Father Gordon," she said demurely, a wicked glint in her blue eyes.

Oh, to hell with self-control. He set down his coffee mug and bent so he could kiss her, could taste the warm savor of French roast on her beautiful mouth. Her arms went around him, and they held on to one another for a long moment, bodies pressed together. She wasn't wearing a bra underneath the oversized T-shirt she had on, and he could feel her breasts, warm and full.

Almost at once, he hardened, although he tried to push the desire away. Oh, he wanted her. That was as much a given as the sun rising in the east each morning. However, while they still had a few hours before they had to leave for the airport, he realized that their time wasn't unlimited.

And neither was his strength. They had a long flight ahead of them, a flight that would take them into the utter unknown. He needed to save his energy.

But as they both came up for air and her eyes met his, he realized those were specious arguments. He needed this—and if the look on her face was any indication, she needed it as badly as he did.

Her hands reached for his. "I can wait for breakfast," she said, her voice husky.

"So can I," he replied. "But I can't wait a second longer to be with you."

Their mouths met again, and again he marveled at how well they seemed to fit, how there was no awkwardness in their kisses, no clumsy attempts to find exactly the right angle. His fingers still entwined with hers, Will led Rosemary out of the kitchen and down the hall to his bedroom. He'd pulled up the covers but hadn't really made the bed.

Maybe he'd had a psychic flash of his own.

Her fingers found the edge of his T-shirt and pulled it up over his head. For a second, he experienced a flicker of self-consciousness. After all, it had been a very long time since he'd been with a woman, and he wasn't in his twenties anymore.

Rosemary didn't seem to notice anything wrong with his physique, though. Her hands trailed up his arms and across his bare chest, and he forgot about the ache in his head, the worry that he wouldn't be enough for her. In this moment, she was the only thing that mattered.

And he would do whatever it took to prove that to her.

The baggy T-shirt Will had been wearing had hidden a very impressive chest and stomach. Not super-defined, just solid and masculine and pretty much perfect in every way. Rosemary ran her fingers over his skin, feeling how smooth and warm it was, how the faint dusting of dark hair on his chest tickled against her fingertips. She pressed her mouth against his flesh and kissed him, tasted the faint flavor of salt on his skin. He released a breath, and in the next moment, they were falling onto the bed, his hands eagerly reaching for her own shirt so he could pull it over her head.

No time to worry about what he thought of her—too thin, breasts too small—because as soon as she was free of the T-shirt, he lowered his head and ran his tongue over her nipple. She moaned out loud, wondering how he'd been able to figure out how sensitive she was there, how a man's mouth on her breast was guaranteed to send waves of delicious pleasure flooding through her body.

Maybe he was psychic, too. Or maybe he simply was paying attention to her reactions.

Whatever the reason, he also seemed to realize this was the time to slide his hand under the waistband of the leggings she wore, moving lower so his fingers could slip underneath her panties and then into her, stroking gently, almost teasing, as if he wanted to make sure she was truly ready for him.

Oh, she was ready. More than ready, really. Impatiently, she grabbed hold of her leggings and underwear and pulled them off, then threw them over the side of the bed so they'd land more or less in the same spot where her T-shirt already lay. Will made a low, growling sound deep in his throat, fingers moving lower still so he could push them deep inside her.

Rosemary arched her back, tremors going all through her body. It was so good, so very good....

However, he paused then, shifting so he could leave a trail of kisses down her stomach, moving ever lower until his tongue slipped into her and she cried aloud, a little glad that the previous night had been cold enough for them to leave the windows all closed. After that random thought, however, she couldn't think of anything else except the sensation of his tongue moving against her, slowly as though savoring her taste, his thick, heavy hair brushing against the sensitive skin of her inner thighs.

It was building in her now, and she knew it wouldn't be very long, wouldn't be very long at all....

Once again, she cried out, her fingers clutching the sheets as the orgasm shuddered its way through her body. It had been a while for her, and yet she was pretty sure that wasn't why the climax had hit her with the force of a speeding train. No, that was all due to Will Gordon and the way he'd made love to her with his tongue. Although she'd allowed herself a few fantasies about him, she honestly hadn't expected a man of the cloth to be so, well, skilled.

But she didn't have time to ponder that conundrum, because he was moving, getting up on his knees so he could remove his sweatpants and the dark blue boxer briefs he wore underneath. It seemed corny to think of a man as magnificent, but that was how he appeared to her then, his erection impressively large, his legs sturdy and tanned, as though he spent more time outside than she'd imagined.

His eyes met hers, and she saw the need in them…but also the hesitation.

"I think I have some condoms in the night-stand," he said, his voice husky with passion. "But if I don't—"

"I have an IUD," she told him, hating how clinical the term sounded—but also knowing they needed to have this discussion. "And I don't know about you, but it's been almost a year for me. I know I'm fine."

Will shot her a rueful grin. "And a bit longer than that for me. I have a clean bill of health, I mean."

"Good," Rosemary said, and lay down against the pillows, her gaze still holding his. "Then there's no reason to stop, is there?"

"None at all."

He moved closer to her, reached down and pulled her against him. For a moment, their mouths met, and she could taste her musk on his lips. But then he pushed her back down, his erection pushing against her…

…and then he was inside, and she gasped again, wrapping her legs around him so she could draw him deeper into her, so she could make sure they were locked together in a moment of intimacy she'd hoped for but had somehow thought might never happen. He began to move in and out, slowly and surely, while she clung to him and wondered if it had ever felt like this with anyone else, to be so close, so perfectly tuned to the other person's movements, to every breath and thrust and sigh.

She didn't think so. It was as if she had only been practicing with those other men, had only played at lovemaking because her heart and mind had never been fully engaged. As she felt Will move within her, she knew she had never loved anyone before him, had kept her heart locked away because she knew that to give it was to risk what she was feeling now, that he had somehow become the whole world to her...and she didn't quite know how that had happened.

Yes, she loved Will Gordon, and her world would never be the same again.

Another orgasm rushed through her, and her legs locked around him, holding him in place as the climax hit him as well. He moaned, and she could feel him spill into her, could feel his heat and his need and his passion—and yes, his love—in that single shimmering moment.

Somehow, he retained enough control to lower himself gently onto her, although she could feel the way his heart pounded within his chest, the heat of his breath against her cheek. She held on to him and waited as he returned to himself, to her and the room that had been their universe for the past half hour, or however long it had been.

At long last, he raised himself slightly and stared down into her eyes. A faint sheen of perspiration gleamed on his forehead, and color flared in his cheeks. She thought she'd never seen anyone so amazingly handsome in all her life.

One hand cupped her cheek. "I love you," he said simply.

"I love you, too," she replied, knowing there was no longer any reason to hide from this. She trusted Will, knew he would never do anything to abuse her heart or her trust. A smile touched her mouth, and she added,

"Now, let's go get some demons."

Chapter 14

GREENCASTLE, INDIANA, WAS THE SORT OF picture-perfect place that looked as though it should have been the backdrop for a bunch of Hallmark Channel holiday romances. Rosemary thought the downtown section of Glendora where her store was located had its fair share of small-town charm, but—at first glance, at least—Greencastle could run rings around Glendora when it came to being adorably cozy.

"Not the sort of place I'd expect to see a bunch of demons hiding out," she said under her breath as she and Will emerged from their hotel that morning to get their bearings.

Despite their early morning activities at his house the day before, they'd managed to catch their plane at Ontario International with no delays and a minimum of fuss. Unfortunately, when they'd landed in Dallas Fort Worth for their layover, they'd ended up spending almost three hours there instead of the hour and some change they'd been promised, and so they hadn't rolled into Greencastle until after midnight. By that point, they were both so exhausted they fell into bed without doing much more than brushing their teeth and getting out of their travel clothes, although Rosemary had summoned just enough energy to cast a warding spell on their hotel room. She might have been tired, but she wasn't so tired that she was about to sleep in the heart of the demons' stronghold without some protection.

Whether it was the wards, or whether the descendants of the Underhill Trust demons hadn't yet discovered they had interlopers in their midst, Rosemary and Will slept soundly that night. He'd gotten a room with two queen beds, but of course there hadn't been any question of them sleeping separately. No, she'd curled up next to him as if she'd done that very same thing hundreds of times before, and fell asleep almost as soon as her head hit the pillow.

Now it was past ten-thirty, and the streets were probably about as busy as they would ever be. It was much cooler here in Indiana than it had been back in Southern California, and she was glad she'd brought her brown suede jacket with her. Also, she was inwardly relieved that the clothes she'd packed to take with her to Will's had been her most practical items—jeans and T-shirts in a couple of different sleeve lengths, a few pretty floral tops, several sweaters. She had a feeling her sequined skirts from India and jeweled flip-flops would have attracted way too much attention in this small town, but in jeans and a brown jacket and brown flats, with her unruly hair pulled back in a scrunchie, she hoped she looked fairly anonymous.

Will looked down at his phone; he'd brought up the Yelp app to hopefully guide them some-place where they could get breakfast. "That way," he said, pointing down the street. "It looks like there's a restaurant serving breakfast a few blocks down."

"Lead on," Rosemary replied, and hoped she sounded lighthearted and like a casual tourist, not someone who'd come here specifically to find footage that proved the existence of demons…and therefore the existence of Heaven and Hell.

Will reached over to clasp her fingers with his free hand, and they began to walk toward their destination. It was too bad that she couldn't allow herself to relax and enjoy the walk, because the day was a lovely one, sunny but cool, the trees here showing autumn finery of yellow and red and gold that wouldn't appear in Southern California for another month. In some ways, though, the town appeared alien to her, just because she wasn't used to seeing so many brick buildings. In earth-quake-prone California, brick structures were a rarity, whereas here they seemed to predominate.

But she did take some pleasure from the sensation of Will's hand encircling hers, the feeling of closeness even that casual touch awoke within her. Everything had been happening so quickly, she had to consciously remind herself that he'd told her he loved her just the day before. Their relationship had taken a quantum leap that morning, and yet she hadn't had much time to savor the moment, to realize that she wouldn't have to face the demons alone.

No, as he'd said, whatever happened, they were in this together.

They approached the restaurant that was their apparent destination, an attractive space with awnings covering the windows. Across the street was a tall, official-looking building with an honest-to-god clock tower in it, an architectural feature Rosemary had only seen in the movies before that moment. However, she didn't have the opportunity to pause and try to figure out what the building was, because Will had gone ahead and opened the front door to their destination.

It smelled good in there, warm and with a scent of chocolate and spice drifting on the air. The restaurant was the sort of place that made you want to relax at once, although she knew that wasn't a very good idea. Everything here in Greencastle might appear idyllic and friendly, but this town was home to several generations of demon offspring. She needed to keep up her guard, no matter what.

A pleasant-faced woman approached and asked if they wanted breakfast or lunch. Will and Rosemary both replied, "Breakfast," and the woman guided them to a table off to one side, handed them a couple of menus, and told them their waitress would be with them in a moment.

Rosemary murmured a thank-you and sat down, and Will did the same. A quick glance around told her they were the only diners here except for a large group seated in a separate dining area to the back of the space. Sunlight slanted in through high windows bordered in stained glass, and soft, unobtrusive music played in the background.

"This feels a little too much like a vacation," she murmured as she glanced down at the menu. Meat-heavy, as she'd feared, but she figured she could get the sampler platter and then see if she could exchange the bacon for some fresh fruit.

Will glanced up at her, and gave a small nod. "I know. And I wish it were. But…."

The words trailed off because their waitress, a woman around Rosemary's age with her fair hair pulled back into a French braid, had approached their table. "What can I get you?" she asked, tone brisk but pleasant.

Rosemary and Will placed their orders—almost the same thing, although he didn't bother to replace the bacon with something healthier—and the waitress withdrew. He sent a quick glance in her direction, but she'd already disappeared into the kitchen.

"Fred sent me a list of the local demons last night," he said quietly. "It reads like a who's who of Greencastle's prominent citizens, so we're going to have tread lightly."

"What about Caleb's father?"

"Daniel Lockwood? He's president of the First Indiana Bank and Trust here in town."

"Figures," Rosemary replied, her lips twisting in an ironic grin. So much for Caleb's stories about his modest upbringing and even more modest bank account. No, it probably wasn't quite the same thing as having the CEO of Wells Fargo as your father, but she still had a feeling the family did very well. "Any brothers or sisters?"

"No." Will had his phone out, but he held it down against his leg, nearly under the table, so she couldn't see exactly what he was reading. The notes Fred Peñasco had sent, she assumed. "Actually, the interesting thing is—well, as long as this list is accurate—that it doesn't look as though any of the cambions had more than one offspring each. All sons, too."

Interesting. Did that mean demons only carried XY chromosomes? It sure seemed that way, although Rosemary had to admit that her high school biology class was long behind her, and she might have been forgetting some of the finer points of sexual reproduction. The more important thing, though, was that the half-demon children of the original Underhill demons only had one child apiece, so her visions of having to confront an army of part-demon adversaries appeared to have been exaggerated. Still, even with Caleb out of the picture, that meant she and Will might be up against as many as thirteen of the part-demon creatures, which wasn't very good odds if they all possessed the same kind of supernatural talents Caleb had.

"So, we're not quite as outnumbered as we thought," she murmured, then pasted on a smile as the waitress came back with their coffee before departing again.

"It doesn't look that way," Will said. He picked up his coffee and took a sip, then gave an approving nod.

Good. She needed a decent cup of coffee, still felt far too draggy even though they'd gotten nearly eight hours of sleep the night before. And the coffee was good—hot and rich and fragrant, not bitter at all. Maybe after she'd drunk the whole cup, she'd start to feel a little more human. And if she was feeling this way….

She sent Will a probing look. "How are you doing?"

"Fine," he replied, and drank some more coffee. "Really. No headache at all this morning. I was a little worried about what spending hours in a pressurized cabin might do to my head, but I'm not noticing any ill effects at all."

"Well, that's good news," Rosemary said, allowing herself to enjoy some measure of relief. All during the flight, she'd worried what she would do if Will had some kind of a relapse at ten thousand feet, but it seemed her fears had been exaggerated. "Still, we can take it easy at first. Maybe wander around, get the lay of the land… figure out the most likely places that hard drive would have gone."

Will's mouth twisted in a grimace, although his next words told her it wasn't because of the coffee. "With Daniel Lockwood as the president of the bank here, I wouldn't be surprised if it went straight into one of his bank's safety deposit boxes."

Oh, that would definitely make their task a lot harder. Rosemary had seen enough caper movies to know that neither she nor Will possessed the necessary skill set to infiltrate a bank vault.

"Well, let's hope that isn't what happened," she said lightly. "After all, I have a feeling these... people...are the types who like to keep their valuables where they can see them."

Will tilted his head to one side, as if considering that possibility. However, he refrained from replying because their waitress returned then with their plates of food, and asked if there was anything else they needed.

Since Rosemary's breakfast looked as though it contained enough food to feed her for an entire day, she said that no, she was fine, and Will murmured something along the same lines. Once they were alone again, he spoke.

"We'll just have to see. Anyway, I have the addresses of the cambions and their offspring, so after breakfast, we can drive around and see what we can find."

Because of course they'd had to rent a car at the airport the night before, so they were already mobile. Their rental vehicle was a silver Toyota RAV4, something unobtrusive enough. With any luck, no one would even notice them driving around without any clear destination.

Will picked up a triangular slice of wheatberry toast, then took a bite. It was almost as if he'd guessed at what she'd been thinking, because he said, "It's lucky that this is a college town. They're probably more used to strangers coming and going than a lot of other small towns in this part of the country."

True enough. Rosemary had done some research on Greencastle while the shuttle took them to the airport, and she supposed she should have recalled that DePauw, a small liberal arts college, was located in the town. That probably explained the excellence of the food here at the restaurant, not to mention the various bars and gastropubs they'd passed on the way to get breakfast.

"Well, but we should still be kind of careful," she said. "It's a lot easier to be anonymous in a car."

"Exactly," Will responded. "It's much better for us to do a casual drive-by than walk through a neighborhood where everyone knows each other, and try to act as though we belong there."

She nodded, and they dug into their meals in earnest after that, as if motivated to eat quickly because they had a goal in mind. Even with substituting fresh fruit for her bacon, Rosemary couldn't eat all of her breakfast, but that was no problem, since Will offered to finish it for her.

Men and their appetites. She wondered where he put all of it, since he was trim and had absolutely zero sign of a beer belly, but clearly, burning off large amounts of food wasn't a problem for him.

After they were done, they walked the couple of blocks back to their hotel and retrieved their RAV4 from the parking lot. No one was around —although the lot was about half full, mostly cars with out-of-state plates—and she couldn't help being relieved that there wasn't anyone around to see the two of them climb into their rental vehicle. The less chance of being connected to it, the better.

She remained silent as Will guided the Toyota away from Greencastle's quaint downtown, toward the south and west and the residential neighborhoods located there. Even at this time of year, the landscape looked brilliantly green to her California-bred eyes, although the trees were turning. However, frost hadn't completely yellowed the grass, and it all looked verdant and lovely, and completely unlike the sort of place where a bunch of demons might be holed up.

Well, to be fair, the true demons weren't here anymore. They'd allowed their mortal bodies to die and had gone back to Hell, but, as Caleb had proved, their descendants were just about as tricky to deal with.

Will and Rosemary turned down a street where the lots were large and most of the houses set far back from the road. "I thought we'd go past Daniel Lockwood's place first," Will said, his tone quiet, as though he feared they might somehow be overheard even from inside their rented car. "I figure he would probably be the likeliest person to have the footage, since it wasn't at Caleb's place in Eagle Rock."

Rosemary thought that theory sounded logical enough, especially since Caleb had actually mentioned his father to her during their confrontation at the house Colin Turner and Madeline Nash had once owned. For all she and Will knew, Daniel was the one who'd been pulling the strings all along. It would have been odd for him to approach her directly, so he'd sent his handsome son to do his dirty work, figuring she'd be putty in Caleb's hands.

And she had been…until she'd gotten cold feet about sleeping with him. Before that, however, she'd gone along with pretty much all his suggestions. Some kind of demonic mind control?

If that's what it had been, then those mind-control powers weren't infallible, because even while Caleb was trying to charm her into leading him to the missing footage, she'd found herself falling for Will Gordon instead. Maybe even demons couldn't find a way to defeat the human heart, not when it was intent on the person who was clearly your soul mate.

Although maybe she shouldn't go quite that far when it came to describing Will Gordon. She knew she loved him, had never experienced this sort of pure emotion for any other man, but "soul mate" might be a bit of a stretch. How could she think of him that way when there was still so much she didn't know about him?

She did her best to push those doubts aside. If nothing else, she knew she wanted to be with Will, no matter what. That had to mean a whole hell of a lot.

He said, breaking into her reverie, "That's it."

All he'd done was incline his head, as if he'd thought that even pointing would give too much away, but Rosemary knew immediately which house he meant. It was large and square, composed of red brick like so many of the other buildings in Greencastle, with white trim and several chimneys and prim rosebushes marching their way up the herringbone path that led to the front door. In fact, the place looked almost exactly the way she imagined a house that belonged to a bank president in a small Midwest town should look, and her mouth curved in amusement.

"Right out of Central Casting," she remarked. "Or at least, whatever location agents use in place of Central Casting."

"True," Will said. He'd been looking slightly grim a moment earlier, but right then, his lips quirked in an echo of her own smile. "What I'm more worried about is how open it is—there are a few trees on the lot, but they're not close enough to the house to provide any cover."

She sent him a quizzical glance. "Even if there were, what exactly were you planning to do? I'm sure a place like this has an alarm system. Unless you're hiding your history as an international jewel thief from me or something."

Her remark made him laugh outright. "No, I don't have anything that interesting on my resume, unfortunately. I suppose I had a vague idea of being able to get close enough to look in a window or something."

"Assuming the demons don't have the equivalent of Michael's wards put in place to keep us humans out."

His expression sobered. "Yes, assuming that. It's hard to know exactly what their powers encompass, since they're so 'other.' And even when they have a lot of human blood mixed in the way Caleb does, they're still forces to be reckoned with."

That was for sure. Rosemary recalled how Caleb had summoned fire to surround his hands, had used those flames as a weapon against her and Will. How he'd disappeared into thin air right before her eyes. Her own powers had grown by leaps and bounds over the past few days, but she was pretty sure she would never be able to pull off a trick like that.

She held back a sigh, since she knew allowing herself to feel hopeless definitely wasn't going to help their current situation. "I suppose we should drive around the block and see if we can get any information about the back of the property. These lots are big enough that they might not have any rear neighbors."

"Good idea."

They'd been driving slowly, a little bit under the posted speed limit of thirty miles an hour, but Will sped up slightly as they made their way down to the next intersection. He turned right and right again. As Rosemary had thought, the street here didn't have any houses on one side, because the large lots of the homes on the next street over backed up here. It seemed land wasn't at a premium in Greencastle the way it was in Southern California.

Interestingly, the back gate to Daniel Lockwood's property stood open. Not that it was probably a good idea to drive in, because even as she and Will watched, a white van with the logo of a local catering company painted on the side entered through the gate and began to make its way along the narrow lane that hugged the wall and appeared to dead end at a large, multi-bay detached garage.

"Is he having a party or something?" Rosemary murmured. "That's kind of odd behavior for a man whose only son has just been murdered, don't you think?"

Will nodded, his dark brows drawn together in a frown. "Maybe he hasn't found out yet."

"But they're part-demon. Wouldn't he just…know?"

"Maybe…or maybe not." His fingers were tight on the steering wheel, and she could tell he wanted nothing more than to pull over, park their rented RAV4 at the curb, and hurry through the gate before it closed again. However, he continued to drive along without speeding up or slowing down, gaze now on the road ahead of him again, as if what was going on at the Lockwood house was of no interest to him. "We really don't know how connected the demons are, whether they can communicate by thought or instinct or some other means we can't begin to guess at. But I can see how Daniel Lockwood might want to keep such a thing quiet for a while, just because people always have questions whenever there's an unexpected death. After all, we really have no idea whether anyone here in Greencastle even knew Caleb was in California at all."

True. Coming here to Indiana made Rosemary think they were basically flying blind during a sandstorm. Sometimes you had to take a leap of faith, though. She wanted to believe that her own psychic abilities would have piped up and told her that no, going to Greencastle to retrieve the *Project Demon Hunters* footage was a spectacularly bad idea, but she'd experienced no such inner warnings. Besides, Michael had certainly been on board with the plan.

Then again, as much as she liked Michael, she had to admit that sometimes he wasn't the best indicator as to whether something was a good idea or not....

"Well," she said, trying to sound positive, "at the very least, that's one piece of intel we didn't have ten minutes ago. It could be something we can work with. I mean, if Daniel Lockwood is hosting a catered party, then it's probably not some kind of quiet family dinner. Maybe we can try to find out what's going on."

"Good idea," Will replied. "Still, since we're out and about, we might as well get an idea of where the other demons are hanging out."

She figured doing a little more recon couldn't hurt, if for no other reason than to know where the rest of the crew was lurking. "Sure."

He touched his phone screen, and the map program he was using switched over to the next address. It wasn't very far, just two streets down and a block over, another large home on a substantial lot, although not quite as big as Daniel Lockwood's. Was he first among equals, or had the cambions decided amongst themselves that for appearance's sake, he should have the biggest and most expensive house?

Since none of the other homes they drove past came anywhere close to his, she had to think something like that must be going on here. Oh, all of them were nice houses, much bigger than hers, even the ones that belonged to the younger generation of demon offspring. But there also didn't seem to be anything about them that would make them stand out to the casual observer.

About an hour later, they'd finished making their circuit, and Will headed back to the hotel since they really didn't know where else to go. Rosemary had snapped a few pictures and made some notes, but she had to admit that the idea of casing thirteen different houses—well, all right, eleven, because it seemed the two youngest quarter-demons still lived at home—and trying to figure out which of them concealed the stolen hard drive made her head hurt.

Or maybe it was something else. As they pulled into the lot at their hotel and Will parked the car, she began to realize the buzzing in her head wasn't mere overload. No, she was definitely getting an image. A formal study with a big mahogany desk and mahogany bookcases filled with leather-bound volumes she had a feeling no one had ever read.

Sitting in the center of the leather-backed

blotter on top of that shining, expensive desk was the hard drive.

She must have gasped aloud, because Will immediately looked over at her and asked in urgent tones, "Are you all right, Rosemary? What's the matter?"

"Nothing's the matter," she said, knowing she was probably smiling like an idiot. "It's just—I know where the hard drive is. It really is at Daniel Lockwood's house."

Chapter 15

WILL DIDN'T BOTHER TO ASK HOW SHE KNEW such a thing. Not when the woman sitting in the passenger seat of their rented vehicle was a psychic who'd exhibited some pretty impressive displays of her talent over the past few days.

"Where in his house?"

"On his desk," she said, her big blue eyes dreamy and focused on something far beyond the interior of the RAV4—something probably a half mile away in the impressive brick house they'd surveilled not an hour earlier. "It's just sitting there where anyone could see it. Arrogant, isn't he?"

Since demons tended to be a prideful lot, Will didn't argue with her assessment. "I suppose he figures it's safe enough there. Who else is in the house?"

Rosemary's brows drew together. "There's a woman…she looks like she's probably around my mother's age, so I have a feeling she's Daniel Lockwood's wife."

Did that unknown woman have any idea who she'd been married to for the past several decades? Probably not; the cambions had worked way too hard to conceal their true natures to let themselves indulge in those sorts of confessions. "What's she doing?"

"Talking to the caterer." Rosemary paused there, her frown easing slightly, although now she appeared to be concentrating, as if she needed to focus on what Lockwood's wife was saying. "There's…they're having a party tomorrow night. A charity fundraiser for the library." She broke off there, her gaze focusing on Will with a sudden intensity that was somewhat jarring after her dreamy aspect of a moment earlier. "It's tomorrow night, Will. We have to go."

"We what?" he said, not sure he'd heard her correctly.

"It's the easiest way to get inside Daniel Lockwood's house," she replied. "Why bother to try breaking in when we can just show up at a party?"

"A party where there'll be dozens of witnesses or more."

"Even better," Rosemary said, apparently not deterred at all. "Since it's a charity event, not everyone there is going to be part-demon. There could be people from outside Greencastle. Can you think of a better way to get in there without being noticed?"

Will had to admit she had a point. "I suppose that could work...."

"I know it'll work. They're still selling tickets at the library. We can go over there and buy some, and then we're set."

She made it sound so easy. However, he had a feeling there were some practical considerations they needed to take into account, including something that might have seemed frivolous on the surface but could be a problem when it came to blending in. "Please tell me it's not black tie."

For a second or two, she just stared at him. Then she shook her head, although she sent him a rueful smile. "No, it's 'cocktail attire,' but I sure didn't pack any cocktail dresses for this trip...and I'm assuming you don't have a suit crammed in your carry-on luggage, either."

"No," Will said. "But we're actually not that far from Indianapolis. Let's go get those tickets and confirm we're on the right track here, and then we'll go shopping."

Rosemary's blue eyes sparkled at that suggestion. He could tell she was looking forward to such an expedition, if for no other reason than it would get them out of Greencastle for a few hours, thereby lowering their risk of detection by the demons.

He reached over and touched his phone, typed in "library" and let the app navigate them over to the building in question. Like so many of the other structures in town, it was red brick, sturdy and simple but well-preserved. It didn't look as though it was in need of a charity fundraiser for its upkeep, but maybe this particular event was focused more on raising money to supplement the library's collection.

The tickets weren't cheap—a hundred and fifty dollars each. However, considering where the money was going, Will had no regrets about the purchase. After all, he reminded himself, most of the people who lived in this town were regular mortals, just like himself and Rosemary. They certainly deserved a library they could be proud of.

But now that they had the tickets in hand, and had confirmed that the event in question would be held on Wednesday, October 23rd, at 7 p.m., it was time for them to get out of Greencastle and find something appropriate to wear. Will had his doubts whether he'd be able to find a suit off the rack that would work—he'd always needed to get them tailored in the past—but maybe a sport coat and a nice pair of trousers would work. After all, the small college town didn't appear to be a hotbed of high fashion.

They drove out of downtown so he could get on I-70 heading east. They hadn't been driving very long before Rosemary let out a chuckle and pointed at the road sign they were approaching. "Looks like they have a Monrovia here, too. I guess I wasn't expecting that." Her expression sobered. "I wonder why Caleb didn't mention it when he was trying to win me over with his 'innocent Indiana boy' act."

Hard to say for sure. Will was actually quite relieved that he couldn't begin to guess at some of Caleb's thought processes. "Did he ever say where exactly in Indiana he was from?"

"No. I'm sure that was on purpose. I doubt he would want any attention focused on Greencastle."

No, probably not. It had taken Fred Peñasco some time to ferret out that particular detail. Will wondered how Michael's friend had managed it, considering he'd had a false name to go on and not much else. Or maybe he'd gone in reverse, had kept picking away at the Underhill Trust crew and then had backfilled the data from there.

"Well, we're here despite Caleb's best efforts," Will said, and was gratified to see Rosemary's expression brighten somewhat. "And now that we know where the hard drive is, our job will be that much easier."

"Unless Daniel Lockwood really does plan to spirit it away to a safety deposit box so it won't be in the house while he's having the fundraising party," Rosemary returned, some of the sparkle going out of her eyes.

"No, I don't think he'll do that. He might have a safe on the property, though."

"In which case…?" she said, and let the question trail off into the ether.

"In which case, we'll figure something out," Will said firmly. At least he sounded confident, even if he didn't exactly feel that way.

If Rosemary picked up on any of his unease, she didn't show it. Quite possibly, she'd decided that it really wouldn't help their cause to allow themselves to be defeated before they'd even made the attempt, so she fell silent then and seemed to be content to watch the countryside passing by outside the windows. He guessed it all must look very foreign to her eyes, so used to Southern California's urban sprawl or its golden-brown hillsides, which usually only sprouted with green for a short month or so during the region's rainy season. Here was mile after mile of open farmland, now bare after the harvests had been gathered in, although the roadside itself was still bordered with green grass, a little yellow here and there from frost, but still lush enough. In a way, it reminded him of the countryside around the town in Massachusetts where he'd grown up, although the land was flatter here and everything felt more spread out.

Soon enough, though, they reached the outskirts of Indianapolis. They'd decided to go to the Keystone Fashion Mall even though it was on the north side of the city and a little out of the way, just because it offered more high-end stores and thus probably more chances to find something that would work for both of them. He got off the freeway at Keystone Avenue and wound around the shopping center until he was able to find a parking space near Nordstrom.

Rosemary eyed their destination with what looked like some unease. "I don't think I've ever shopped at a Nordstrom in my life."

"Not even Nordstrom Rack?" he asked. The discount store was his go-to for shoes, since he knew he could always find something there to fit his size-thirteen feet.

"Oh, well," she said, relenting. "That's different."

Yes, it was, but Will knew that if they wanted to blend in at all, they needed to look the part. True, all the locals would know at once he and Rosemary were from out of town, but the library assistant who'd sold them the benefit tickets had proudly told them people were coming from Indianapolis for the event, and so he figured they could just pass themselves off as some DePauw alumni who'd come back to show a little love for the college town. Or at least, he hoped the story was convincing enough that no one would question it too much.

Well, unless the part-demons in attendance were able to sniff them out the moment they walked through the door.

First things first, though.

"Any demons around?" he asked Rosemary as they entered the store through the cosmetics department, only half joking.

She paused and stared at him for a second, clearly trying to gauge his expression. Then she shook her head. "No, I'm not sensing anything. But then, I couldn't tell what Caleb was, so I'm probably not the best person to ask."

Although Will thought she was being too hard on herself, he decided he'd better let the comment go. Besides, he'd found himself checking the rearview mirror far too often on the drive over to the mall, and he hadn't been able to detect a single vehicle that looked even remotely suspicious. He thought they were safe enough here.

Which was why he said, "I think it's all right if we split up. We'll get this done more quickly."

Her mouth pursed in amusement. "What, you

don't want to watch me try on ten different dresses and fifteen pairs of shoes?"

"Would you really need to look at that many?" he asked, feeling vaguely alarmed. Surely the process couldn't be that complicated....

Rosemary laughed outright, and gave him a good-natured smack on the arm. "Maybe. All right, I won't subject you to my shopping obsessions. Meet back here when we're done? I'll try not to take too much time."

"That sounds perfect," Will said, although he'd begun to wonder whether splitting up was a good idea after all. True, a Nordstrom in Indianapolis didn't seem like the sort of place that would be fraught with peril—well, except to his bank account—but he also didn't want to make such an amateur mistake. "Or maybe—"

"It's fine," she cut in. "We'll be fine." She went up on her tiptoes and kissed him on the cheek. "Now, shoo. And don't buy anything unless it's at least thirty percent off."

The place where she'd pressed her lips against his skin seemed to tingle slightly, and he wished he could give her a real kiss. However, that would have to wait until they were alone together. "I'll do what I can."

He offered her a smile and then headed off toward the men's department, following the signs. Rosemary lingered where she was for a second or two before nodding to herself and going over to the escalator. She was soon lost from view, and Will made himself keep going. With any luck, he'd find something suitable quickly enough. Although their plan was to meet back in the cosmetics department, he figured he would go in search of her if he was done within fifteen or twenty minutes. From the way she'd been talking, he guessed her own shopping would take much longer than that.

The prices were a bit staggering, that was for sure. Yes, he wore jackets in his capacity as a minister, but he'd gotten in the habit of going to downtown Los Angeles for that sort of thing, since he could save a lot of money by picking things up in the Fashion District rather than paying department store prices for them.

Well, he didn't have that option here, so he'd just have to do the best he could.

However, fate appeared to be smiling on him, because on a sale rack he found a dark gray Ted Baker suit in a thirty-eight long marked down to under three hundred dollars. Will figured he couldn't do much better than that—the suit fit him perfectly—and so he bought it and a white dress shirt and a tie patterned in gray and silver and burgundy. He'd been needing new dress shoes for a while anyway, and so he didn't feel quite as bad about that purchase.

All through this shopping frenzy—well, it felt like a frenzy even though he knew he was being quite careful with his spending—he couldn't help wondering if they were crazy for attempting to crash a fundraiser at a cambion's house. Then again, he'd thought the same thing about their trip to Indiana in general, but so far, their luck seemed to be holding. Surely if Daniel Lockwood or any of the other demon offspring had realized they had a pair of interlopers in their midst, they would have moved against him and Rosemary before they had a chance to leave town.

Then again, maybe they'd planned to do something about them, but then decided to hold back since their prey had headed out of Greencastle. Maybe even now, the part-demons were lying in wait for the strangers to return.

Not a very comforting thought, but one Will knew he'd have to keep in the back of his mind, just in case.

He paid for his shoes and added the bag to the ones he was already carrying, then glanced down at his watch. Twenty minutes had passed, give or take. Time to go in search of Rosemary.

He hoped she was having as much luck as he had.

In general, she loved to shop. Right then, however, Rosemary found herself frowning as she stared at the racks of cocktail dresses. Had she ever in her life bought a cocktail dress?

She didn't think so.

And honestly, what kind of dress was she supposed to wear to a benefit cocktail party that just happened to be held at the home of a half-demon who would probably tear her apart limb from limb if given the chance?

Well, nothing too tight, in case you have to make a quick getaway, she thought, and made herself go over to the closest rack and start pushing her way through the size-fours.

And since it was a cocktail party at a small town in Indiana, nothing too short or too revealing, too flashy or sparkly or…well, memorable in any way, which sort of took all the fun out of shopping in the first place.

However, she found a few likely candidates, although she had to put one back after she glanced at the price tag and saw it was nearly eight hundred dollars. No way was she going to spend that much, not when she had no idea whether the dress was even going to survive the evening.

Her favorite was possibly a little too memo-rable, a slate-blue lace Tadashi Shoji midi dress with a nude lining, but Rosemary slung it over her arm anyway. It was definitely more her style than the discreet sheath-style gowns she'd been choosing before she found the lace gown; with any luck, she'd get to wear it again when she was safely back in Southern California and she and Will were able to go out for an intimate dinner together.

That was probably getting a bit ahead of herself, but Rosemary figured it couldn't hurt to have something to look forward to. Yes, a nice dinner with him in his new suit. Of course, she hadn't seen him in the suit yet, but since Will looked amazing in pretty much anything he wore, she guessed he would be even more spectacular in a good suit.

The blue lace dress fit her perfectly, which seemed to be a sign from the heavens that she was supposed to buy it. Shoes were more problematic, just because she was not a high-heel person—to put it mildly—although she knew she couldn't wear a designer cocktail dress with flats. Luckily, she located a pair of jeweled ankle-strap sandals that had a delicate kitten heel, low enough that she thought she probably could do a creditable job of running from demons in them.

That difficult task accomplished, she smiled a little to herself as the salesclerk rang up the shoes and put them in a bag. After that, she took a quick trip to the accessories department to pick up a small evening clutch and a pair of dangly earrings. She'd just turned around to head toward the escalator when Rosemary saw Will approaching her, a garment bag draped over one arm and several smaller bags hanging from the other.

"I thought you told me to meet you down-stairs," she said, her tone only a little accusing. Actually, she was glad he hadn't come any earlier, just because she didn't want him to see her in her new finery until it was time to get ready for the party.

Which she knew was silly. It wasn't like she was trying to hide a wedding dress from him or something.

Probably the wrong thought to have, though, because her mind wandered away for a second or two in order to contemplate the idea of marrying Will Gordon, and what kind of dress she would have, and that was even more ridiculous. Yes, they were in love, but she was kind of getting ahead of herself. Better to see whether they survived the following evening before she started wondering about wedding gowns and floral arrangements.

"I figured I'd get done before you did," he responded calmly, although his gray eyes glinted at her, and his mouth had that amused lift in one corner. "Not by much, though."

"No," Rosemary said. "I lucked out." Or maybe it was more that Will had lucked out, since now he didn't have to worry about waiting around for her. Either way, it had been an effective targeted strike. They began to walk toward the escalator, and she went on, "So…back to Greencastle?"

"Actually, I was thinking about that," Will replied. "It might be better to stay here for the afternoon. The less time we're in Greencastle, the less chance of running into someone we don't really want to see."

His suggestion made some sense. Of course, they would be walking into the lion's den the next evening…so to speak…but there was something to be said for not tipping their hand until the very last minute. They'd been lucky when they went out to breakfast and hadn't crossed paths with anyone who looked even remotely suspicious, and yet Rosemary didn't know how long their luck would hold.

"Sure," she said. "So…what? Lunch? I'm not really hungry yet."

"What about a movie? There's a theater right here in the mall."

Going to the movies was not something she would have necessarily thought of—that sort of activity seemed awfully prosaic, considering their reason for being here in Indiana—but on the other hand, it did sound pretty safe. They could go see whatever seemed convenient to fill the time they had, and then grab a very early dinner after that. At some point, of course, they'd have to head back to Greencastle, but she realized that the vague notion she'd had of sampling whatever night life the small college town had to offer probably wasn't a very good idea.

Besides, she guessed they'd be perfectly able to find something to occupy themselves in their hotel room.

"Sounds like a plan. But let's put this stuff in the car first."

Will agreed that was a good idea, and they went downstairs and out to their rental, and stowed everything in the cargo area before pulling the little privacy screen closed so no one could see what they had stashed back there. Rosemary would have been worried about wrinkles, except she'd spied an iron and ironing board in their hotel room closet, and so she knew they could repair any damage if necessary.

That task handled, they went back to the mall. The theater there seemed to specialize in foreign and indie films, but there was a comedy playing that looked good, and Will seemed agreeable. They bought a pair of tickets and some water and popcorn to tide them over, and took their seats.

There weren't many people in the auditorium, which didn't surprise Rosemary too much, since it was a little after two o'clock on a weekday afternoon. Actually, she was glad of the sparse attendance, because it allowed her to take a quick scan of the other movie-goers and determine that they all looked pretty harmless.

Maybe she actually would be able to relax and enjoy herself.

When the credits began to roll, Will reached over and laid his hand on top of hers where it sat on the armrest. Just that light touch was enough to send a happy little shiver through her.

Somehow, she had the feeling that nothing terribly bad could happen as long as he was at her side.

Will was relieved to see that Rosemary appeared to have lost herself in the movie—she laughed along with the other audience members, and watched the somewhat ludicrous events unfold with wide eyes. Clearly, she was doing her best to give herself a chance to relax and forget the real reason why they'd come so far from home.

For himself, he wasn't quite that transported. Oh, he supposed if he'd watched the film under normal circumstances, he would have been diverted enough by it, but his mind couldn't quite stop attacking the problem of their attendance at the charity cocktail party the next evening. He tried to reassure himself that if the Greencastle demon contingent had been able to detect his or Rosemary's presence, they would have already descended, but he didn't know that for sure. Demons liked to toy with their victims, after all, and maybe they were both being sucked into a false sense of security.

Unfortunately, he couldn't think of a better way to get access to the hard drive. He trusted Rosemary's vision, and so he found no reason to think that the footage wasn't there in Daniel Lockwood's home. Getting access to it probably would be difficult, and Will knew that inwardly he was counting on her inner vision to come to their aid once again. If it failed them, he wasn't quite sure what they would do.

Luckily, he was pretty good at improvising.

The movie ended, and Rosemary seemed to have noticed that he hadn't been paying it much attention, because she didn't attempt to discuss it, only led him over to a mall directory so they could figure out where to eat. After a bit of discussion, they decided on a restaurant called Seasons 52, just because it wasn't a place either one of them had heard of before, and also it offered plenty of options to get an interesting glass of wine with their food. Maybe having a drink wasn't the best idea, but Will knew he was tense enough that he could definitely use one.

Because the restaurant wasn't located in the mall itself, they went back outside and moved the car to their chosen destination. At only a little past four-thirty, the place wasn't too crowded, although there were enough people enjoying happy hour specials that it certainly didn't feel empty, either.

The hostess guided them over to a table in a corner, a spot Will approved of because he could keep an eye on the people coming and going in the dining room. Under different circumstances, he would have enjoyed their surroundings, because the interior was warm and dim, with good use of natural materials and a friendly, intimate feel.

Right then, however, he couldn't quite prevent himself from giving a quick, narrow-eyed glance at everyone in the room, making sure that none of them looked suspicious in any way. Rosemary obviously noticed, because she said in an undertone, "Will, this place feels totally safe."

"You're sure?" he asked, allowing himself to experience a twinge of relief—although he still didn't relax all the way.

"I'm sure," she replied. "Or at least, as sure as I can be. But choose a wine, because I think I see our waiter heading over here."

Quickly, Will bent his head and perused the wine offerings. Splitting a bottle seemed to be too much of a risk, especially since they had to drive back to Greencastle after this. The tempranillo by the glass sounded interesting, so that was what he ordered after the waiter had approached. Rosemary asked for pinot noir, and the man said he'd be back in a minute with their drinks.

"Are we snacking or eating for real?" Will asked as he picked his menu up again.

"Eating for real, I suppose," Rosemary said. "I know it's early, but I don't see the point in going someplace to eat after this."

No, she was probably right. He decided on the pork tenderloin, figuring it would have some heft to it but wouldn't be as heavy as a steak. When the waiter returned with their wine, Rosemary requested the roasted chicken, which didn't surprise Will too much; he'd already noticed how she did her best to avoid red meat.

Once they were alone again, she raised her glass. "To making it this far."

There was something he could drink to. Will lifted his glass of tempranillo and clinked it against hers, then took a swallow. Yes, that was definitely a decent glass of wine.

However, as he lowered his glass and glanced over at Rosemary, he realized that she hadn't drunk any of her own wine. Instead, the glass remained frozen halfway to her mouth, her eyes wide with…fear? No, that wasn't it. More like…shock.

Immediately, worry pulsed through him, and he looked in the direction where she was staring. A man was approaching their table, quite purposefully. He didn't look like any of the men from the files Fred had sent him, and so Will didn't think the strange man was a cambion—and since he appeared to be in his late fifties or early sixties, he definitely couldn't be one of their children, either.

The stranger paused next to their table. For a few seconds, his gaze lingered on Rosemary, who continued to stare at him in shock.

At last, though, she apparently managed to find her voice.

"*Dad?*"

Chapter 16

ALL ROSEMARY COULD DO WAS SIT THERE, frozen in shock, body numb. It was like one of those dreams where it was impossible to move, where it felt as if the very air had congealed around her.

How could he be here? How was this even possible? The man standing in front of her was recognizably her father, even though she hadn't seen him in more than seventeen years. Older, yes, his hair now completely gray and with new lines etched around his eyes and mouth, but even with all those changes, she would have known him anywhere.

Except…he'd died ten years ago.

"I know this is something of a shock," her father said. "Do you mind if I sit down?"

"Um…." Her mouth didn't seem able to form more than that single syllable.

Will came to her rescue, thank God. "I'm Will Gordon," he said. "And you're…?"

"John McGuire," her father replied. "Nice to meet you, Will." Once again, he looked over at Rosemary. "Is it all right if I join you?"

Mutely, she nodded, then watched as he pulled out one of the empty chairs at their table and sat. He looked happy and healthy enough, skin slightly tanned, hair still thick despite all the gray. In fact, in his button-down shirt and khaki pants and deck shoes, he looked as though he'd just wandered into the restaurant after getting in a good round of golf earlier that day. Irrelevantly, Rosemary thought he probably would have fit right in with the Greencastle demons, those bankers and lawyers and businessmen.

"What's going on?" she asked, thoughts racing around and tripping over themselves. This shouldn't be possible, but that was definitely her father sitting across from her at the table she'd been sharing with Will. He even sounded the same, with a warm-toned voice that had always seemed infinitely soothing.

Well, except for the times when she'd overheard him arguing with her mother.

The words spilled out, even though she realized as soon as she spoke that she probably should have phrased them a little more diplomatically. "You're supposed to be dead."

Her father paused and glanced around them, but because the restaurant wasn't too busy yet, no one else had been seated close enough to be within earshot. "I know," he said. "It was...necessary."

Will lifted an eyebrow and leaned forward slightly, his wine apparently forgotten for the moment. "Are you in the witness protection program or something like that?"

"No," her father said, then paused. "Well, not exactly." His gaze flicked back to Rosemary. "You see, I had to stay away to make sure you would be safe."

Her fingers rested on the base of her wine glass. The cool surface beneath her fingertips gave her something solid to focus on, something to tell her this was really happening, that she wasn't suddenly having the mother of all nightmares. "I don't understand. Safe from what?"

Another one of those pauses as he took a quick glance over his shoulder. Their waiter happened to be passing by, and he apparently took that random look as an invitation to come over and inquire if the new addition to their group also wanted a glass of wine. Her father appeared to think that over for a moment, then asked if he could have a martini instead—Grey Goose, light on the vermouth, and a bowl of lobster bisque. That important business handled—and with the waiter heading off toward the kitchen—John said, "From anyone who might have taken too much of an interest in my children—the children I was never supposed to have."

A spark of fury rose in her at those words. "What, you're saying you didn't want us?"

"No," he replied calmly. "That's not what I meant at all. I'm saying that I should never have fallen in love with your mother or started a family with her. That was not what I was sent here to do."

"Sent where?" Rosemary snapped. Once again, she wondered if she was having some sort of a nightmare, one of the infuriating kinds where everyone spoke to her as if they were making perfect sense but all she heard was gibberish. "To do what?"

"To observe," her father said. "To keep watch."

"On whom?" she demanded, but next to her, Will's eyes lit up in comprehension, and he leaned forward in his seat.

"On the Underhill Trust demons."

Her father looked pleased that Will had figured it out so quickly. "Yes, exactly. You see, by myself, I didn't have the power to send them back where they came from, but they left on their own eventually. However, their offspring needed to be watched as well, and so…here I am."

Rosemary picked up her wine and took far too large a swallow. Maybe she should have been more concerned about keeping a clear head, but right then, she knew she needed some alcohol to steady her nerves. "That doesn't make any sense, though. Michael Covenant told me they were brought to this world in the 1940s or something like that. You're not that old."

"Well—" He had to stop there, because the waiter had returned with his martini. After murmuring a brief thank-you and pausing for a moment while their server walked away, her father said, "I'm older than I look." He sipped at the martini, gave a small nod of approval, and then added, "You see, I'm actually an angel."

An incredulous laugh escaped Rosemary's lips. She'd been expecting excuses for his disappearing act—and for faking his own death—but did he really think she was going to buy a story as ludicrous as that? "Oh, really?" she responded, her tone dripping sarcasm. "You're an angel. Seriously, that's the best you can do?"

"It's the truth."

She sent an imploring glance over at Will. Right then, she really needed him to speak some words of wisdom, because she could tell she was getting dangerously close to exploding. And while lashing out at her father might have felt good, she knew she couldn't do anything that would attract too much attention.

However, Will had that thoughtful expression back on his face, one which told her he might actually be seriously considering what her father had just said.

Had the entire world gone crazy?

She took a large, entirely disrespectful swallow of her pinot noir and asked, "Did Mom know?"

"Of course not," her father replied. Then he clasped his hands on the tabletop—hands bare of rings, which seemed to tell her he had never remarried—and went on, "I know this must sound fantastic to you. I honestly hoped you would never find out about me. But circumstances have changed all that."

"What circumstances?" Rosemary inquired, although she had an uneasy feeling she already knew the answer.

Apparently, Will did as well, because he said, "*Project Demon Hunters.*"

Her father nodded. "Exactly. I suppose I should have realized you couldn't escape fate forever."

"'Fate'?" she echoed, but he couldn't respond immediately, because the waiter appeared with their food at exactly that inopportune moment. After everyone had been given their respective meals and the man had mercifully gone away, she went on, "What are you talking about?"

"Eat," her father said. "You're going to need all your strength."

Never in her life had she been less enthusiastic about consuming a meal, but she made herself cut off several pieces of roasted chicken and force down a bite. "Are you trying to tell me this was all meant to be?"

"In a manner of speaking, yes." He took several swallows of bisque, during which time Will silently cut himself a few pieces of pork tenderloin and ate them in silence. Once again, she wished he would step in, but he'd obviously decided— correctly, as much as she hated to admit it—that this was a matter she and her father needed to hash out on their own. "Tell me, Rosemary—have you noticed any recent changes in your powers?"

How in the world could he have known about that? As much as she would have liked to say she hadn't experienced anything different at all, she knew that would be a complete lie. Maybe some people would have said it was all right to lie to her father, since he'd lied to her mother and to his children, had made them all believe he was dead, and yet she knew if she did such a thing, she would be no better than he was.

"A few," she muttered, then made herself take another bite of chicken.

Although he must have noticed the sulkiness of her reply—uttered in much the same tone she'd used when she was a child and had gotten in trouble for some minor transgression or another—he didn't seem annoyed with her, but rather nodded in a pleased way. "It's because of your exposure to demon-kind—specifically, Caleb Lockwood. Your angelic nature began to exert itself because of being in the presence of a creature antithetical to someone with your blood."

Angelic nature? Once again, she had to quell the urge to let out a derisive laugh. She was no angel. Far from it.

However, Will didn't seem nearly so skeptical. "That glow within you when you cast the wards on my house," he murmured, and her father nodded.

"Yes, that sounds about right. That part of you woke up because it knew you were in need of extra protection."

Well, he was right about waking up—she definitely wanted to wake up from this nightmare. Over the years, she'd allowed herself a few wistful daydreams about her father coming back into her life, and—even after her family received news of his death and she tried to tell herself that she could handle the loss because he'd been absent from her life for years—to still hope deep down that maybe it had all been some kind of horrible mistake and he'd been alive all along.

Oh, her father was obviously alive. However, now that she'd been confronted by that particular reality, Rosemary honestly didn't know how happy she actually was about his miraculous return to the world of the living.

"So, if that's really true"—and she paused there for a moment, as though to let him know she still didn't quite believe any of it—"then how come Caleb couldn't detect what I was?"

To her surprise, it was Will who responded. Voice quiet, he said, "And the light shineth in darkness; and the darkness comprehended it not."

Rosemary only stared at him blankly, but her father smiled, looking absurdly pleased.

"A very good quote," he said before adding, "John, chapter one, verse five. Your mother raised you girls to be complete heathens, didn't she?"

"Pagans," Rosemary corrected him, her eyes narrowed. "I didn't exactly see you trying to take us to Bible study, Dad."

He shrugged and sipped from his martini. "Well, your mother had very distinct ideas about that sort of thing, and since I'd represented myself to her as being fairly agnostic, I suppose she would have found it odd if I'd suggested that you go to church. Anyway, as Will just pointed out, we beings of light can see those of the darkness, but the reverse doesn't hold true. Caleb would have thought you were only a normal young woman and nothing more."

"Well, I told him I was a psychic," she pointed out, but her father didn't look terribly concerned.

"Oh, but that's different. Those powers come to you from your mother, and from your mother's mother. They're entirely separate from the gifts that have recently awakened in you."

As Rosemary mulled that particular revelation, Will spoke. "Was that part of what drew you to Rosemary's mother? Her psychic powers?"

Her father smiled. "No, her charms were enough on their own."

"But not enough to keep you around, I guess," Rosemary said. The words fairly dripped acid, but she found she really didn't care. Even if her father really was what he claimed to be, his origins didn't change the fact that he'd walked out on them, had allowed his wife and daughters to believe he'd been dead for the past ten years.

"Rosemary," Will murmured, but her father lifted a hand.

"It's all right. I suppose I deserve that on some level, but I did what I had to do."

"Why?" she shot back. "If the de—I mean, if our friends over there in Greencastle can't even recognize us for what we are, then I don't see why you felt the need to abandon your family for some sort of mythical 'protection.'"

He gazed at her evenly. It was hard to look back at him, to meet his eyes and see the very real sorrow there—sadness for what she and her sisters and mother had suffered. Voice quiet, he said, "Do you think Belial's cambions are our only enemies? There are many forces of darkness in this world, and I couldn't take that risk."

There didn't seem to be much she could say in response to a statement like that, so she lowered her eyes and made herself take a few more bites of her meal. As far as she was concerned, Daniel Lockwood and the rest of his little cabal were plenty to deal with. She really didn't want to think that there might be more evil-doers lurking out there in the world, just waiting for a chance to wreak havoc.

"But that's neither here nor there," her father continued. "Now that these new powers have awakened, you're not as vulnerable. You can protect yourself."

Rosemary didn't know about that. Then again, she'd managed to fight off Caleb, if only just barely. "So, I'm good," she said. "What about Isabel and Celeste?"

"They should be safe. They haven't drawn the attention of these dark forces the way you have."

"But if they did?"

He was quiet for a few seconds, fingers tapping against the stem of his martini glass. "Then their own powers would awaken as well, and they'd be able to mount a defense. However," he went on, a slight frown deepening the line between his brows, "they are not quite as strong as you. The gifts that are handed down—whether from angel or demon—aren't inherited evenly. The main reason Caleb Lockwood was sent to California to entice you into locating the *Project Demon Hunters* footage wasn't simply because he happened to be Daniel Lockwood's son. No, it's also because he was the strongest one of his generation."

"Well, then, I guess it's a good thing he's dead," Rosemary remarked, and her father looked at her in surprise.

"He is?"

For some reason, knowing that her angel father wasn't all-seeing made her feel a bit better about the situation. "He died on Saturday night. Drowned."

"Interesting. Daniel has shown no sign of mourning his son."

"Would he?" Will asked. "That is, it doesn't seem to me as though those of demon-kind have too much caring or compassion within them."

Rosemary's father ate a spoonful of lobster bisque, his expression thoughtful. "It's true that they don't experience emotions the same way we do, but they still have some familial loyalty. But with Caleb out of the picture, that makes our own situation a bit easier."

Well, that was true. After all, she wouldn't have to worry about avoiding him at the party. She'd already planned to blow-dry her hair straight and get a flat iron from the local drugstore in an attempt to alter her appearance somewhat, but she knew Caleb would have seen right through such a simple disguise.

She began to comment, but at that moment, the restaurant's hostess led a group of three—two men and a woman who looked as though they'd just gotten off work—to the table next to them. So much for privacy. Although Rosemary had no reason to believe their new neighbors would listen in on their conversation, she knew they couldn't take the risk. Mouth tight, she glanced over at Will, and he gave her a small nod, as if indicating that he knew the discussion couldn't continue.

Her father's mouth pursed, but then his shoulders lifted slightly and he reached for his spoon with a resigned air. They all ate in silence for a moment or two, and then he said, "You're staying at the DePauw Hotel, correct?"

Rosemary nodded.

"Then I'll meet you there in an hour and a half. Enjoy the rest of your meal."

He got up from the table, took his wallet out of his pocket, and then dropped two fifty-dollar bills on the table. Even as she began to protest, he sent her a quick smile and walked away.

For a moment, she could only stare after him. Then she looked over at Will, who appeared as flummoxed as she was. He released a small breath. "Go ahead and finish your dinner," he said. "Then we'll get on the road."

———

Will glanced over at Rosemary. She was still huddled in the passenger seat of their rented RAV4, jaw tight, her gaze fixed on the twilight landscape passing by outside the car windows. They hadn't said much of anything as they finished their meal, and she'd remained silent as he guided them back to the interstate and headed south and west toward Greencastle.

Finally, he said, "Do you want to talk about it?"

"Not really," she replied, her voice small and tight, not sounding like herself at all.

He could understand that. So many people preferred to retreat into themselves when confronted by the sort of life-changing shock Rosemary had faced earlier this evening, and yet Will knew she needed to talk this out, needed to understand that what her father had said hadn't changed anything about what he felt for her…or who she was as a person.

"You have every right to be angry—" he began, but she didn't let him get any farther than that.

"Damn straight I do," she cut in. Her arms were folded across her chest, and she still wouldn't look over at him. "I don't give a crap who or what my father says he is—he had no right to do that to my mother, to the rest of us."

"No, he didn't," Will said. Possibly, as John McGuire had tried to point out, there had been extenuating circumstances, but that still didn't excuse walking out on your wife and three children. Or rather, while marriages broke up all the time, Will couldn't quite understand the cruelty of allowing Glynis and her daughters to believe John was dead.

However, Will had read the Bible enough times to also realize that God's love could sometimes be cruel, that sometimes acts were committed that seemed incomprehensible to the human heart, even if the motives behind them might have been pure. But since he had a feeling that Rosemary probably wouldn't be too receptive to a comment along those lines, he decided to put that notion aside for the moment.

"It doesn't change anything," he said, and she

finally looked over at him, her face pale in the half-light of gloaming and the faint illumination from the dashboard instruments.

"What doesn't change anything?"

"Knowing who—what—your father is. It doesn't change how I feel about you."

Her mouth curved, but there was something almost bitter in that smile, something that didn't look very Rosemary-like. "If he's even what he says he is," she replied. "Let's just say he hasn't done much to make me trust him."

While Will could understand her reaction, he somehow realized that Rosemary knew her father had been telling her the truth. She just didn't want to acknowledge that truth quite yet.

"Maybe," he allowed. "But I don't see how he could know so much about the Underhill Trust and *Project Demon Hunters* and everything else if he didn't have access to some fairly well-developed supernatural powers."

Her fingers tightened on her elbows as she held herself. The glance Will allowed himself before he returned his attention to the road told him she looked very small and fragile, cold and scared, and he wished he was able to take her in his arms and let her know that he loved her no matter what, and that they'd figure all this out one way or another.

At last, she released a small gust of a breath. "I

know. I mean, I understand that on some level, but...." The words slipped away, and she sighed again. "I guess I'd just rather have it be only regular human psychic powers ramping up rather than some weird angelic thing that I don't know how to control. If that's even possible. I mean... how can I be part angel?"

"If you're going to make that argument, then you also have to ask, how could Caleb be part demon?" Will pointed out. "We know what he and the other Greencastle demons are. If we can acknowledge their existence, then we also have to acknowledge that angels exist as well, and can mingle with humans in the same way that demons have." He didn't add that there was Biblical precedent for this sort of situation, mostly because he guessed she wouldn't want to hear about that sort of evidence. Besides, Rosemary was perfect, completely unlike the twisted Nephilim who were supposed to be the offspring of angels and humans.

She frowned. "I suppose you're right. I just—I don't want this, Will! I don't want to be some kind of a freak!"

"You're not a freak, Rosemary," he said, praying she could hear the sincerity in his voice, could get past her hurt and fear to understand that nothing had changed who she fundamentally was as a person. "You're amazing and strong and talented and beautiful. You're the woman I love. All the rest of this—we'll figure it out together. It's going to be okay."

A silence then, during which he could only hear the sound of the wind whistling outside the windows of their small SUV. Then at last, her hand stole onto his arm and gripped it. He could feel the desperation in that touch, the need to know that he truly meant what he'd said. Bits and pieces of her life were falling apart all around her, and she clung to him now like a drowning swimmer might cling to a lifeline.

Still hanging on to him, she said, "I'm so angry with him, Will. And I hate it. I'm not—I'm not an angry person."

"I know you're not. You have every right to be angry. But you can't let that anger get in the way of what we're here to do."

She gave his arm a final squeeze, then released it and slumped back in her seat. "I know. And maybe—" She broke off there and was silent for a few seconds, as if she was turning over something in her mind. "Maybe he's coming to talk to us at the hotel because he has a plan to help us."

Will had been thinking much the same thing, and he hoped they were right. Of course, it could be that John McGuire had said he would meet them at their room because he felt he still had unfinished business with his daughter, but the situation was tense, and Will thought it might be better if they focused on practical considerations for the time being. After all, he couldn't think of a single thing Rosemary's father might say—a single excuse he could offer—that would even begin to erase what he'd done to his family. Maybe he'd been acting in their best interests, but if that was truly the case, he needed to do a lot more explaining.

If Rosemary was even willing to listen to those explanations. Judging by the way she'd reacted to her father's reappearance, probably not.

"That would make sense," Will said. "Obviously, he's been observing Daniel Lockwood and the rest of them for some time now. He must know a lot more than we do, and should be able to offer some helpful advice."

"Unless my father tells us the whole plan is crazy and that we need to head back to Southern California, stat."

Such an eventuality seemed distinctly possible, but Will only shrugged. "Or maybe he's going to tell us that he's got it handled and that he can spirit the hard drive out of there for us."

Rosemary's mouth quirked ever so slightly. No, it wasn't exactly a smile, but it was maybe half the way there, and that was probably as much as he could ask for at the moment. "If he was going to do us a favor like that, then you'd think he could have handed the damn thing to us back at the restaurant."

True enough. Well, they'd be back at the hotel soon, and he supposed they'd find out then. Since he really didn't have a reply to her remark, Will settled for shrugging slightly. Rosemary seemed to take his gesture as a signal that the conversation was over, because she settled herself back in her seat and fell silent. However, judging by the brief glance he gave her before looking back at the road, she didn't appear angry, more…thoughtful, her fine brow furrowed slightly as she regarded the ever-darkening landscape beyond the car windows.

Roughly half an hour later, they were back in Greencastle, and he pointed the RAV4 toward their hotel. As he parked, Will sent a wary look around their surroundings, but he didn't see anyone nearby. In fact, the parking lot appeared nearly empty, and he wondered if John McGuire had even shown up yet. Maybe he could travel instantly from place to place the same way Caleb had apparently been able to.

However the man was getting there, Will didn't see any need for himself or Rosemary to linger. They got out of the car and hurried into the hotel, then went over to the elevator so they could take it to the third floor where their room was located. The only person to take note of their progress was the same bored-looking clerk who'd checked them in the night before, and he barely glanced up from his iPad as they passed.

As soon as Will and Rosemary entered their hotel room, he saw his question had already been answered—John McGuire sat in one of the chairs at the table over by the window, and looked up as they arrived.

"You made good time," he said.

"Obviously, not as good as you," Rosemary returned. The frown was back, digging a small line into the fair skin between her brows. "Whatever happened to knocking on the door like a normal person?"

John tilted his head slightly and sent her a look so mild, Will couldn't really interpret what he might be thinking. "It was better not to risk being seen," he said. "I knew you couldn't have gotten back here any faster than you did, so I knew I wouldn't be interrupting anything by popping in like this." A pause, and then he added, "You should try it yourself."

"Try what?" Rosemary said, although Will got the feeling she was being deliberately obtuse.

"Traveling like I do."

Her eyes widened. "I can do that?"

"If you put your mind to it." John got up from his chair and came toward them, although he seemed to understand that his daughter wasn't in the mood for any fatherly displays of affection, since he stopped several feet away. "In fact, it's something you should practice now, because it's going to be the best way for you to leave the Lockwood house tomorrow night after the hard drive is back in your possession."

"I'm not leaving Will behind—"

"I'm not suggesting that you would," John said mildly. "You're certainly strong enough to take him with you."

That comment didn't seem to convince Rosemary. She crossed her arms and sent him a narrow-eyed stare. "I know for a fact that Belial had to put Audrey on an airplane to get her out of Tucson and over to his house in Colorado. Are you saying I'm somehow stronger than he was?"

"In some things, yes," her father replied. "Angels are stronger than demons."

"I'm not an angel," she retorted. "I'm only half angel, according to you. So, I don't really see how that could make me more powerful than a full-on demon."

"In some ways, you aren't." John shook his head, as if annoyed at his daughter's stubbornness. "I'm afraid there are some things you'll just have to take on faith."

Her mouth tightened as she said, "I think that's more Will's department."

While he wanted to say, *Leave me out of this,*

Will knew he needed to act as peacemaker if he possibly could. "I think we have to acknowledge that all this is a little beyond our scope. But if your father says you have these skills, Rosemary—then I think you should at least try."

John looked at him approvingly. "Exactly. Try it yourself, just to see. All you have to do is imagine where you want to go, and you'll be there."

This piece of encouragement didn't seem to help much, because her expression was still dubious and more than a little angry. But then she let out a breath and said, "Fine."

And she disappeared.

While this had been the hoped-for outcome of the exercise, Will couldn't quite stop himself from taking a step back. She had been standing there by the foot of the bed just a second before, and now she was gone. He looked over at John, who was now smiling.

"See? I knew she could do it."

A second or two passed, and then she reappeared in the same spot she'd occupied just a moment earlier. Her eyes were wide, but with wonder this time.

"It worked," she said, the disbelieving tone of her voice at odds with her words.

"I know," John replied. "So, where did you go?"

"Back to Will's house in Pasadena," she said. "I thought that should be safe enough, since the place is warded and the demons—hopefully— wouldn't be able to detect my presence there."

"Good choice," her father told her. "Especially since I assume that's where you'll be going when you leave Daniel Lockwood's house. Now, try it with Will."

Despite his confidence in Rosemary and her abilities, he couldn't quite hold back a nervous tickle of anticipation. It was one thing to stand there and watch her come and go, but to be taken away like that, to disappear into nothingness and emerge somewhere else?

Will wasn't quite sure how he felt about that.

However, he tried his best to seem confident and relaxed as he went over to her and took her by the hands. "Do I need to do anything?" he asked.

"No," John said. "Except don't let go."

Will was about to reply that of course, he wouldn't do anything so foolish. But he wasn't given the chance, since Rosemary's slender fingers tightened on his and the hotel room vanished around him. In the next moment, before he had time to blink or even process the enormous blinding darkness that had filled the space between one breath and the next, he felt something solid beneath his feet. He looked down and saw the polished oak of his living room floor, saw the edge of the Persian carpet that covered part of the surface.

And then he lifted his head and saw Rosemary staring at him with a sort of tremulous awe.

"I did it," she whispered. "We're here."

Yes, they were. Back in his house, surrounded by the books and the antiques and the other items he'd carefully collected over the years to make this place his home. The relief he felt at standing in his own house disappeared quickly enough, though, because he knew this was only an exercise. They hadn't come back here to stay. Still....

He went over to her and took her in his arms, held her close. Her heart was beating quickly, whether from excitement or stress or the exertion of what she'd just done, he couldn't know for sure. He kissed the top of her head and then said, "You are the most amazing woman I've ever known."

She looked up at him, and her blue eyes glinted in a way that made him happy, that told him she had begun to return somewhat to herself. "Well, I'm guessing you haven't had too many half angels cross your path."

"No, probably not."

They kissed again, and then she said, "I wish we could stay here."

"I know." His fingers tightened on hers. "But we sort of left your father waiting in our hotel room."

That reminder actually made her grin. "True. Except after what he's done, I don't think being left to cool his heels for a while is that bad a punishment."

Possibly, she was right, although Will didn't think they were the ones who should be meting out such punishment. "Well, we also need to plan, so we should probably head back."

"All right. I don't like it, but…okay."

Since they were already holding hands, there wasn't anything Will needed to do except hold on and try not to wince as the world disappeared around him once again. They reappeared in the prosaic surroundings of their small hotel room; the only thing that seemed to have changed was that John McGuire had sat down once again in one of the chairs by the window.

"Very good," he said. "Tomorrow night, be ready to get away as soon as you have the hard drive. As a precaution, you should send your luggage back to Will's house when you leave for the party."

"I can do that, too?"

"Yes."

Now Rosemary looked pleased. "No more TSA lines," she said. "I am totally down with that." Her expression sobered almost immediately, though, and she went on, "What else do I need to know?"

"Only that you can use your powers to ward yourself and Will," John replied. "Or rather, think of it as a minor enchantment you can use to wrap around yourself."

"Like a disguise?" Will asked, and the other man shook his head.

"Not exactly. It's more that anyone with demonic blood in attendance will simply ignore you, and won't have any need to notice you or interact with you in any way. Of course, it's not infallible—you need to do whatever you can to avoid attracting attention. Slip in, blend, mingle...and then get out."

Arms crossed, Rosemary asked, "If it's so simple, why don't you do it? You must be more powerful than I am."

Her father didn't even blink. "My task is to observe. I'm already walking the line by giving you this advice. If I were to interfere directly —" He broke off there, mouth tight, then said, "I'm afraid this is something you'll have to do on your own."

Will wanted to ask more questions, but something in John McGuire's expression told him that answers would not be forthcoming. Instead, he glanced down at Rosemary. "You okay with this?"

"No, but I'm not going to waste time arguing." She closed her eyes briefly, as if doing her best to inwardly visualize what her father had told her about using her powers to create enough misdirection that the demons wouldn't even know she was there. "I saw the hard drive in Daniel Lockwood's office," she went on. "But what if he's moved it?"

"He wouldn't have taken it out of the house," John replied. "It's too valuable to him. But locked doors aren't much of a hindrance to us."

No, obviously not, what with the way both he and Rosemary were able to transport themselves pretty much anywhere they liked. However....

"What if he put it in a safe?" Will asked.

A lift of the shoulders. "Like I said, locks are really not a problem for us. The most important thing is to avoid detection. If the hard drive really is locked away somewhere, then it might be some time before he even realizes it's missing."

That sounded like a best-case scenario, but Will figured they might as well allow themselves to be cautiously optimistic. After all, what was the point in even attempting such a maneuver if you were pretty sure it was doomed to failure from the start?

"Okay," she said. "Anything else we need to know?"

John shook his head. "Just be careful, and be quick. After that...I suppose it's up to fate. Best of luck."

And he disappeared.

Rosemary blinked. "Well…that was abrupt."

Will had been thinking much the same thing, but he only said, "I suppose he thought he'd done what he needed to, and wanted to give us some time alone. It's clear he's focused on making sure we get the hard drive—and don't get caught."

She didn't look terribly convinced by that argument, but she didn't protest. Instead, she came over to Will and wrapped her arms around him. "All right," she said. "We're alone. Now what?"

In answer, he bent and kissed her, tasted her sweetness and felt her lithe, lovely body press up against him. "Oh, I could think of a few things."

The wicked glint had definitely returned to her big blue eyes. She grinned, and led him over to the bed.

And he proceeded to show her that truly, nothing between them had changed.

Chapter 17

ROSEMARY SET DOWN THE STRAIGHTENING iron and eyed herself critically in the mirror. It had been a while since she'd done this to her hair, but all the hours of fighting her unruly mane when she was in high school and still cared about such things must have remained in her muscle memory, because her hair actually looked pretty good, lying shiny and sleek over her shoulders. It also felt longer than normal, the straightening process having added a couple of virtual inches to her chestnut-brown locks.

Between that and the smoky eye makeup—courtesy of a quick run to the local Walgreens earlier in the day, because of course when she was at Nordstrom the day before, she'd completely forgotten about getting any cosmetics to supplement the mascara and lip gloss she'd brought along on this trip—she wouldn't say she was completely unrecognizable, but even someone who knew her probably would have had to look twice to confirm her identity. She honestly didn't know whether any of the Greencastle demons would have recognized her on sight even if she was looking like herself. But this disguise, subtle as it was, did make her feel a little bit better about walking into Daniel Lockwood's house.

She put the cosmetics in her overnight bag and then went out into the main part of the hotel room. Will stood in front of the mirror there, frowning a little as he fussed with his tie. In her opinion, there was nothing for him to be frowning at—he looked damn amazing in that suit. How he'd managed to find one that fit him so well at such short notice, she had no idea. Maybe God had been smiling down on him…if you believed in that sort of thing.

"You look good," she said. "Too bad we're not going out on a hot date."

His gaze moved from the reflection in the mirror over to where she stood, and she could see the admiration in his eyes. "You look incredible." A pause, and then he quickly added, "Although I think I like your curly hair better."

She chuckled. "Is that the truth, or are you just trying to be polite?"

"It's the truth," he said, and his eyes met hers

in the mirror and held. "You're perfect just as you are, Rosemary. But I do have to say I like that dress."

Her fingers brushed against the skirt. She really liked it, too—liked the way it followed the lines of her body without being too clingy, appreciated how its soft gray-blue hue echoed the color of her eyes. No, it wasn't particularly sexy or revealing, but she should have known that Will was the sort of man who would appreciate its subtle appeal.

"Me, too," she replied. "And hopefully, I'll be able to wear it again on a real date. Are you almost ready?" And she glanced at the clock, which told her it was a little after seven. Technically, the fundraising cocktail party had started on the hour, but she knew they definitely didn't want to be among the first to arrive. No, they should appear in that comfortable zone about twenty minutes or so after the festivities had begun; that way, they had a better chance of blending in with the other couples and groups who'd be showing up at around the same time.

Will gave his tie a final tug and then nodded. "As ready as I'll ever be." He paused before adding, "I'm still not entirely happy about the car situation."

Neither was she, but while her newly acquired and ever-growing powers seemed vast to her, they weren't quite up to the task of snapping her fingers and sending their rental back to where they'd got it in Indianapolis. No, they'd decided about the best they could do was to leave it here at the hotel and then call the local Enterprise office —since there actually was one in Greencastle— after they were safely back in California to have someone come by and collect it. Because they'd already scoped out the neighborhood where Daniel Lockwood's house was located, Rosemary knew she could have herself and Will appear in the shadow of a big tree located in his right-hand neighbor's yard.

Speaking of snapping her fingers....

"And you're packed?" she asked.

He nodded.

Not really a snap of her fingers, but more a mental twist. Just a slight bend of her thoughts toward her overnight bag and Will's duffle, and they were sent from the hotel room all the way back to California, where they now sat on the floor in his bedroom.

With any luck, the rest of the evening would go as smoothly.

That little detail managed, Rosemary went over to him and entwined his fingers with hers. His skin was warm against her flesh, reassuring her. She knew her own hands must feel like ice, because she was chill with nerves, but there was no backing out now. They had to get that footage away from the Lockwoods.

A slight tightening of her fingers, and the hotel room was replaced by cold night air and the shadow of an oak tree that sheltered them from any unfriendly eyes. Her heel was resting on a tree root, and she stumbled for the barest second before Will's grip strengthened and he held her in place.

"Are you all right?" he asked in a murmur.

"Fine," she said, a little annoyed with herself for her clumsiness. "Next time, I'll do a better job of sticking the dismount."

He chuckled—but she noticed how he maintained his hold on her hand, how he helped steady her as she walked across the grass of the neighbor's lawn and to the street. Unlike her own neighborhood back in California, there wasn't any sidewalk here; the best they could do was make their way along the edge of the street, past the parked cars that had already begun to take up all the available space. In a way, that was good, just because with so many cars already here, probably no one would notice that they hadn't come in their own vehicle.

Lights gleamed from every window of the Lockwood house, and graceful outdoor candle lamps hanging from wrought-iron hooks illuminated the front walk. Rosemary and Will fell in behind a group of three older couples, obviously good friends, judging by the way they chatted as they headed up the path to the door.

To her relief, the man at the front door was obviously not Daniel Lockwood, nor any of the other Underhill Trust demons. She heard one of the men from the group in front of her and Will call him Thomas, and guessed from a few other things they said that he must be the head librarian here in Greencastle. He didn't seem surprised to see a couple of complete strangers walk in, only greeted them warmly and thanked them for contributing to the library.

They smiled and said it was their honor, and then they were safely inside. The house seemed huge—she guessed it was nearly twice the size of Michael Covenant's extremely spacious home—but the ground floor still seemed crowded, with well-dressed people ranging from their thirties all the way up to their seventies or more bustling about, chatting and nibbling hors d'oeuvres and drinking wine or champagne or cocktails.

As soon as she and Will emerged from the shelter of the oak tree in the neighbor's yard, Rosemary had conjured the enchantment her father had spoken of, the one that would make the two of them unobtrusive, unmemorable. She still hadn't seen any of the Underhill Trust demons, but she assumed they had to be around somewhere.

Will snagged them a couple of flutes of champagne from a passing waiter's tray and then murmured as he handed one of them to her, "Any idea where the hard drive is?"

"Mmm," she replied noncommittally, then took a sip of champagne. Probably water would have been safer, but the champagne would help them to blend in. As she sipped again, she let her thoughts drift, moving to the vision she'd had the day before, of the hard drive sitting in the middle of that huge polished mahogany desk.

This time, though, as the image of the desk and the library which surrounded it swam up in her mind's eye, she could see that the desk's surface was completely empty, with even the blotter that had occupied the space now gone.

"Not there," she said in an undertone, her tone terse. Maybe it had been expecting too much to think that Daniel Lockwood would have left the damn thing out there in plain sight while he hosted an intimate party for two hundred guests, and yet the pang of disappointment that went through her was almost physically painful.

However, Will only nodded, his expression resigned, as if he'd been expecting such a thing. "Do you know where he put it?"

Rosemary wanted to snap that no, of course she didn't. But she realized that her powers or her sight or whatever she wanted to call those strange abilities must also have been enhanced, and now was the time to make them work for her, rather than believing that they came and went at their own whim without any control on her end.

Another sip of champagne, and she shifted so her back was to most of the people in the crowded living room where they stood. Will seemed to understand what she was doing, because he moved as well, doing his best to block her from any casual passersby. To most people, it would only have looked as though they were sharing an intimate conversation, but of course she knew there was a far greater purpose to what she did now.

Once again, she visualized Daniel Lockwood's library/office, but only so she could place where it was in the house—at the back, at the end of the hallway that bisected the ground floor. From there, her consciousness moved out—into the living room where they stood now, and into the family room on the other side of the hallway from Lockwood's office, the enormous dining room, the equally large kitchen and accompanying nook, with a table large enough to accommodate a sit-down Thanksgiving dinner, the powder room and full bath off the family room. In all that space, though, she didn't get one whiff of the hard drive, which meant it wasn't down here at all. That made sense, she supposed; the half-demon would want to keep his treasure far away from the regular humans who were milling about the house, drinking and chatting, never realizing that their host wasn't exactly what he pretended to be.

All right. If it wasn't down here somewhere, then the drive would have to be hidden upstairs in one of the bedrooms. If she hadn't acquired her handy new talent of being able to wish herself wherever she needed to go, Rosemary might have worried about how she was supposed to sneak upstairs, even with as crowded as the house currently was. However, she knew she could simply hide herself in a bathroom and then zap herself up to the hard drive's hiding place... assuming she was able to track down where Lockwood had hidden the damn thing.

There seemed to be five bedrooms upstairs—four rooms of various sizes and the master suite, which was enormous, with a separate sitting area and a walk-in closet bigger than her living room and a bathroom that could have swallowed all of hers and Will's room back at the DePauw University Hotel. Briefly, she allowed herself to wonder why someone with only one child would need a house this big, but she realized there was nothing practical about such a place. It existed only for show, to prove to everyone else in this small town how successful its owner was.

Something about the master bedroom was

drawing her, though, making her realize that all those other rooms were completely irrelevant. She saw it then—the hard drive sitting in a drawer amongst a collection of leather- and velvet-covered jewelry cases in various shapes and sizes. That vision was followed by a flash of Daniel Lockwood himself putting the drive there, stacking the cases on top of and around it. Most likely, his wife didn't even know it was there, hiding amongst all the various gifts he'd given her over the years.

"I've got it," she murmured, and Will sent her a relieved smile.

"Where?"

"Upstairs," she said, still in an undertone. Then she lifted the champagne flute to her lips and took another sip. Speaking more loudly this time, she said, "Darling, could you hold this for me? I need to go to the ladies' room."

He blinked, looking a little surprised at her request...a surprise that quickly morphed into dawning comprehension. "Sure, sweetheart. You know where it is?"

"Down the hall, I think." Rosemary handed him her glass and gave him a feather-light kiss on the cheek, not heavy enough to leave any of her lipstick on his skin. "I'll be back in a jif."

She turned away and headed toward the powder room, heart pounding even though she tried to reassure herself that this was all going to be fine, that no one had noticed either one of them yet. Or at least, while she'd been the recipient of several smiles as she passed, she knew it was just because people were being generally friendly and not because anyone had recognized her or thought there was anything out of place about her actions.

Of course, the powder room was occupied. She held back a curse and continued to the other bathroom, the one opposite the family room. To her relief, no one was inside, so she went in and closed the door but didn't lock it. After all, she needed to make sure that whoever came here next could get in without any trouble. Leaving behind a locked bathroom with no one in it was sure to attract attention.

She didn't stop to think about what she was about to do. That seemed like the quickest way to psych herself out of the whole thing. And she sure as hell wasn't going to pause to ponder how she was acting like it was no big deal to vanish herself from one spot, only to appear in another. Maybe once this was all over, she'd be able to sit down and process everything that had happened during the past twenty-four hours or so, but now was definitely not the time. Onward and upward.

Here goes nothing, she thought, and sent herself upstairs.

Will stood in his corner and did his best to act nonchalant, as though there was nothing terribly strange about him loitering there, a champagne flute in either hand. But then, to the casual observer, there probably wouldn't be. Anyone who'd been paying any attention at all would've overheard Rosemary saying that she needed to go to the bathroom. Most of the men attending the party had probably been put in a similar position by their significant others at one point in their relationship.

No, it was more that he knew Rosemary wasn't powdering her nose or doing anything quite so innocuous. It was all he could do to prevent himself from glancing up toward the ceiling, as though he could somehow see through all those inches of plaster and lath to spy on what she was doing on the floor above him.

He was slightly relieved to note that none of the Underhill Trust half-demons—and he'd recognized several of them at the party, thanks to the photos and information Fred Peñasco had sent him—appeared to have given him a second glance. Rosemary's little spell seemed to be working, and thank God for that. If forced to a confrontation, he would do what he needed to, but Will had to admit it was unnerving to be standing here on his own. Funny how he'd come to rely on her amazing gifts after such a short amount of time.

"Enjoying yourself?" came a voice from over his shoulder, and he startled, nearly slopping some champagne on his hand from Rosemary's glass, since it was more filled than his own.

Will looked over to see an older man, probably in his late sixties, standing a few feet away. No one he recognized, he saw at once, and he did his best to get his heartbeat down to a more normal level. "It's a very nice party," he replied honestly. And it was. The champagne was excellent, and what he'd seen of the hors d'oeuvres seemed to indicate they were both varied and plentiful. His own church had hosted some of its own fundraisers in the past, but they'd never had the kind of budget Daniel Lockwood apparently had at his disposal.

"You're not from around here," the man said, and once again, Will experienced a start of panic. However, he did his best to offer the stranger a confident smile.

"No," he said easily. "My wife"—he held up the champagne flute, as if to explain her absence —"went to DePauw and found out about the fundraiser from a friend of hers. She thought it would be nice to give back to the community, so here we are."

The man nodded. "Wonderful college. We're lucky to have it." He added, "I'm Sam Mackenzie, by the way. Vice president at the same bank as Daniel."

"Nice to meet you," Will said, inwardly thanking providence that the entire management of the bank wasn't staffed by demons. That would have made this conversation a lot more awkward. "I'd shake hands, but—"

Sam chuckled. "I understand. Anyway, I'm just making the rounds and wanted to say welcome. Be sure to say hello to Daniel if you get the chance. He's always happy to see alumni come back and participate in our events here in Greencastle."

"Oh, definitely," Will replied. Of course, he knew he was going to do everything in his power to avoid Daniel Lockwood and the rest of his cabal, but it wouldn't have been very politic to say such a thing out loud. "Once my wife gets back and reclaims her champagne, we'll start to wander."

"Good to hear." Sam nodded at Will and then headed back toward the dining room, and Will allowed himself an inner sigh of relief.

All right, Rosemary, he thought. *Whatever you're doing…better hurry.*

The master bedroom seemed more lavish in reality than it had in her vision. Rosemary allowed herself a quick glance around at the dark, traditional furniture—purchased from Ethan Allen, or someplace even more expensive?—at the coordinating blue silk curtains and comforter, at the dark-framed pictures on the wall. Landscapes, most of them, all oil paintings, all original. It looked like a movie set rather than a place where people actually lived.

Well, so does the rest of the house, she thought as she made herself go over to the large dresser. It was topped by a three-paneled mirror, and she caught a glimpse of herself in it, looking far more chic than she probably ever had before. Her face was pale, though, or at least, she thought she appeared a bit peaked, despite the heavy evening makeup she wore.

Or maybe that was just her guilty conscience.

She tried to tell herself there was no need to feel guilty. After all, she was only in here to take back something that had been stolen from her… or at least, stolen from Colin Turner. But since he wasn't around to take action and protect his property, she had to take care of the situation for him.

Still, she had to stand in front of the dresser for a few seconds to steel herself to open the drawer and reach inside. Thank God her inner vision had told her to look in the top right drawer, so she wouldn't have to waste time searching the entire enormous piece of furniture.

Wrapping a fold of her skirt around her finger so she wouldn't leave any prints, she took hold of the heavy brass handle and pulled open the drawer. Just as she'd seen in her mind's eye, it was full of small leatherette and velvet cases, no doubt each one with its own expensive trinket. For a demon, Daniel Lockwood seemed to do a pretty good job of pampering his wife. Or maybe it was only that he'd bought her the jewelry because that was what was expected of a man in his position.

No time to worry about it now. Still with her skirt protecting her fingertips, she reached in and pushed two jewelry cases aside and grabbed hold of the hard drive. Just as she was rearranging the boxes so it wouldn't look as though the contents of the drawer had been disturbed, a woman's voice carried over to her, clear and sharp.

"What are you doing in there?"

Rosemary whirled, inadvertently slamming the dresser drawer shut with her hip. Standing in the doorway of the master suite was the same woman she'd seen in her vision the day before. Daniel Lockwood's wife…Caleb's mother.

She was somewhere in her fifties—probably late fifties, if Caleb had been telling the truth about being twenty-nine—but her fair skin was smooth and taut, her highlighted dark hair thick and plentiful. Looking at her even, elegant features, Rosemary could see where her son had gotten his looks.

"I—I got lost," she said, knowing how stupid that must have sounded. "I was looking for the bathroom."

"In my dresser drawer?" Mrs. Lockwood asked, elegant brows lifting slightly. "What's that you have in your hand? Were you trying to steal from me?"

The supercilious tone in her voice seemed to indicate she thought that was exactly what was happening. Rosemary wanted to retort that it was actually her son who was the thief, but something stopped her. Although neither of Caleb's parents looked as though they were mourning their son too much, she didn't want to rub his loss in the other woman's face. Also, she had a fairly good idea that Lockwood's wife knew nothing about her husband's true origins…or his extracurricular activities.

And then she realized, with that same strange knowing that had led her here in the first place, that she could reach out with her gifts and get the truth from this woman, could exert a gentle influence to prevent her from calling for help. Only a breath of an intention, and Mrs. Lockwood seemed to relax, her dark eyes going blurry.

"You won't remember any of this," Rosemary said, and the demon's wife nodded.

"Remember what?" she asked, staring vaguely up at the ceiling.

"Nothing at all," Rosemary replied. She began to move toward the doorway, intending to go past Mrs. Lockwood and down the stairs, but something made her pause. Lowering her voice, she said, "Do you know?"

Now those unfocused dark eyes shifted toward her, although Rosemary still had the impression that the woman was looking at something else entirely. "Know what?" she said.

"About your husband. What he is."

A faint line appeared in the unnaturally smooth skin between Mrs. Lockwood's brows. She didn't look as though she'd had a facelift—not yet, anyway—but obviously, her aesthetician had a free hand with the Botox. "He's a banker. What else is there to know?"

"He never said anything about where his father came from?"

The frown deepened. "Daniel's father is dead. He left him a lot of money…a lot of lovely, lovely money."

Well, that seemed to explain why she'd married her half-demon husband. Incongruously, Rosemary wanted to smile. No, she didn't have a golden lasso, but this strange talent of hers seemed to be just as good when it came to getting people to tell the truth.

"And you married Daniel because of that."

"Of course," she said. "Wouldn't you want to live in the biggest house in town and be married to the richest man?"

"Not if it meant being married to a half-demon," Rosemary replied, to which Mrs. Lockwood stared at her blankly before giving a tipsy-sounding laugh.

"A what? Daniel may have his faults, but he's no devil."

Demon, Rosemary thought with some weariness, but it seemed obvious to her that the woman who stood at the entrance to the master suite had absolutely no idea what she'd been married to all these years. How she'd managed that, Rosemary didn't know, but she supposed that someone who'd been given everything she desired out of life might not have wanted to peek behind the curtain to see the truth behind what was actually happening in her world.

Obviously, the two of them deserved each other.

And she needed to get out of there. Mrs. Lockwood wasn't a problem, but someone might come up here in search of her, and she needed to be long gone by then.

"Of course, he's not," Rosemary said cheerfully. "Well, I need to go downstairs and collect my husband. But I think it's probably a good idea if you stay up here for a few more minutes, just in case."

"Yes, I'll stay," Mrs. Lockwood said in a dreamy tone that was probably very different from her normal speaking voice.

Rosemary smiled and then ducked out, the hard drive now tucked into the little evening bag she carried. It didn't quite fit, and she couldn't close the kiss-lock clasp on the thing, but with it tucked under her arm, it should be difficult to tell that she was carrying anything other than the usual lipstick, cell phone, and credit card.

Hurrying—but doing her best not to look as if she was in a hurry—she descended the stairs. As much as she would have liked to simply vanish herself and Will out of there, she couldn't do that without physically touching him. Besides, this whole venture was predicated on flying low and avoiding notice. If one of the partygoers simply disappeared in the midst of everyone else, it might attract just a little attention.

When she got to the bottom step, she looked around but didn't see him. He definitely wasn't off in the corner where he'd been standing when she disappeared to go to the bathroom, and a mixture of irritation and worry spiked within her. Was it too much to ask that he stay put so he'd be easy to find? Then again, maybe stubbornly standing in one place would have attracted its own kind of attention.

Well, the house was big, but it wasn't so big that she shouldn't be able to track him down. Purse still clenched tightly under one arm, she headed toward the dining room, figuring he'd probably gravitated to that space, if for no other reason than all the food arrayed on the long table there.

Someone touched her arm, and she nearly jumped out of her skin. However, she realized in the next moment that it was only Will, who'd approached her from behind.

He bent toward her and murmured, "Did you get it?"

"Yes," she said quietly. "Let's get out of here."

She looped her arm through his—somewhere along the line, he'd gotten rid of one of the glasses of champagne he held—then took the remaining glass and downed its contents before depositing it on the tray of a passing waiter. A quick look around to make sure no one was paying attention to them, and then she began to move toward the front door, Will keeping pace and doing a remarkably good job of looking unconcerned and not as though his companion had just taken a valuable artifact from the homeowner's bedroom.

"Going so soon?"

Oh, shit. Rosemary ground to a halt and saw Daniel Lockwood standing near the foyer, arms folded, but a pleasant smile on his lips nonetheless. He was very tall, she realized, taller than he'd seemed in his pictures. Handsome, of course, his dark hair streaked with gray and a set of broad shoulders filling out the navy suit he wore. At least his wife was nowhere in evidence.

Had he been able to figure out who they were? Or was this just horrible bad luck, with the half-demon playing concerned host regarding a couple of partygoers who were ducking out far too early?

Will's fingers tightened on her arm, but he managed to smile and say, "It's a wonderful party, but my wife isn't feeling well, so we've decided to head home. But thank you for hosting—it looks like your fundraiser was a raging success."

Daniel Lockwood smiled thinly, although the smile never reached his eyes. In that moment, Rosemary noticed with an odd, jarring clarity that his eyes were pale blue, very unlike his son's. "Oh, it was. If nothing else, it allowed me to know who my true enemy is."

"Excuse me?" Will said, looking nonplussed.

Who knew that an Episcopalian priest could be such a good actor? Unfortunately, she knew his acting was to no avail, since their cover was clearly blown. Fear pulsed through her, but Rosemary told herself to stay calm.

Not that she had any other options.

"You're not going to do anything in front of all these people," she told the demon.

"What people?" Lockwood asked, his tone now silky.

It was as though a strange, shimmering veil had dropped around the three of them. Rosemary could still see the interior of the house, could see people as they talked and ate and drank and laughed, but she couldn't hear them…and she somehow knew, with an odd, chilling certainty, that they couldn't hear or see anything of what she and Will and Daniel Lockwood were doing.

"Give it back," he said, and she clenched her purse more tightly against her body.

"Give what back?" she replied.

A brief, humorless laugh. "The drive you stole from my wife's dresser. Did you think I was foolish enough to leave it completely unguarded? As soon as you broke through the wards I set on it, I knew who you were and what you had done. So hand it over, please."

Damn it. She'd been so certain they had the upper hand here that she hadn't even stopped to think whether the hard drive had been protected in some way. Of course, even if she had been able to detect Lockwood's wards, she wasn't sure whether she would have been able to disable them.

"No," she said, a little startled at her own courage. "That's Colin's footage—and Michael Covenant's, as his co-producer—and they both wanted it released. Better get ready for a whole lot of people to start believing in God."

The half-demon scowled. "You really think it will be that easy?"

"Well, if it isn't, then you have nothing to worry about, do you?"

His hand shot out toward her purse. In almost that same moment, though, he gave a yelp of pain, and the tanned skin on the back of his hand began to bubble. Rosemary stared, not sure what was happening—until she saw the vial in Will's hand.

Holy water. He must have hidden it in the inside pocket of his suit jacket.

Obviously, the blessed liquid affected half-demons, unlike their offspring. The strange, shimmering barrier that had blocked them away from the party began to fade, the sounds of the gathering starting to seep in. That was the only encouragement Rosemary needed. Will's hand was still holding her arm, and so she laid her other hand on top of his fingers and shut her eyes, imagining the safety of his living room, thousands of miles away from where they currently stood.

A blink, and they were gone.

Chapter 18

"I THINK WE'RE SAFE," WILL SAID, AND Rosemary slowly eased her grip on his fingers.

She looked around the living room, her face still pale. Because it was two hours earlier here in California, the sun hadn't quite gone down yet, and there was enough light remaining that it was easy enough to see surroundings that were happily familiar to him—and hopefully, would be soon for her as well.

"Are you sure?" she said. "What if he tries to follow us?"

"And leave a house full of party guests?"

She planted her hands on the hips of her pretty, lacy gown—although he noticed she still had her evening bag clenched under one arm—and shot him a disbelieving look. "Do you really think Daniel Lockwood is going to care about his guests when someone's just walked off with the hard drive he worked so hard to steal?"

While Will had to admit she had a point, he still thought they should be safe…for the moment, anyway. "He cared enough to put that shield or whatever it was around us when he tried to stop us from leaving. He didn't want anyone to hear what he was saying."

Rosemary gave a reluctant nod. "I suppose that's true. I know his wife still doesn't know what he truly is."

"How do you know that?" Will asked. Inwardly, though, he wasn't all that surprised. Daniel Lockwood had worked very hard to present a perfect image to the people of Greencastle, a flawless façade that had them believing exactly what he wanted them to believe. It didn't seem too strange that he would have handed the same lie to his wife that he'd told everyone else.

"Because she found me getting the hard drive out of her dresser"—she paused there, as if noticing Will's flare of alarm, and spoke quickly —"and I put kind of a whammy on her or something to stop her from calling out for help."

"A whammy?" Will repeated, a little amused by her use of the word, although he certainly didn't like the idea of her getting caught in the act.

"A hex, a spell, an enchantment…whatever

you want to call what it is I can do." Rosemary shrugged, then went on, "Anyway, she seemed open to confessions, and so I asked her about Daniel Lockwood, whether she knew what he was."

"And she said no."

"Yes." She was silent for a moment, then said, "It just seems so strange that she could be with him for all those years and never notice anything strange about him, but...."

At first glance, it did seem odd, but there were extenuating circumstances involved. Will went to Rosemary and took her by the hand, led her over to the couch. "You have to remember that Daniel Lockwood is half-demon, but he was born in this world and grew up here just like any normal human, so of course he's going to have an easier time fitting in than a full-blood demon like his father might have."

"I suppose you're right." She glanced around the living room, tension obvious in every line of her slender body. "I still keep thinking he's going to bust in here at any moment."

Will threaded his fingers through hers and squeezed them gently. "Even leaving aside the question of running out on a hundred-plus guests who paid for the honor of attending his party... you warded this house, remember? It's guarded by your super-duper angel energy."

He'd said those words halfway as a joke, but Rosemary didn't seem inclined to smile. She looked over at the front door and then at the windows, which were mostly shielded by the curtains but let in an odd beam of light here and there. "Yes, that energy," she said. Her voice sounded almost defeated, not like the tone of a woman who'd succeeded against all odds in stealing back the much-desired *Project Demon Hunters* footage. "I'm still not sure what I'm supposed to do about that."

"Don't do anything," he told her. "At least, you don't have to do anything right away. Give yourself some time to absorb everything your father told you."

Rosemary let out a breath, and her shoulders hunched. "My father." A pause, and then she added, "I have absolutely no idea what to say to my mother about that."

Yes, that was one piece of information she really couldn't keep a secret. Glynis McGuire deserved to know the truth about her ex-husband, if nothing else. Isabel and Celeste needed to know that their father was still alive...and very much more than a mere mortal.

"You can figure that out later. Not too much later," he said quickly, when it looked as though Rosemary was about to open her mouth to protest. "But still, they're not even expecting you back from Indiana until late tomorrow at the very earliest. Take the rest of this evening to decompress, to relax—and congratulate yourself."

"For what?" she asked, looking confused.

"That," he said, and pointed at her evening bag, which she'd finally set down on the coffee table. A corner of the hard drive protruded from the flimsy beaded purse, looking very out of place. "We got the footage, Rosemary. Or rather, you got it. That's something to be proud of."

A tired smile touched her lips. "I guess we did go into the lion's den and make it back out alive."

"Exactly. So give yourself a little time. What would you like to do?"

Her head tilted slightly to one side as she considered the question. "Get out of this dress and into something more comfortable," she said.

That sounded like a very good idea. And even though he was used to wearing the equivalent of a suit for most of his working days, he thought that trading it now for a sweatshirt and a pair of jeans would make him feel much better about life. "We definitely need to do that. What else?"

Once again, she smiled, although her expression now had much more life to it, and the smile was a genuine one. "Well, we went to that damn party with all that great food, and I didn't get to have a single bite. So…let's order some food in, and I hope you have a bottle of wine we can crack open."

"I can manage that." Will got up from the couch, then extended a hand to Rosemary so he could help her up as well. "And after that, we can call Michael and give him the good news."

———

Rosemary sat at the large dining room table and watched her mother carefully. Since she really had no idea how best to tell Glynis the truth about the man she'd married, she'd basically just blurted it out, then waited in tense silence as her mother sat there, fingers clenched on the tabletop. It was just the two of them; Rosemary had wanted to tell her mother about John McGuire first, if for no other reason than they could then decide how best to break the news to Isabel and Celeste.

At last, her mother lifted her hands from the table and folded them in her lap. She looked very tired, but also in a way at peace, as if the news that her husband had left her because outside forces had compelled him to do so rather than because he didn't love her anymore had put to rest an inner torment she'd carried with her for years. When she spoke, she asked a question Rosemary hadn't been expecting.

"How did he look?"

After staring at her mother in surprise for a second or two, she found her voice. "Good," she managed. "Older. But still very much like himself."

Her mother's mouth curved slightly. "I'm surprised an angel would allow himself to age."

Rosemary had wondered about that as well. However, she'd thought of one possible explanation. "Well, if he's here pretending to blend in, then I guess I could see how he would have to age like any normal person would. I mean, he aged while you were married, didn't he?"

"Yes, but it's generally not as obvious when you're talking about someone aging from their mid-twenties into their mid-thirties." She sighed and reached for the mug of herbal tea that had been sitting in front of her, then took a sip. "So, he went back to Indianapolis."

"That's where you met?" That was another thing she'd always wondered about. Her mother had always said she'd met John McGuire at an education conference—she'd taught high school history before taking early retirement at the time of her mother's death—but she'd never provided any details about where that conference had taken place. In the past, Rosemary had always assumed it was because her mother was too bitter about the breakup to want to revisit a time when she and her former husband had been young and in love, but now the thought crossed her mind that possibly Rosemary's father hadn't wanted her to provide that information.

"Yes. At the airport, of all places." Another smile, one that awoke a spark of happiness in her blue eyes. "I missed my flight…and the rest is history, I suppose."

There were so many questions Rosemary wanted to ask, and yet she sensed this wasn't the time. Her mother needed a chance to absorb this new and strange information, to come to terms with the realization that so many things she'd taken as the truth had been built on false foundations.

"But," Glynis went on, her tone now brisk, "I have to believe that if he came forward to help you, then maybe at some point he'll be able to be a part of our lives again."

This seemed like an overly optimistic view of the situation—after all, her father hadn't said anything along those lines, had made it sound as though he could only help out up to a point. Tears stung her eyes, and she didn't know for sure whether they were for her mother, or for herself. Somehow, Rosemary managed to say, "I suppose that could happen. In the meantime, we have Daniel Lockwood and his half-demon buddies to worry about."

"I thought you said you were safe," her

mother responded, now looking worried. "You've protected Will's house, haven't you?"

"Yes," Rosemary said, relieved to have the conversation shift to more practical concerns. "And his car, and Michael's house, and my place in Glendora, even though I don't plan to be staying there any time soon." After she and Will had eaten and allowed themselves a night to merely sleep, she'd gotten up the next morning and warded the hell out of anything she thought needed protecting. She'd even slipped over to the store long before either Celeste or Isabel would be there to open up, and had cast wards on the entire building before heading over to their houses as well to do the same thing there. And before she'd rung the doorbell at her mother's house, she'd warded her home as well. With all that handled, Rosemary thought she'd protected the people and places she cared about as best she could, but she still didn't know for sure whether it would be enough.

"And have you seen or heard anything from this Daniel Lockwood?"

"No." Everything had been oddly quiet since their return from Indiana, which hadn't reassured her at all. Will had called Michael to let him know the hard drive was safely back in their possession, and Michael was apparently hatching some sort of plan to get himself and Audrey away from Tucson

so they could come upload the footage themselves, but none of those schemes had solidified
just yet. Rosemary felt as though the situation was
in an odd holding pattern, although she wasn't
quite sure what they were holding for.

The next shoe to drop, probably.

"Well, then, it sounds as if you've won this
round." Her mother smiled again before sipping
at her tea once more. Rosemary realized she'd been
neglecting her own cup, and lifted it to take a
swallow. "And I'll talk to Isabel and Celeste. I
know this has been hard for you, and maybe it
will be easier for them if they hear it from me."

"You're sure?" Rosemary asked as relief crept
through her. Yes, maybe it was cowardly to have
her mother make that particular revelation to her
sisters, but she knew they would be full of questions…and she just didn't have any real answers to
give them.

"Yes." Her mother got up from her seat and
came around to where Rosemary was sitting, and
laid a hand on her daughter's shoulder. "It's all
right. You take care of yourself and Will. I like
that man."

"I do, too." That was about all she would
allow herself to say. Of course, her feelings for
Will had gone far beyond "like," but she thought
her mother understood.

After that meeting, Rosemary drove back to

Will's house. Earlier that day, they'd retrieved her car from the garage at Michael's house, and she knew she'd be going back soon to pack more of her things. Although no formal agreement had been made, they'd both held the assumption that she'd be staying with Will for the foreseeable future. What exactly would happen with Michael's place, she wasn't sure—she felt a little guilty for backing out of her agreement to act as caretaker while Michael and Audrey were living in Tucson —but in the interim, she would do her best to go by every day and check on the property to make sure all was well.

Will wasn't home when she got there, but she'd been expecting that; he was well enough to drive, after all, and that meant he needed to get back to at least some of his duties at the church. However, Rosemary wasn't too put off by the solitude that greeted her, because she could tell that her wards were working—for the moment, anyway—and besides, he'd said he should be home by five-thirty at the latest. That was less than an hour off.

So she busied herself with putting away some more of her personal belongings in the drawers Will had cleared for her, and then went into the kitchen to take an inventory of the items in the refrigerator. He'd offered to take her out for dinner, but she knew they couldn't go out to eat or order takeout indefinitely. At some point, they'd need to start making their meals here.

Which was fine. She actually liked the idea of getting all domestic with him, of making a home together here. Maybe they were jumping the gun, but this felt right, felt better than any other relationship she'd had in the past. Just that morning, she'd met his next-door neighbor, an older woman named Lucille who had a pair of adorable little terrier-mix dogs, and both Lucille and the dogs had taken to her right away, making Rosemary feel as if she already belonged here in a way she never quite had in her house back in Glendora.

A quick inspection told her there wasn't much in the fridge except some frozen Mexican food from Trader Joe's. They could still cobble together a meal from those odds and ends, but it would probably be better if they went to the store instead. Well, she'd sit down and make a list while she was waiting for Will to come home.

She'd just settled herself on the couch with her phone to start putting together a shopping list when someone knocked at the front door. Almost at once, her heart leapt into her throat, but she told herself not to be silly—if Daniel Lockwood was going to show up with revenge in his heart and mayhem in his mind, he sure as hell wouldn't knock politely and wait for someone to answer the door. Anyway, as she'd headed out to her mother's earlier, she'd seen a couple of high school–age kids making the rounds of the neighborhood with a box of those fundraising chocolate bars, and so she just assumed it must be the two of them finally showing up at Will's house.

Anyway, the place was warded. Daniel Lockwood couldn't even make it past the boundaries of the property, let alone walk up the porch steps.

Rosemary set down her phone and went over to the door. As she opened it, her breath caught. Malicious dark eyes laughed down at her.

"Hi, Rosemary," Caleb Lockwood said. "Miss me?"

***

Project Demon Hunters concludes with
Unbroken Vows.

Also by Christine Pope

THE WITCHES OF WHEELER PARK

(Paranormal romance)

Storm Born (April 2020)

Thunder Road (June 2020)

Winds of Change (July 2020)

PROJECT DEMON HUNTERS

(Paranormal Romance)

Unquiet Souls

Unbound Spirits

Unholy Ground

Unseen Voices

Unmarked Graves

Unbroken Vows

THE DEVIL YOU KNOW

(Paranormal Romance)

Sympathy for the Devil

Charmed, I'm Sure

A Wing and a Prayer

THE WITCHES OF CANYON ROAD*

(Paranormal Romance)

Hidden Gifts

Darker Paths

Mysterious Ways

A Canyon Road Christmas

Demon Born

An Ill Wind

Higher Ground

Haunted Hearts

THE WITCHES OF CLEOPATRA HILL*

(Paranormal Romance)

Darkangel

Darknight

Darkmoon

Sympathetic Magic

Protector

Spellbound

A Cleopatra Hill Christmas

Impractical Magic

Strange Magic

The Arrangement

Defender

Bad Blood

Deep Magic

Darktide

THE DJINN WARS*

(Paranormal Romance)

Chosen

Taken

Fallen

Broken

Forsaken

Forbidden

Awoken

Illuminated

Stolen

Forgotten

Driven

Unspoken

THE WATCHERS TRILOGY*

(Paranormal Romance)

Falling Dark

Dead of Night

Rising Dawn

THE SEDONA FILES*

(Paranormal Romance)

Bad Vibrations

Desert Hearts

Angel Fire

Star Crossed

Falling Angels

Enemy Mine

TALES OF THE LATTER KINGDOMS*

(Fantasy Romance)

All Fall Down

Dragon Rose

Binding Spell

Ashes of Roses

One Thousand Nights

Threads of Gold

The Wolf of Harrow Hall

Moon Dance

The Song of the Thrush

THE GAIAN CONSORTIUM SERIES*

(Science Fiction Romance)

Beast (free prequel novella)

Blood Will Tell

Breath of Life

The Gaia Gambit

The Mandala Maneuver

The Titan Trap

The Zhore Deception

The Refugee Ruse

STANDALONE TITLES

Hearts on Fire

Taking Dictation

Night Music

Golden Heart

* Indicates a completed series

About the Author

USA Today bestselling author Christine Pope has been writing stories ever since she commandeered her family's Smith-Corona typewriter back in grade school. Her work includes paranormal romance, fantasy romance, and science fiction/space opera romance. She makes her home in Arizona.

Christine Pope on the Web:
www.christinepope.com

facebook.com/ChristinePopeAuthor

twitter.com/ChristineJPope

pinterest.com/ChristineJPope

www.ingramcontent.com/pod-product-compliance
Lightning Source LLC
Chambersburg PA
CBHW021133260626
47169CB00005B/1581